BEAST

MEGAN CREWE

For Jenny,
who always believed

1

For the rest of this story to make sense, you have to know that Davey and I had been best buds forever.

My first memory is of the two of us sneaking out of kindergarten to play in the pouring rain. In the chaos of post-snacktime washing up, I tugged Davey's shirt and tipped my head toward the door, and his face lit up with a conspiratorial grin. We snuck down the hall and out into the deluge.

We'd just transformed a muddy patch in the yard into a makeshift Slip'N Slide, laughing and sputtering with our inevitable falls, when the door thudded. "Boys!" Mrs. Mitchell yelled.

She marched us inside, muttering about calling our parents. I was too giddy from the adventure to care. My dad would probably just tweak my ear and call me a rascal in the tone that told me it was a compliment.

Standing there dripping by the row of cubbies, Davey started to shake. His eyes welled up, and my giddiness faded. I remembered what I'd seen of *his* dad: the rough snap of his voice, the clench of his fingers when he hustled Davey out of the room.

"It was my idea, Mrs. Mitchell!" I said. "Davey shouldn't be in trouble. It's not fair."

Mrs. Mitchell's eyes narrowed. "The two of you are about to lose your computer time for the rest of the month. Should I make that two months just for you, Max?"

I raised my chin. "Yes. He didn't even want to come—I made him. It's all my fault."

That wasn't true, but I meant the words with every fiber of my five-year-old being.

I would have done anything for Davey. I'd have died for him, if it could have made a difference. If you believe any of this, believe that.

2

The lake was the best place to party, hands down. Getting out there was kind of a hassle, so everybody moaned when I told them the plan, but it was the middle of May and already sweltering. No one wanted to be packed into Reuben's apartment or someone's parents' house, bumping against each other and swapping sweat every time they went to grab a beer. I reminded the girls that they'd be able to dance under the stars, and the guys that they might be able to talk the girls into skinny-dipping, and that got them all on board.

Saturday evening, I told Mom I needed the car to "take Vicky for a moonlight picnic" and swung by the liquor store with my doctored license. When I honked the horn at Davey's, he came out of the house halfway through a sneeze. Pollen season was in full swing. His eyes were red and his hair was sticking out like he'd taken a shower followed by a nap, but at least he'd picked a shirt that made him look more slim than scrawny. Sometimes he got the attitude that there was no way he'd be getting lucky, so why even try. I maintained that you couldn't win a game unless you were playing it.

"Spring sucks," he said as he climbed in. He snuffled. "Screw trees. Screw flowers. I vote that our next war be declared against all plant life."

I snorted and pulled away from the curb. "You look like a flower with that hair. My mom keeps a comb in the glove compartment—make yourself presentable, man."

He grimaced at me, but he got out the comb. "I spent the last half hour trying to find the allergy pills. Stupid cat swatted them under the dresser."

After a few quick swipes at the rumpled brown strands, he slumped back in the seat and tugged a piece of paper out of his pocket. A small smile crossed his face. "Hey, I thought you'd like this one. Remember how Mr. Peck ripped into Reuben for touching his car yesterday?"

I glanced over and cracked up. Davey's comic doodles were something else. He'd drawn Mr. Peck like an evil Elmer Fudd, which wasn't far from the reality, with a foot-high comb-over and sparks shooting out of his mouth. Our teacher jabbed a finger at the shaggy-haired Reuben 'toon, who was standing beside the car gazing obliviously into the distance. The glints on the car's windshield formed eyes, which it was rolling at its owner.

"Good one," I said. "You gotta show Rube that. And Vicky, when we pick her up—she'll get a laugh."

"How long have you stuck with her now, Max?" Davey said. "I'm starting to think you're settling down."

"It's only been three months," I said, which admittedly was some sort of record. "We're not getting *married*. She's just got a little more to her than some. No point in cutting a

good thing short."

"Not like you'll have any trouble finding a replacement when you want to." Davey shook his head. "What about that girl you said you're setting me up with? Is she going to be there tonight?"

"Patience, my Padawan. That sort of delicate operation takes time."

"So why am I coming? I hate these things."

"Because you always come," I said. "I've got to have someone there making me look good."

He glared at me, and I knocked his shoulder with my fist. "I'm the only thing standing between you and a lonely life of online porn. Shut up and enjoy yourself, all right?"

We found Vicky sitting on the front steps of her porch with Shannon and Tyler and a couple cases of beer. She had on the pink dress she'd modeled for me in private the week before, that fit tight on top and loose at the bottom in just the right way, and her sun-streaked hair was pulled back in a ponytail, leaving her tanned neck and shoulders bare. When she leaned through the open window to kiss me hello, her mouth tasted like cherry lip gloss. I wondered exactly how pissed Davey would be if I called a ten-minute timeout and carried her upstairs to her bedroom.

She pulled back, smiling. "Hey, handsome." Then she glanced past me. "Hi, Davey!"

"Hi," Davey said, not quite meeting her eyes. He always clammed up when Vicky was around—his standard reaction in the presence of feminine hotness—but she never let on that she noticed. Like I'd said to Davey, there was more to Vicky than being hot. She was a sweetheart too. I'd lumped her in with the airhead types until a party around Valentine's Day when Davey had spilled his cup of beer on her. She'd spent the whole time he was frantically apologizing reassuring him that it was no big deal instead of fretting over her clothes. So I'd asked her to dance and offered to drive her home. We'd spent quite a bit of time in this car since then.

Vicky slid into the seat behind me, Shannon and Tyler shoved the beer in the trunk and hopped in beside her, and we were off.

Once we got out of town, I pushed my foot down on the pedal and let the engine roar. The lake lay fifteen minutes down that straight, lonely road. For the first five, it was fields of corn or grazing grass. Then the trees started multiplying until there was thick forest on both sides.

The car was just slipping into the sharp shadows of the pines when Vicky gasped.

"What the hell was that?" Tyler said.

I eased off on the gas. "What's up?"

"There was something back there," Vicky said. "By the trees. I think I saw blood."

"Probably a dog that got hit," Shannon said.

"It was bigger than a dog," Tyler said.

I switched to the brake. "Guess we should go back and take a look then."

Tyler pulled a face. "You want to gawk at roadkill?"

"What if it's a person who got hit?" I said. "You want to leave them to bleed to death?"

Naturally, there were no complaints after that.

The gravel rasped under my shoes as I got out. I squinted at the trees. Imagine if we did find a body in the woods. No one would ever forget this party.

"It was a little farther up, on the other side," Vicky said. She and the others followed me as I crossed the road. The sun was sinking, making our shadows stretch out beside us like starved giants.

At about ten paces, the smell hit me: rancid and cloying. My stomach lurched. I knew before the buzzing of the flies reached my ears that we were too late to do anything for whoever or whatever was lying there.

Shannon stopped, coughing and shaking her head, and Tyler stayed with her. Vicky walked on beside me, tensed. Davey straggled along behind, like he didn't really want to come but couldn't think of an excuse not to. I pulled my phone out of my jeans pocket, my fingers tight around the plastic case. If it was a person, we'd need to report it.

We crunched along the gravel past a bunch of saplings all leaning together, and stopped dead at the sight of the carcass.

All that remained was a mess of meat and innards and skin. It was hardly recognizable as anything at all, but one leg jutted out: brown fur matted with blood, a hoof at the end.

"It's a cow," I said.

Vicky put her hand over her mouth and stepped back. Davey's breath hitched. "Something must've really wanted a hamburger," he muttered.

I'd started inhaling through my mouth instinctively, but the stink of decaying meat coated the roof of it and tickled up into my nose, along with something pungent and sour, like old sweat. I cleared my throat and spat on the ground. Nothing newsworthy about a dead cow. But now I was glad. To see a human being chewed up like that would have been…

I suppressed a shudder.

"What did that?" Vicky said, her shaky voice muffled by her hand. "A car wouldn't have torn it up that badly."

"Maybe a bunch of coyotes ganged up on it," I said. "Or a couple found it after it'd already gotten hurt."

"Well, that's a good enough look for me!" Davey turned and headed back to the car. Vicky grabbed my hand. She glanced back once as we walked away, and shivered.

"At least it wasn't a person, right?" I said, squeezing her fingers.

"Yeah," she said. "It just looked so… vicious, you know?"

No one said much the rest of the way to the lake, but as soon as I'd parked at the edge of the clearing, all memory of the cow carcass seemed to vanish. Shannon and Tyler raced across the sparse grass to the sandy patch at the edge of the water, giggling. Vicky and I hauled the coolers out of the trunk. A few leftover logs still lay on the fire pit. I dragged Davey over to the edge of the forest so we could scavenge for kindling.

A low cliff, pockmarked with caves, loomed beyond the trees. I nudged Davey. "Remember the time we went spelunking?"

"I remember how you insisted on saying that word every five minutes," he said dryly. "And that you convinced me to try to squeeze through the gap at the back of one of the caves."

I laughed. "Right. How long did it take you to wiggle out again?"

"Long enough that your parents were about ready to call the FBI by the time we made it home." Davey's smile faltered. No doubt he was remembering, as I just had, how his dad had freaked out too. The next time I'd seen him, not all of his bruises had been from the rocks.

I clapped Davey on the back. "Well, we both survived." And in a few months we'd be far away from that asshole.

"Is Ash coming?" Davey asked while we walked back to the clearing with our loot.

"Unless she's gotten too cool for her big brother's shindigs," I said. "Hey, last one to the pit has to get the fire started!"

I didn't even try to win. I loped over to the pit and turned around, grinning. Davey came panting after me. He dropped his kindling beside the stones with a sigh.

"It'll give you something to do while you're working up

the nerve to dance." I gave him a little shove. "I'll help. Go grab the lighter."

By the time we had a decent fire going, the sky was dark except for the pale circle of the moon and a smattering of stars overhead, and the rest of the crowd had started to show up. I counted eleven vehicles as I set my phone in my speaker dock on the roof of Mom's car and let the music blare. More headlights flashed from down the road. Ash and her group staked out some of the blankets by the fire pit. Reuben and Crystal roared up on her Vespa, the two of them already stoned and carrying baggies of pills. Bottles were clinking, hot dogs sizzling over the flames, and couples splashing in and out of the water. It was everything a Max Weston party should be.

Vicky danced with me, and then with her girlfriends, and then with me again. Davey sat slouched on a log near the fire, poking at the coals with a stick. After a while, Vicky tugged him to his feet and got him dancing too.

All Ash's friends had stood up. Ash and Emmett, her boy-of-the-month, swayed to the music beside another couple. The other sophomores raced across the sand, shrieking, in a drunken game of tag.

Emmett kept trying to slide his hands up Ash's loosely buttoned shirt. Each time she laughed and slipped out of his reach. She raised her arms in the air, her silver bracelets flashing and her eyelids dipping low as she lost herself in the song. Emmett watched her with a narrow stare. Then he headed for the coolers.

I ambled over so I reached them just as he did, as if by chance. "Here," I offered as he picked up a bottle sealed with a plastic rim. "I've got that."

He glanced up, and I could see he recognized me—as his girlfriend's older brother, as the host of the party, it didn't matter. He gave me a short nod and a shorter smile.

I pulled out my Swiss Army knife, opened the blade, and applied it to the plastic. I took a little longer with the cutting than I needed to while Emmett waited. He was the type, all tattooed shoulders and ape-like posturing, to take any appearance of a knife as a show of force. I flipped it back into the sheath and handed over the bottle.

"Having fun with Ash?" I said lightly.

His eyes flicked away. "Yeah," he said and stalked off.

Reuben ambled over, bobbing his head and trying to focus on me at the same time. "Max! The lake. Rockin'. Best idea ever!"

"Thanks, man," I said. Every time I talked to Reuben I found it harder to believe he was the same guy who used to climb out onto his roof with me and Davey to discuss the state of the world, the nature of the universe, and whether any of us stood a chance at getting into the boobalicious school secretary's pants. Somewhere in the last couple of years he'd lost track of the concept of moderation. It was like the more drugs he shoved in one end, the more everything else that used to be part of him emptied out the other.

"Look at that friggin' moon!" he shouted. He spread out his arms and turned in a circle, his face tipped to the sky. Then he staggered and caught his balance against a car. "You gotta try this new stuff Crystal picked up. Forgot it—she went back to the 'partment to get it. So awesome."

"Sure, Rube," I said, even though I never do pills at a big

thing like this. Someone's got to keep his head. I took a swig from the beer I'd been nursing for the last hour. "You let me know when she gets back."

He might have said something else, but I glanced across the clearing then. Emmett was drawing Ash down onto his lap. Her expression would have been unreadable to just about anyone. Her lips curled in a coy smile, and her eyes were masked with smudges of dark blue shadow that matched the streaks in her hair. But I knew her. Her jaw twitched as he talked into her ear, and the angle of her shoulders was tight as she flipped her bangs out of her face.

I raised my beer to Reuben in parting and circled around the fire.

"Hey, Em," I said from behind them. "Gotta borrow my sister for a second." When she looked up, I raised my eyebrows at her. "You told me you put the bug spray in the trunk, but it's not anywhere I can see."

Ash hadn't said anything about bug spray, but she didn't show it. She sighed and scrambled off Emmett's lap.

"It's got to be in there somewhere. Be back in a sec, Em."

Emmett scowled and said nothing.

"Why're you letting him piss you off?" I asked as we walked to the car.

Ash swiped her palms past her eyes. "He says he doesn't like the crowd here. He wants to go to some stupid party one of his friends in town is having instead. His friend who always looks at me like he's about to eat an ice cream sundae off me."

The bit with the knife had done more than I'd expected.

Which meant Emmett was an even bigger wimp than I'd guessed.

"So let him go. Who needs him? There are plenty of rides."

"I know, I know," she said. "I was just… I don't want to be a total bitch."

"Sure you do." I knocked my elbow against hers. "Bitches rule the world."

She laughed. "It's stupid, right? I still get thinking like a loser sometimes. But I know how to handle it. If I don't want to do it, just don't."

"Exactly."

Ash sauntered back to Emmett to tell him what was what. His scowl deepened. He touched Ash's arm, but she shrugged him off and walked down to the water. *Good girl.* A few minutes later, he and a couple others from her gang took off.

The rumble of the engine had just faded when another sputtered out of the trees. The light of the fire wavered over the windshield of Jena's dad's ancient jeep. She hopped out alone.

I couldn't help grinning. "His Royal Scholarliness couldn't make it?"

She gave me the quintessential Jena look, the one she'd been making at me for ten years: head cocked and left eyebrow slightly raised. In the darkness, with the breeze ruffling her dark brown hair and her tank top showing off her lean arms, she could have been a warrior princess. The kind of warrior princess who'd wear ripped jeans and read Nietzsche for fun.

"Joss had to do some extra research for his bio report," she said, as if Lover Boy would have lowered himself to mundane pastimes like dancing and drinking if he'd only had room in his schedule. The number of times her boyfriend of one year had accompanied her to one of our crowd's parties was exactly zero.

"No problem," I said. "I can show you a good time."

Her eyebrow arched a little harder, like I'd known it would. "Oh really?" she said. "What have you got up your sleeve tonight, Max?"

"What more do you need?" I asked. "We've got a full moon and a starry sky, the biggest bonfire the beach has seen since last year, more alcohol than a whale could drink, and a lake I hear is the perfect temperature for swimming… if you're interested in getting wet."

I smirked at her. She laughed and smacked my shoulder. "You never change, do you?"

"You wouldn't want me to," I told her, but who really knew, these days? Jena and I used to be almost as tight as Davey and me, but ever since she started dating the indomitable Joss, she was hardly around.

Vicky came up beside me and hooked her hand around my elbow. "Hey, Jena!" she said. "I was starting to think you weren't going to make it again."

Jena glanced around at the thinning crowd. "I guess I'm kind of late, aren't I?"

"What's late with these things?" Vicky smiled. "Come on, I saved a couple of the lemon spritzers for you just in case."

We sat on the sand to talk, and somewhere in there a

joint ended up in my hand. I let myself take a couple of tokes before passing it on: just enough to relax a little. Time stretched in a haze of color and laughter and the stars creeping overhead. After a while I noticed I was lying on my back and the sand was making my shirt damp. The breeze had gotten almost cool.

I pushed myself upright. The only cars left were mine and Jena's jeep. The fire wasn't much more than a few flames flickering over the embers, and the last song on the playlist was fading out. Vicky and Jena were standing by the water, still chatting. Reuben had splashed right in with his clothes on and was trying—and failing—to float on his back.

Ash's gang had all departed except her and her friend Sofia. They sat on the blanket shoulder to shoulder as if propping each other up. Sofia's dark eyes followed me as I walked over. I winked, and her lips curled upward.

Davey was hovering over the fire on the other side. "'Bout time to get going?"

I glanced toward the lake. Jena was checking her watch. It couldn't be that late, could it? There was still so much night for us to own.

"Let's get the fire really going one last time," I said. "Go out with a bang."

I turned back toward Davey, but he wasn't looking at me anymore. Ash was stretching her arms over her head, her chest rising, and he was all but ogling her across the fire pit.

"Davey!" I said, and he startled. "Wake up, man. More firewood. There was tons over by the caves. I'll make sure we don't lose the flames completely."

He stood up. "Right, right." He sounded a little woozy,

though I hadn't seen him drink much. Maybe the walk would clear his head.

As he headed off toward the trees, I took his spot by the fire. I prodded the one log that wasn't totally burnt through until the unblackened end touched the flames. Somewhere behind me, Reuben sloshed out of the lake. Vicky and Jena's voices grew louder as they ambled over. I got up to tell them we were going to hold out a little longer.

Before I opened my mouth, Davey started screaming.

3

The scream was made of pure pain and terror. Nothing in it proved its maker was even human, but somewhere below conscious thought I must have registered the direction and who'd gone off that way, and the understanding shot straight to my legs. I was running before the cry broke off.

The moonlight hardly penetrated the forest. I stumbled toward the sounds of snapping twigs, ripping cloth, and gasped breaths. The piney air stung my throat. Branches scraped at my arms and whipped past my face.

There. A massive shape thrashed on the ground ahead of me. Part—the bottom part—was Davey. An arched back and a mass of stringy hair shuddered over him. The creature's mouth jerked at his shoulder as its claws raked across his chest. His arms flailed. The only noise he was making now was a stuttered whimpering.

I didn't think, just kept running. "Get off him!" I yelled, and threw myself at the thing.

I rammed into its sinewy body with a shove of my hands, putting my entire weight into knocking it off Davey. A sour stench filled my nose. The creature swayed and shoved me back. I staggered, caught my balance, and lunged forward again. My fingers wrenched across coarse greasy skin and shreds of cloth. Shouts echoed through the trees around us: Jena's voice, Vicky's, Reuben's.

The thing glanced up for the first time, its eyes wide, and my heart started hammering twice as hard as before. The eyes were an animal's, slit-pupiled and yellow. The fangs it bared at me would have made a lion cower. But beneath the lank, matted hair, the nose and the blood-flecked lips and the sickly pale skin looked... human.

Then it kicked me in the chest and bolted.

I careened into a tree trunk, and an ache radiated through my ribs. I teetered and hurled myself back toward Davey. The creature had already outdistanced me. Its hunched form charged through the underbrush into the shadows by the foot of the cliff.

Davey moaned. I crouched beside him, all my attention narrowing onto my best friend. He was gulping for air. Blood streaked across his face and drenched his shirt. Ragged edges of skin and flesh gaped through the tears in the fabric.

"We have to stop the bleeding," someone—Jena?—said. "I'll get one of the blankets."

"What the fuck?" said someone else, almost definitely Reuben. "Oh man, oh man, oh man."

I peeled off my shirt. As I pressed the fabric against Davey's chest, Vicky knelt down by his head. She smoothed her hands over his hair.

"It'll be okay," she said. Her voice slurred a little, shaking even as she tried to sound soothing. "Hang in there."

Davey's eyes stayed fixed on me. His lips moved as if he

were going to say something, but instead he just sucked in more air. How much pressure was enough? What if I pushed too hard and messed him up worse?

Jena hurried back. She tossed a blanket over Davey. He winced, and she grimaced. "I'm so sorry, Davey."

I helped her ease him onto his side so we could wrap the blanket tightly around him. "We've got to get you to the car, bud," I said. "Then it's straight to the hospital—they'll fix you up, no problem." With the blood mostly hidden by the thick cloth, it was easier to believe that.

"Should we call an ambulance?" Vicky said.

The fanged, not-quite-human face of the thing I'd wrestled with flashed through my mind, and my back stiffened. "I don't know if we're safe here. We can get him to the hospital faster ourselves." Reuben was hovering over us, his hands twitching. I motioned to him. "Come on, Rube. Grab his ankles. I'll take his shoulders."

Reuben tried, but his brain was so fried from the giant cocktail he'd mixed inside his body that he lost his balance in the simple act of bending over. Jena swooped in. "Here, I've got him."

Everywhere I touched made Davey flinch. In the end, I managed by grabbing the edges of the blanket and lifting him as if he were on a stretcher. My fingers and arms were burning from the strain before we'd made it out of the trees. Fifty push-ups a morning clearly didn't cut it.

Vicky and Reuben wobbled along beside us. "Keep looking at me, Davey," Vicky said. "Try to stay awake, okay?" I'd have to stop teasing her about the hospital melodramas she was hooked on if they'd taught her how to deal with a situation like this.

Ash and Sofia hurried over. My sister's eyes widened when she saw what we were doing. I jerked my chin toward her.

"Ash, get in the car. Vicky, can you sit with Davey in the back? Keep talking to him like you're doing?"

Jena laid Davey's legs as far across the seat as she could reach and ran around to the opposite side so we could heft him all the way in. A whining noise that sounded more animal than human slipped from his throat. His face was damp with sweat.

"Sorry, buddy," I said. "We've got to get you inside."

Vicky squeezed in after him, placing his head gently on her lap. "Call me as soon as you know he's all right," Jena said. "I'll take the others home."

I nodded and jumped into the car. We hadn't put the fire out, and we were leaving behind the coolers and the blankets and who knew what else, but those concerns felt incredibly distant compared to Davey's ragged breaths behind me. I started the ignition and hit the gas.

Something thumped off the trunk. Ash squeaked, and my pulse stuttered. Then I figured it out.

"The speaker dock. Guess I might be getting a new phone!"

My sister let out a sputter of a laugh. She folded her arms over her chest as the car bumped off the dirt track and onto the road.

"What happened to him?" she said.

"Something in the woods attacked him. We scared it off."

"Something? A bear? A wolf?"

I had to swallow before I could answer. "I don't know. It was just some kind of… beast-thing." That ran on two legs and had a face almost like a man's.

Ash stared at me for a few seconds before her eyes started to drift. Her head lolled against the window.

Davey stirred. His voice mumbled behind me. "…last time I do what you tell me…"

"Shhh," Vicky said. "We're on the way. It won't be long."

In town, the streets were empty. I zoomed through two red lights. Why had they decided to build the goddamned hospital all the way at the other end? Maybe we *should* have called for an ambulance.

But then we'd have been sitting there by the lake waiting for it, watching Davey bleed, wondering if the thing was going to come back for the rest of us.

"Hey," Vicky said. "You're looking a little more awake."

"Driving freakin' fast," Davey muttered.

"We're almost there. Right, Max?"

"Yep."

The blanket rustled behind me. "Where we goin'?"

"The hospital, remember?" How out of it was he? "Like Vicky said, we're almost there. You'll be okay soon."

A lurch of movement filled the rear view mirror, and Vicky yelped. Davey pitched forward. He grasped the edge of the driver's seat by my shoulder. Ash broke from her doze with a flinch.

"Davey, what are you doing? You'll hurt yourself," Vicky pleaded, and I said, "Davey, man, we'll talk, but you've got to lie down." Davey ignored both of us. Sweat or blood, probably both, had plastered his hair to his forehead.

"No hospital," he said. "Don't take me there, Max. You know how my dad blew up when I had to go after those bad pills Reuben got. He'll kill me, he really will."

When Davey's dad had come to the hospital to pick him up, he'd spent an hour shouting at one of the administrators about the co-pay and dragged Davey to the car without so much as a "How are you?" I didn't like to think about how much worse it would have been once they'd gotten home. But right now there were other, more important considerations. Like:

"What do you think is going to happen if I *don't* take you to the hospital? You're already dying, you idiot. Now lie the fuck down so you don't make it worse!"

He hesitated. Then he let Vicky guide him back down on the seat. "I'm not dying," he said petulantly. "I'm not even bleeding anymore. Look, Vicky."

Dried blood crackled as he pulled the blanket up. Vicky was quiet for a moment. "Max," she said, "he really doesn't look that bad."

The memory of his ripped-up chest rose up behind my eyes. How could he not look bad? I gritted my teeth and yanked the car over to the curb.

"If you die because we stopped to talk about this," I said, "*I* am going to kill you."

Davey managed to chuckle. I hit the overhead light and turned, bracing myself. Ash peered over the back of her seat.

At first I just blinked, as if maybe if I cleared my eyes I'd see what I'd expected. Davey had pulled the blanket off his shoulders. His skin was mottled with ugly red marks, but they looked shallower and less ragged than before. More like he'd been mauled by a cat than by a creature the size of a man. And he was right. Other than one cut near his neck that was still oozing a bit, he wasn't bleeding anymore.

"I think he's okay," Ash said.

I closed my eyes, shook my head, and checked again, but nothing had changed.

"Is that what he looked like to you before?" I asked Vicky.

Her chin wobbled. "I don't know. It was dark."

And she'd been drinking and smoking up.

The joint. Had I dragged a little deeper than I'd meant to? Or it might have been purer stuff than Reuben's usual wares and gone to my head more than I'd realized. Or… It *had* been dark in the woods. I'd thought I'd seen blood all over Davey, his skin gouged, but some of those impressions could have been dirt or shadows playing tricks.

I inhaled. "Okay, so you're not bleeding. You were before. Maybe you lost too much. And any of those scratches could get infected, and then what?"

Davey pushed himself farther up in the seat. "I feel okay. I mean, it hurts like hell, but I'm not dizzy or woozy or whatever. If I was blood-deprived, wouldn't I feel it?"

True, he didn't sound like a guy who'd just lost half the liquid contents of his body. He sounded weirdly normal.

"If we go into the E.R. like this, we'll probably have to wait hours before anyone even checks him over," Vicky said.

I sat back. "And they'd have to call his dad. Which will just make a bigger problem." If I'd known back at the lake that he was only hurt, not dying, I'd never have rushed him to the hospital in the first place.

"There's the twenty-four-hour CVS," Ash said. "They'd have bandages and antibiotic stuff, wouldn't they?"

Vicky smiled. "That's right!"

We could get a bunch of people involved who'd make everything more complicated, or we could do pretty much the same things they would ourselves, faster. The answer was obvious.

"You're staying over at my place, Davey," I said. "I'm not buying you a tube of antibiotic cream and kicking you out on the curb." Someone should be keeping an eye on him in case he was worse than he looked.

"'Course," he said, and that settled it. I'd panicked, I'd made a mistake, but we were back on track.

"All right." I took the car out of park. "Let's do this. I've always liked playing doctor."

Vicky giggled, and so did Ash. Right then it seemed like everything would be all right.

4

When I woke up just before noon, Davey was zonked out in the sleeping bag beside my bed. He was snoring, so he was definitely still alive. The night felt like a messy blur. Had I really tried to rush him to the emergency room? I'd have to watch it with the weed next time.

I rubbed my eyes, grabbed some clothes, and headed for the shower.

Ash was coming out of the upstairs bathroom. With her hair wrapped in a white towel and her face scrubbed clean, she looked younger, more fragile—like she had all the time a couple years ago. She'd built up more armor since then.

She crossed her arms loosely over the front of her T-shirt when she saw me. "Is Davey okay? I can hardly remember what happened."

"Oh yeah," I said. "Sleeping like a log."

But I returned to my room ten minutes later to find Davey sitting up in the sleeping bag. He looked pale, but not necessarily more so than usual. I plopped down on the bed.

"How're you doing?"

"Sore," he said with a crooked grin. "And hungover. Otherwise, just great!"

I socked him in his good shoulder, a little lighter than I normally would have. "I'll get the Tylenol. And you should probably put on more of that antibiotic cream."

We got to work peeling back the sterile pads we'd taped all over him last night. The adhesive crinkled, and he winced. "Ow, that stings."

"It wouldn't be so bad if you shaved your back now and then."

I lifted the first bandage, and for the second time in twelve hours I sat there staring at Davey's half-naked body.

When I went still, Davey glanced over at me and then craned his neck trying to see his shoulder. "Is it that bad?"

I snapped myself out of it. "No, I just can't believe how good you look with the hair ripped off. You really should start waxing."

He elbowed me and reached back to dab the antibiotic cream on the wound. Which when we'd bandaged it had been a dark red gash. His fingers slid over a patch of seamless pink skin—the kind of pink you'd expect to see under a scab that's just fallen off after a cut has had days to heal. A nervous energy started to fizz in my chest.

"Some big goddamned dog," Davey said. "I used to like dogs, but I think I'm adding them to the list of things I hate now."

I opened my mouth, closed it again, and gave him a slanted smile. If he didn't remember anything more disturbing about the thing that'd attacked him, why freak him out? I wasn't totally sure how much I'd only imagined anyway.

"Yeah," I said. "Dogs suck."

He bent over his abdomen. "Weird. Those scratches closed up fast, didn't they? Do you think it's the cream? I've never used this stuff before."

"It is kind of weird," I said. Davey's brow knit, and I added, "Probably it's the cream. We got it on there really fast." Hell, maybe it *was* the antibiotics.

"They still hurt, that's for sure." He grimaced as he rubbed a mark slashed across his left collarbone. "At least it looks like I'm going to survive to make it to New York."

I prodded him with my knee. "You'd better. I'm not fending off the roaches on my own."

I'd gotten into NYU on a scholarship, and Davey had barely edged in at the Bronx Community College, so the plan was to share whatever sorry apartment we could afford with whatever miserable jobs we could scrounge up and not complain, because hell, we'd be living in New York City. Davey's dad just about shit a brick when we told him, and even though Davey had stayed over at my house that night for cool-down time, he'd shown up at school two days later wincing every time he got bumped in the hall.

But there was nothing that asshole could do to stop us. The one good thing Davey's mom had done after she left was set up a college fund, and no one but Davey could touch that.

Davey patted the last bandage back into place. His head drooped. "Guess I should go home."

I grabbed my laptop off my desk. "You can hang out here if you want. I've got that politics paper to write, but it'll only take an hour or two."

"Crap. I forgot. There goes the rest of my weekend."

"You need to learn to bullshit better. Teachers don't care how much time you spend on it as long as it sounds pretty."

He rolled his eyes. "Yeah, yeah. Not everyone's a master of persuasion like you, Max. Unless *you* want to write it for me."

"And what would you learn from that?" I shook my head in mock exasperation.

I lent Davey a shirt and walked down to the door with him. He stopped in the front hall. "You know, I was thinking maybe I should submit a couple of my drawings to the newspaper, for that last issue before we graduate. It would be kind of cool to see them in print. If the editors think they're good enough."

There was a sort of question in his voice. "Of course they're good," I said. "Good enough that the teachers might recognize themselves. How smart would it be to piss them off right before finals?"

"Oh. Right. I hadn't thought about that."

I cuffed him lightly on the head. "So it's a good thing you've got me to do the thinking for you."

He glanced around once as he tugged on his sneakers, as if he were looking for something.

"Are we going to do that Tarantino marathon this week? His new one is out Tuesday."

"Next weekend it is." As he headed out, I added, "Stay out of the woods!"

He gave me the middle finger and ambled away, hands in his pockets, shoulders slouched, like always.

"Was that Davey, Max?" Mom said from the kitchen.

I walked over to the doorway. She was spreading mayo on two pieces of rye bread, smoked turkey and Swiss on the cutting board beside her. Dad's favorite.

"Yeah," I said. "He stayed over."

"I thought you had a date with Vicky. You got in pretty late."

She didn't bother to glance up. Going through the motions of being a responsible parent.

"We ended up hanging out after I dropped Vicky off," I said. "Did Dad start a new project?"

She arranged the turkey on the bread, raised her head, and smiled. "It's got him too busy to come out to eat. You know your father. But a creative mind needs fuel."

These days, Dad spent most of his creative energy on ranking up in *League of Legends*, not putting together new masterpieces of sound. It was hard to tell whether Mom had managed not to notice this or was willfully un-knowing it.

"He's lucky he's got you looking after him," I said, because that was exactly what she wanted to hear. She smiled a little brighter. As she breezed out of the room to his studio down the hall, she started to hum the song Dad had composed for her when they were first dating, "Lady by the Lake."

I grabbed a Pop-Tart, but after one bite, the red jam against the pale pastry made me think of the blood on Davey's skin last night. I chucked it in the garbage and went upstairs.

The blanket and the remains of Davey's shirt were bundled in the back of my closet where I'd shoved them last night. I uncrumpled them in the daylight streaming through the window.

The shreds of his shirt were more red than blue. The middle of the blanket, the part that had been on top of Davey, was soaked through with blood, stiff now that it had dried. A metallic scent rose off it, thick and coppery as old pennies.

I grimaced and folded the blanket over so I didn't have to see the stain any more. The fizzing in my chest expanded: worry, and underneath it, a quiver of something like excitement.

Davey *had* been bleeding to death. And then he'd been okay, just like that.

I drove out to the lake to pick up the things we'd left. The speaker dock had taken a dent to the side, but my phone still worked. I called Vicky and Jena to let them know Davey had recovered, leaving out the 'faster than the speed of light' part, and poked around the edge of the woods for a few minutes without venturing too far out of the baking heat of the sun. There was no sign of the creature that'd attacked Davey.

What made sense was that it'd been some dirty, crazy bum, mutated by the joint I'd smoked and the darkness. But I already knew not everything about this situation made sense.

Monday morning, I walked into school with a tickle of nervous anticipation in my gut. I scanned the hall for Davey. We had first period together, English, but he tended to show up two seconds before the last bell rang. I started to text him as I headed down the hall.

A tap on my shoulder interrupted me. Mr. Blythe, the music teacher and choir director, looked down his thin nose at me. I'd never taken music, but Ash had gotten private vocal lessons from him when she was in junior high.

He cleared his throat. "Mr. Weston. Could I have a word?"

It was one of those questions teachers asked when they were really giving you an order. "Sure," I said, as if I were doing him a favor. "What's up?"

He motioned for me to follow him into the music room. The chairs were empty—he must have had prep first period.

"I wanted to speak to you about your sister," he said.

I kept my hands loose by my sides and a smile on my face, but inside I tensed. I had a feeling I knew what was coming. "What about her?"

Mr. Blythe fingered the songbook propped up by the piano. "I'm concerned. I was always impressed by Ashley's vocal maturity and enthusiasm, so I was surprised that she dropped her lessons. When I approached her about joining the choir last year, she told me she was no longer interested in music. I thought it might be a passing phase, but she still hasn't come around."

I shrugged. "If that's how she feels, you've got to respect it, right?"

Mr. Blythe settled his gaze on me with a sharpness I didn't like. "Certainly. I have observed, however, that she looks to you for... guidance, quite a bit. I find it hard to believe that someone with that much love for music would lose it completely. Perhaps if she received encouragement from a person she looks up to, like her older brother..."

My hand clenched around the impulse to sock him right in that snooty nose. He presumed to know what was best for Ash better than I did, did he? Maybe if he'd been paying more attention during those lessons, he'd have realized the music was screwing her up instead of helping her.

I was the one who'd noticed. I was the one who'd put her back together when she was falling apart. She was fine now—happy, *strong*.

Because I wasn't an idiot, I didn't hit him. I didn't even stop smiling. But a little of my anger must have shown in my eyes, because Mr. Blythe's mouth tightened before I said a word. I kept my voice casual.

"What Ash does is up to her. She's the one you should talk to. To be honest, I think it's kind of creepy that you're asking me to try to change her mind instead of bringing it up with her."

He stared at me for a moment. It might have qualified as a glare. I pretended not to notice and glanced at the clock.

"Crap, only three minutes left before class starts. Sorry I couldn't help you more, Mr. Blythe."

"She has real talent, Max," he said. "There are all sorts of opportunities for young people with talent. She'll miss out if she doesn't try for them soon."

I looked back at him before I stepped into the hall. "Like I said, it's up to her."

The conversation stewed inside me. I walked to class, nodding to people I passed, fighting the urge to swing by Ash's first period history to make sure—what? That she was okay? Then I saw Davey ducking into the English classroom.

The bell rang as I slipped in after him. Mrs. Klein

frowned, so instead of talking to Davey, I had to make a face of apology and scoot to my seat, one behind and one over from him. She'd arranged us alphabetically. As she went through the attendance, I studied what I could see of Davey's face. He'd slumped over his desk, and his skin looked not just pale but kind of grayish. I was about to lean over and ask him if he was okay when Mrs. Klein clapped her hands.

"Let's get right to it, folks. Othello, Act III. What did we learn from that first conversation between Othello and Iago? Max?"

I gritted my teeth and tried to think of the fastest way to answer. "Well, it's clear that—"

Davey's shoulders shuddered. I paused.

"Max?" Mrs. Klein said. And Davey vomited the entire contents of his stomach onto his desk.

5

The mess of liquid and mush slid across the wooden surface to splatter onto the floor. The girl sitting at Davey's right squealed and skittered into the opposite aisle. Davey wavered, peering at what had come out of his mouth in a daze.

The sour, sickly smell of stomach acid and half-digested cereal made my own stomach lurch. I slid out of my chair and put my hand on Davey's back. "I'll get him to the nurse."

Davey rose when I tugged on his shirt. Mrs. Klein blinked, nodded, and started for the phone, I guessed to call a janitor.

In the hall's dim light, Davey looked even grayer. He shuffled along, one arm clutching his abdomen, his eyes glazed. "How long have you been sick?" I demanded.

"Last night," he mumbled.

"For fuck's sake, Davey!" He hadn't healed up, not really —only on the outside. The beast-thing must have infected him with something. "Why didn't you call me?"

"It wasn't that bad then." He let out a mangled chuckle.

"I knew you'd be pissed."

"Of course I'm pissed. You go on all, 'I'm totally fine, just a little sore,' and then—" We came around the corner before the nurse's office, and I halted abruptly. With the cutbacks, we were sharing our nurse with the elementary school down the street this year. She wouldn't be here until the afternoon.

Davey jerked to a halt beside me. Beads of sweat were forming on his forehead. One dripped off and splatted on his sneaker.

"What's wrong?" he croaked.

"No nurse."

He groaned. "Screw it. Maybe I should have listened the other day. If you think I need the hospital, let's just go."

I didn't want to consider how crappy he must be feeling to give in now. His dad wasn't going to be any happier about the emergency room bill now than he'd have been yesterday morning. But Davey obviously needed medical care.

Wait. We did have other options.

"Come on." I nudged him onward. "We'll go to the urgent care clinic. I can foot that bill. You've got your fake I.D. Your dad won't even have to know." Unless the doctor there thought he was so badly off *they* sent him to the E.R., in which case at least he'd be alive. Even urgent care would put a dent in my summer job savings, but living on ramen for an extra few months in New York was worth keeping Davey's dad off his back.

Halfway across the lawn, Davey buckled over with an awful heaving sound, but nothing came out except a little clear liquid he spat into the grass. He straightened up, shivering.

"Just keep walking," I said. "We'll get there."

When we made it to the center, the woman at the reception desk gave us a bored look. Her gaze drifted over Davey's pale, shivering, sweating form, and her lips pursed. She handed over a clipboard with a form.

"Fill the whole thing out," she said. "Get him to write down everything he's taken."

My jaw tightened as Davey took the clipboard. I gripped his shoulder to stop him from walking off.

"He hasn't taken anything. He isn't *on* anything. Some... animal attacked him Saturday night, scratched him up and bit him, and now he's sick."

She shrugged, dismissing us. "Sure, hon. Just fill out the form."

"Look!" I jerked at the collar of Davey's shirt.

My fingers faltered. There was nothing to look *at*. The pale, freshly healed marks of yesterday morning had completely vanished, leaving only faint smudges of scars. As if the mauling had happened months ago.

No doctor was going to believe Davey had recently been infected by those.

A middle-aged man came up to the desk, breathing hoarsely. The receptionist turned to him. I drifted over to the chairs with Davey. My hands clenched on my lap as I sat down.

It didn't matter what they believed. We weren't going to leave here until they agreed to run whatever tests he needed. And if they couldn't get their act together to figure out what was wrong with Davey, we'd just have to sort this out ourselves.

"Do you think this stuff really helps?" The herbal pills chittered against each other in the baggies I was carrying as Vicky and I headed toward my house. We'd swung by her place after school to dig into her mom's stash of supplements. Ms. Curtis made no secret of her skepticism of the "medical establishment."

"My mom always makes me take some when I've caught something. I usually get better pretty quick. They shouldn't hurt Davey, anyway." Vicky frowned. "So the doctor didn't find anything really wrong?"

I swiped the back of my neck. The sluggish breeze was barely shifting the afternoon heat. "She said it looked like a standard stomach bug to her. But they're doing blood tests and some other stuff." After a whole lot of pressing, and me paying up front.

"I hope he's okay. That whole thing on Saturday was so freaky."

She didn't know the half of it. "Well, at least he can relax at my place for now without his dad breathing down his neck," I said. "Thanks for coming over. You were really good with him that night. And he's going to be getting sick of my face before too long." Maybe getting fawned over by a prettier one would cheer him up a bit. He'd managed not to puke since we'd left urgent care, but he could have done a convincing zombie impression without any effort.

I'd set Davey up in my room with an extra pillow and a bottle of Tylenol. We found him lying on top of the sleeping bag where I'd left him, his shirt damp with sweat and his arms wrapped around his abdomen. When I stepped through the doorway, his eyes opened.

"Hey," I said. "How's it going?"

He smiled weakly. "I've felt better."

"Think you can keep anything down? Vicky's brought some of her mom's special cures."

"Guess I can try." He looked past me to Vicky and gave her a limp nod. "Thanks, Vicky."

The fact that he could look straight at her without blinking or blushing meant he was so out of it he couldn't even feel awkward. Was he getting worse? How could the doctor have diagnosed him properly when she wouldn't even believe what had happened to him?

I needed a second opinion. From someone who'd be a little more open-minded... or someone who could even corroborate what I'd seen the other night.

An odd giddiness raced through me. Of course.

"There's leftover soup in the fridge," I said while Vicky started sorting through the pills. "It'd be good for you to get a little food in you along with the herbal magic. I just need to heat it up."

I stepped into the hall and stopped. Ash was standing outside her bedroom, her friend Sofia practically hanging off her elbow.

"Is Davey all right?" Ash asked. She must have heard us talking. Sofia's gaze lingered on me. I didn't want *her* seeing Davey like this—he wasn't exactly the most appealing specimen of manhood at the moment.

"We'll see," I said to Ash. "He's going to hang out here for a bit, but Mom and Dad don't need to know, okay?" They could be pretty oblivious, but they weren't going to lie for me if Davey's dad pitched a fit.

Ash shrugged. "No reason I'd mention it." She shot me a conspiratorial grin and slipped into her room. Sofia hesitated outside. I might as well offer something to distract her.

"Tomorrow," I mouthed. Her face brightened as if I'd promised undying devotion and not just an unspecified period of attention. She ducked her head and followed Ash. I reached for my phone.

It rang four times before Jena picked up. "Hi, Max."

I let out a silent breath of relief.

"I need you," I said, in a tone of exaggerated adulation. "Desperately." It was a running joke of ours, a line from an awful romance movie she'd insisted we watch when we were eleven. One of my life's missions was never to let her live it down. When she laughed, I added in my normal voice, "Seriously, can you come over?"

"Right now?" she said. "What's going on?"

"I have a, ah, situation I could use your expert judgment on," I said. "And probably also your dad's expert medical opinion, if you can pass on your observations." Mr. Roseman worked as a nurse at the old folks home; he ran into infections and other health problems all the time.

"Medical opinion?" Jena repeated. "Is this a goof-off thing or is something really wrong?"

Jena-before-Joss would have already figured it out, because Jena-before-Joss would have been hanging with our usual crowd and heard all about Davey's dramatic exit from class. No doubt Jena-now had been too busy talking about "narrative reality" and "creative ethics" with Joss's gang to pay attention to anything as pedestrian as school gossip. Suddenly I wished she had brought Lover Boy along Saturday night. Maybe the beast thing would have eaten *him*.

"It's Davey," I said. "He's not doing so great. Just come, and I'll explain everything."

She paused, but only for a second. Jena-before-Joss wasn't gone completely. "Okay. I'll be there in a bit."

I nuked the soup and brought it up to my bedroom on one of Mom's serving trays. Davey had managed to sit up, leaning against the side of the bed. Vicky was telling him about how Shannon had nearly set a chair on fire in chemistry class.

"Jena's coming," I said as I set the soup beside him. "I figured we could go over your symptoms with her, and she could talk to her dad, in case there's something the urgent care doctor missed. If we need to, we can get Reuben to score some meds from his pharmaceutal connection." Rube might have become a vacant space of a friend in most respects, but he was good for at least that one thing.

"Cool," Davey said. He eyed the soup like it was an alien being waiting to suck out his brain.

"It's cream of chicken," I said. "My mom's specialty. Have a little to take the pills with, at least."

Vicky offered a little green tablet that was the immune-boosting one, as well as a purple capsule that apparently settled the stomach, and an orange one for fevers. Davey looked skeptical, but he sipped the soup and swallowed them one by one. Then he lay back down.

"Okay, I'm done for the day."

The knocker thumped against the door downstairs. I got up. "That'll be Jena." She must have driven to get here that fast. I jogged down the stairs.

It was Jena. Unfortunately, it was also Joss.

I bit back a *What the hell are you doing here?* when I saw him standing next to her on the porch. His shiny red Mini Cooper was parked by the curb. He was wearing those little rectangle glasses he let sit so low on his nose they couldn't actually be helping him see, and a corduroy blazer he must have been sweating buckets under. The ends of his curly black hair were artfully arranged around the collar in a way that was probably supposed to suggest they'd fallen there at random. Joss was far too high-minded to worry about things like appearances, after all.

Jena looked at me defiantly, as if daring me to complain. As if I'd ever been anything but perfectly polite to Joss's face.

I swept back my arm. "Jena, Joss, good to see you. Why don't you come in?"

"I was at Joss's when you called," Jena said as she stepped past me, even though I hadn't asked. "He's been volunteering at the hospital, remember? I thought he might be able to help."

How could I forget? The incredible Joss was both an aspiring poet and a doctor in the making. I guessed he was going to compose sonnets about the beauty of people's internal organs.

Thankfully, Davey saved me from having to comment out loud. The hall floor upstairs creaked and the bathroom door banged shut, not quite tightly enough to completely muffle the gasp and the splatter of a few spoonfuls of chicken soup plus various herbal remedies being spewed into the toilet. It seemed fair to leave it at, "Crap."

Jena peered up the stairs. "How sick is he? I thought the E.R. said he'd be fine. Have you taken him in again?

"Yeah, about that… Can I talk to you for a minute out back? Alone?"

Jena turned to Joss, who shrugged without so much as a glance at me. He hadn't even bothered to say, "Hello." I'd asked his girlfriend to rush over here on a matter of unexplained urgency, and he just looked bored. Because nothing outside his little sphere could possibly be noteworthy?

"Make yourself at home." I pointed him to the living room couch, waiting long enough for him to notice the Grammy award plaque hanging on the wall. He blinked, and I smiled. "My dad's."

I enjoyed the flash of startled admiration that passed over Joss's face before he flattened it. He'd probably like Dad —one pretentious artist to another.

"How long ago did your dad win that again?" Jena asked as I led her away.

"Twenty years now." And as far as I could tell, that was where his real career had ended.

In the backyard, the sun was glaring down. I walked to the cooler spot at the far end where trees loomed over the chain-link fence. The ravine there ran right through the west end of town and effectively connected Davey's yard to mine. When we were younger, we used to scramble over our respective fences and meet up at the halfway point down by the creek to go tree climbing or salamander hunting.

Jena followed me. "What's the big secret?"

I'd better get the worst part over with first. "I lied about the hospital," I said. "We didn't go."

"What?" Jena said, so loud I winced. "What the hell are you talking about, Max? He was—he was torn to pieces. He was bleeding to death."

"Good. So I wasn't imagining that."

She paused, her dark blue eyes almost black in the shade. "Of course not. Why would you think—"

"He begged me not to take him, Jen," I said. "In the car. And he showed us the scratches and bites, and they didn't look that bad after all. The next morning he was walking around like nothing had happened. All the cuts, they're *gone.* They're nothing but scars. You look at them, and you'll start wondering if you were imagining things too."

"How could they be healed already? At least one of them... I saw *bone*, Max. I swear I did."

"I'll get him to show you. I don't know how it happened, but it did. And..."

"And what?" she said when I halted.

I hadn't meant to bring it up, but it felt right. I could use someone smart on my side who knew the whole story. And knowing Jena, this piece of the puzzle would be what hooked her.

"You're going to think I'm messing with you," I said. "But I'm not. I swear it. Did you see the thing that attacked him that night?"

"Not really. It took off so fast, and the forest was dark. I figured it was a big dog, or a small bear, or something."

"I saw its face," I said. "It looked... partly human.

Unless you know of any bears or dogs that have a nose like this, or a mouth like this." I pointed to my own.

Jena was silent for a moment. "You think he got attacked by a werewolf or something."

I threw my hands in the air. "I don't know. Believe me, I'd rather *not* be thinking that. But whatever it was, it fucked him up in such a weird way the hospital won't know where to start. We *did* go to the urgent care clinic today, but they didn't take him seriously. Maybe there's something supernatural going on. Maybe it's a scientific mystery, and all he needs are the right meds. I just want to know if you're going to help."

"Have you told anyone else what you saw? What does Davey think?"

"He doesn't remember much," I said. "He thinks it was a wild dog, and I don't see how freaking him out will do him any good, especially when we're not sure. Vicky and Reuben were too out of it—they don't realize how badly he was hurt to begin with. If I tried to explain it, they'd tell me *I* need to see a doctor. The head-shrinking kind."

"Well, let's not reject that idea yet," Jena said dryly, but I knew I had her. She turned. "Come on. I won't have anything to ask my dad about if I haven't even seen Davey."

In the morning, Davey managed to swallow five or six spoonfuls of soup without throwing up. A minor victory.

"Both of my 'rents have gone to work," I told him, "so do whatever you feel up to. If you get worse, text me. Got it?"

"Yes, master," Davey rasped, and chuckled, but it wasn't all that funny that he sounded like Gollum without even trying.

Ash came down as I was putting on my shoes. She was wearing an outfit I remembered giving a thumbs up to when she brought it home: a wide-necked, rough-edged T-shirt and an acid-wash jean skirt that ended just above her knees.

"Everything you wear is saying something," I'd told her. "And it should say, 'If you want something from me, you'd better kiss my ass.'" When she'd first started dressing as the new Ash, almost two years ago, she'd looked uncomfortable in her skin. Now she wore the clothes like they were a part of her.

She paused at the bottom of the stairs with a pensive expression, her arms folding in front of her. Her thumb rubbed over the inside of her arm as if by instinct. My chest tightened. I dawdled so we headed out together.

"Mr. Blythe had a talk with me yesterday," I said. "Has he been bugging you too?"

Ash shrugged. "He gave me a pamphlet—this arts school in Richmond. It's the same one Gabrielle goes to."

Gabrielle, who used to come over and play guitar while Ash sang. Who'd stopped talking to her after Ash quit choir and hooked up with a cooler crowd.

"So what do you think?" I asked, as if this were something we were actually considering.

"What would be the point? He doesn't get that I'm not into that stuff anymore."

She looked down, her hair falling across her face. I didn't like that hint of uncertainty.

"You can go for it if you think you're ready."

"No way. Who needs it—everyone acting all artsy and sensitive when there are just as many jerks there as any other school? It's not like I'd get anywhere with music anyway. If I want to sing, I can do it on my own, no worrying what anyone else thinks."

That last bit was what I'd wanted to hear, but the line about it not getting her anywhere set my teeth on edge. After all this time, that asshole's words were still echoing in her head.

Ash *had* been good—like, someday-going-pro good. The problem was how much of herself she put out there to be that good. Scribbling down lyrics straight from her heart to the page, no distance, no defenses. Nothing to protect her when the guy she'd crushed on all year listened to the song she'd written for him and laughed in her face. Got his friends to quote the lyrics mockingly back at her. Nudged them and snickered whenever he'd passed her in the hall.

The truth was, I hadn't noticed anything was off. My introspective little sister had just gotten even more introspective. But she'd been hurting herself for months before the day I accidentally walked in on her in the bathroom and caught her with the nail scissors clutched in her shaking hand, etching little lines of blood on her arm.

She hadn't stopped shaking the whole time she was pouring out the story. "I tried to talk to the school counselor, but she said if he's stopped, I should just stop thinking about it," she'd said between sobs. "But I can't. Why would he do that? What's *wrong* with me?"

That was what killed me the most. She'd blamed herself instead of the jerk.

What if I hadn't walked in right then? How much further would she have taken it? Thinking about that made me feel sicker than Davey had looked yesterday.

"Is everything okay?" Ash asked.

I shook myself back to the present. "Sure. I'm just thinking everyone better watch out next year, with you ruling the school when I'm gone."

She laughed and blushed a little. There. I'd fixed her, hadn't I? I was making sure she'd be too tough to let anything mess her up like that again.

We parted ways at the school doors. I dropped off Davey's sick note at the office—the secretaries never looked too hard at those—and found Vicky waiting by my locker. She leaned in for a kiss.

"Hey," she said. "How's Davey doing?"

"He seems stable." Stable in a pretty crappy state, that was. How long were those test results going to take to come in?

A movement down the hall caught my eye. Ash's friend Sofia was standing by the drinking fountain in a billowy black shirt-dress that only made her arms and legs look thinner. She was watching me.

Right. I'd told her, *Tomorrow*. My heartbeat kicked up a notch.

Vicky tugged the collar of my shirt straight with an affectionate smile, oblivious. I hesitated.

What she didn't know wasn't going to hurt her. It wasn't like I made a habit of two-timing—I was doing this for Davey's benefit. It was one concrete thing I *could* do right now.

"Sorry about my stomach," I said, though it hadn't made a sound. "I was up so late researching symptoms and antibiotics I slept in, no time for breakfast. And I've still got to finish up that lab report."

"Aw, you poor thing." Vicky pecked my cheek. "How about I go grab a snack from the corner store for you?"

"Seriously? You're the best, Vick."

She squeezed my hand and set off down the hall. I caught Sofia's gaze and motioned toward the stairwell.

The staff restroom in the basement was never left locked. I tested it gingerly—it's always possible an actual staff person might be using it—and stepped inside without looking back.

Sofia pushed past the door a few moments later. She'd

tucked her bobbed hair behind her ears in a childish way that contrasted with the crimson lipstick on her mouth. It gave her a little-girl-playing-dress-up quality that wasn't really my thing, but I wasn't here to dispense fashion advice.

"I don't have a lot of time," I said. "You wanted something?"

She lifted one shoulder in a careless half-shrug. "You," she said. She was trying her best to sound confident, but the little tremor in her voice gave her nervousness away. "I want you."

Even if she was far more Davey's type than mine, I got a thrill out of those words. I smiled and leaned past her to slide the deadbolt into place.

"Okay," I said, close enough to breathe in her sugary perfume. "You've got three minutes of me. Better make it worth it." I stepped even closer, like a dare.

She blinked and then bobbed up on her feet to kiss me. So of course I kissed her back.

I'd come up with this plan last month, when I'd gotten a little more drunk than usual at the party Ash had thrown while our parents were off in Paris for their anniversary, and noticed Sofia watching my every move. I'd given her a few minutes in a secluded corner then, and she'd been even more stuck on me since.

It wasn't like she was in love with me—she hardly knew me. Just a minor infatuation. She got to make out with the guy she was lusting after. I got to make out with a cute girl. When the time was right, I'd tell her how little any of this meant to me and send Davey in to soothe her wounded feelings.

After Sofia had gotten over any illusions she'd had about me, what could be better for her than an awkwardly goofy guy who actually liked the idea of getting sweet on someone? And Davey wouldn't hit the college scene as a guy who'd never been kissed outside of a game of Truth or Dare. Heck, maybe *they'd* fall in love and be set for life. It was genius, pure and simple.

But it'd only work if Davey got better. The image of him pale and shivery popped into my head, and suddenly I was noticing the aftertaste of cheap coffee in Sofia's mouth and the bumps of her ribs through the thin fabric of her dress.

She felt almost as fragile as he'd looked. My stomach turned. I drew back and popped the deadbolt.

"Time's up."

Sofia stared up at me. She let go of my shirt, her cheeks flushing. When she reached for her tote bag, it tipped over, spilling binders and textbooks onto the floor. I knelt down to help shove them back in.

"Sorry," she said, blushing deeper. "Big test first period. Mr. Shorney scares me."

"Oh, you don't need to worry about him," I said. "Shorney's completely obsessed with patterns. Just relate everything you talk about to some other historical period, and he'll cream himself even if it's not one hundred percent accurate."

"Oh. Awesome. Thanks!" She ducked her head and darted out the door.

I rubbed the traces of that red lipstick off my face. She and Davey really would be the perfect summer romance: a couple of neophytes learning the ropes. All was well that ended well.

Dad's motorcycle was standing in the driveway when I made it home after school. I suppressed a groan and went in.

He was standing by the living room window, a Mike's Hard dangling from one hand.

"Hey, Dad," I said. "Did they finally fire you?"

He took a swig from the bottle and turned toward me. "Not yet, surprisingly enough. I did get called into the V.P.'s office for another rant about my 'creative interpretations' of company policy." He made air quotes with his fingers and grinned. He'd passed forty a couple years back, but he still had this rakish air that made it obvious why Mom had fallen for him, and maybe why she'd stuck around through all the other girls who'd fallen for him since.

His eyes slid back to the window. "I got an idea for a song just after lunch. Told the manager I had a client house call to make and skedaddled."

I would have asked why he wasn't in the studio hammering it out, but I didn't really care. Dad had his fantasy that he was still some hotshot yet underappreciated songwriter, like Mom had her fantasy that she was the great woman behind the great man. It rarely paid off to try to shake up their preferred flavor of melodrama. So I just said, "Cool," and started for the stairs.

"Hey, Max," Dad said, "is there any particular reason I ran into Davey upstairs a couple hours ago? I think he's still in your room."

Crap. At least I'd been anticipating this possibility since the moment I saw his motorcycle.

"Oh, that." I rolled my eyes. "Davey had a little 'misstep' with a girl he was messing around with who's in a bunch of his classes. We figured it'd be best to give her a day of cooling off time before he comes face-to-face with her again. You know how chicks are."

Dad nodded sagely. "Sometimes that's just what you've got to do." He raised his bottle to me. "Tell him good luck."

"I will."

When I opened my bedroom door, Davey was sprawled on top of the sleeping bag, his eyes closed and his mouth slightly open. The bowl of soup on the floor was empty, which meant at least he'd eaten something. One of the controllers for my old Nintendo system was lying on the corner of the sleeping bag. I guessed he'd been keeping himself entertained too.

He couldn't be feeling *that* bad then. I leaned over to poke his shoulder. "Hey, Davey, wakey—"

Before I'd even touched him, his eyes popped open. He jerked upright, and his hand lashed out to shove my arm away. Pinpricks of pain bloomed on my wrist.

He sat there blinking at me while I stared back at him. I glanced down at my arm. Three thin lines of blood were welling up where his nails had scraped my skin.

"Holy shit," he said. "Did I do that? I was just—I must have been having some dream…"

"Okay." I laughed even as I held my body perfectly still. "Note to self: next time wake up Davey with a bucket of cold water thrown from across the room. And note to Davey: trim your fingernails, man."

"Yeah." He examined his hands. The nails didn't look

much longer than their usual bitten-to-the-quick state. Maybe I *had* startled him out of a nightmare.

"How are you feeling?" I said.

"Less pukey. Not great though. But I got a call from the clinic. No signs of infection or anything else abnormal, they said."

"Well, maybe it is just the flu." If it was something worse, we were obviously on our own, but I'd figured as much. "Jena's dad told her what antiviral meds are good for a severe case of that. Exactly how are you feeling not great?"

Davey frowned. "Hot. Like a fever. A little achy all over. I guess that's all standard flu stuff. It's definitely better than yesterday."

The scratches on my wrist were still stinging. "That's it? Nothing weird?"

He looked at me quizzically. "Weird like what? I'm sick. It's not going to feel normal."

I opened my mouth and closed it again, making myself shake my head sheepishly. If I kept pushing, I was only going to look like an idiot.

"Then I'll get Reuben to pick up the antivirals." They'd tackle any weirdo viruses the clinic's tests wouldn't have picked up too, at least. I reached for a change of subject. "Hey, that girl I found for you, everything's just about ready."

"Yeah?" Davey said, with less enthusiasm than I expected.

"She's completely your type. Dark hair, big eyes, waifish. All you'll have to do is swoop in and heal her broken heart."

"Yeah, yeah. You make it sound so easy. What's her

name?"

"Sofia."

"Hmmm." His eyes brightened. "I like that. Sounds Spanish, or Italian, or something." Then he shuddered. Before I could ask if he was okay, my phone rang.

My expression when I checked the screen must have said everything. Davey's shoulders tensed. "It's my dad, isn't it? Shit."

He shifted as if to start rolling up his sleeping bag, moving like a guy preparing for a walk down death row. I waved him still. He wasn't in any condition to go back into the line of fire.

"It's fine. I'll handle it."

I pressed the Talk button with the phone a good inch away from my ear. Mr. Reeve's voice had no volume control, and it was only worse when he was in a bad mood. "Hello?"

Even his breath was loud, crackling over the line. "Max? I'm looking for David. He hasn't been home the last two days."

Thankfully, the school schedule offered me the perfect excuse. "Oh, hey, Mr. Reeve. Yeah. Some seniors went on a camping trip this week to do biology field work. Davey was on that. I bet he forgot to remind you. He forgot just about everything he was supposed to bring except his sleeping bag, to tell you the truth." I winked at Davey, who was braced on said sleeping bag.

A closet door squeaked. "The school should have notified me about this."

"The permission forms went home a while in advance. I think it was the day I was over and you were heading off for some special work dinner? You probably had a lot on your mind."

Davey's dad would rather have eaten his own hand than admitted to blanking on signing his son up for a five-day trip. My little memory jog contained just enough reality to sell the story.

"Right," he said after a moment's pause. "I would've told him to put it on the calendar. Should've known he wouldn't bother. That kid is such a screw up."

My jaw clenched. "He tries."

"Yeah, sure he does. Thank you, Max."

Davey sagged against the side of the bed as I hung up. I exhaled sharply. "There. He's off your back for the rest of the week. But now that my dad's seen you, I don't think staying here is a good idea. Would you mind crashing at Reuben's?"

A hitch of a laugh escaped my best friend. "Anywhere's better than home."

I don't think any of us was sure how Reuben managed to afford his own place, even a cramped first-floor-and-basement apartment where the utilities rarely functioned all at the same time. When his mom had gotten a job offer in Phoenix last fall, Reuben had declared himself unwilling to leave and moved in with Crystal, who'd graduated last year. She worked the night shift at a laundromat, and the two of them dealt, but they inhaled so much of their inventory they must have been barely scraping by. That never seemed to bother Reuben, though.

When Crystal let me and Vicky in Friday after school, he was sitting on the sagging couch next to Davey, gesturing wildly while Davey laughed. Jena was leaning against the ancient radiator by the window. The fan whirring beside her took a slight edge off the heat.

Crystal flopped into a wicker chair and nudged one of her gerbils in the cage on the crate that acted as an end table.

"Check him out." Reuben motioned to Davey. "Good as new, right?"

"Looks like." I gave Davey a thumbs up. Between the rest and the antivirals Reuben had scored, he'd been more himself every time I'd come by.

Jena gave me a pointed look. I pretended not to notice, ducking my head to kiss Vicky on that place under her ear that produced the perfect breathy giggle. Then I patted her on the back. "Why don't you tend to your 'patient'?"

Vicky squeezed onto the couch. Davey didn't even blush when she touched his forehead to check his temperature. I guessed after she'd cradled his head while he was bleeding and watched him puke, he'd realized there wasn't much worse she could see and gotten over his shyness.

Jena sidled up beside me. "So what do you think?" I said. I'd asked her to stop by so I wasn't relying on just my own judgment. The scratches on my wrist were just little trails of scabs now, and I hadn't seen any other reason to worry since, but I couldn't completely shake a lingering uneasiness either.

She frowned. "He does look like he's recovering. This is going to sound strange, though. I don't remember his hair being that dark."

"They're so cool," Vicky was saying.

Davey grinned. "Of course, why wouldn't I? Hey,

Reuben, you got a piece of paper and a pen?"

I eyed him as he bent over with the pen. His hair had always been a sort of dull dun brown, but now it did look… richer, or something.

"It could be just that his face is paler than usual. More contrast."

"That makes sense," Jena said, but she was still frowning. "This probably doesn't matter anymore, but I did find out there's a sort of museum of the supernatural a couple towns over. The people who run it might have some useful info, if we end up needing it."

"Here's hoping we don't."

Davey filled in a few final details and handed the paper over to Vicky. She leapt up. "This is awesome. Thank you! Look, Max."

The drawing was Davey's usual style, sparse and cartoonish, but as always he'd managed to capture enough of the people so anyone could tell who he'd drawn. Vicky was standing on her toes to kiss my cheek, her eyes closed and her hair falling in waves down her back. I had my arm around her, but I was facing forward, my gaze directed out of the page. A crown sat crookedly on my head, and my mouth curved with a cocky smile.

I glanced up at Davey with one eyebrow lifted. When our eyes met, his lips curled into a smirk.

I blinked, and the smirk was gone. Davey lowered his head bashfully as Vicky thanked him again. But every hair on my body was standing on end.

"I'm going to put it in my locker." Vicky glanced at her watch and made a face. "Aw, I'd better go. I'm supposed to be meeting my Spanish tutor in fifteen minutes."

Jena straightened up. "I should get going too."

Vicky looked at me, but my skin was still creeping. Davey was due to go home tomorrow at the latest. I should make sure he was completely ready.

"I'm going to hang out here a while," I said. "Good luck with the Spanish."

7

Davey stretched his arms out on the back of the sofa and then brought one hand to his belly. Its gurgle reached my ears from across the room.

"Man, I'm hungry." He looked bewildered. Considering how his stomach had been treating him lately, I wouldn't be surprised if he'd forgotten what it was like to want to put food in it.

"I'll order some pizzas," I said.

Crystal let the gerbils run around on the floor a bit, Reuben cackling every time he blocked one of them from scurrying under the sofa. When the pizzas arrived, Davey wolfed down six slices of meat lovers. Making up for lost time, I guessed.

Reuben got out a joint. I brought it to my mouth without inhaling each time it passed my way. He talked about the freaky new pills his supplier was promising, and we all discussed the best set-up for the big graduation party I'd throw. Somewhere in there I decided Davey really was okay and didn't say anything when he got ahold of the second joint a few times.

"You want to crash here for the night, Max?" Reuben asked after it'd been dark a few hours.

"Yeah," I said. "Thanks, Rube. I'm not sure I'm up for the walk home."

Davey was already sprawled on the couch, his head propped up on his hand, his eyelids drooping. I relaxed in the chair across from him while Reuben and Crystal look their turns in the apartment's single bathroom. Davey's head bobbed down until it touched the arm of the couch.

"You should bring Ash next time you come," he said in a spacey, half-asleep voice.

"Yeah?" I said easily. "Why's that?"

"Be good to see her. And hear her. Wish she'd sing that song more."

I kicked the side of the couch. "Ash doesn't sing anymore, lame-brain."

"Sure she does. You know, that one, 'the lights come on when you…'"

The one she'd written for the jerk in eighth grade. Davey must have grabbed the joint more times than I'd noticed. "That was two years ago, bud."

"Just a few months," Davey mumbled. "You went out to get drinks. She didn't know I could hear her from the hall. Think that was when I knew it…"

"Knew what?" I shifted forward, but all that came out of his mouth was a whistled snore.

"The john's yours," Reuben hollered.

I nodded, but didn't get up. Footsteps creaked down the basement stairs to the bedroom, and I looked at Davey.

He'd asked about Ash at the party. I'd seen him checking her out, but I'd thought it was a momentary thing. Maybe it hadn't been the first time.

I pressed the heels of my hands against my forehead. My best friend ga-ga over my little sister? Davey could hardly look after himself half the time. Sure, he'd never hurt Ash on purpose, but accidentally…

She'd gone through enough crap already. She shouldn't be anyone's training wheels.

I heaved myself to my feet. I might not have been stoned, but it was late, and I was tired. Maybe this would all look better in the morning.

When I woke up, Reuben's bedroom door was still closed, but the mid-morning sun was streaming through the grimy window over the washing machine. I rubbed the musty smell of the laundry room futon from my nose and headed upstairs.

The couch held nothing but a warped impression of Davey's body. Water was gurgling through the pipes in the bathroom. I ambled into the kitchen.

Whoever was in the bathroom had been frying up some bacon. The greasy pan sat on the stove next to the half-empty package, the temperature off but the strips still sizzling. They looked perfectly done, crispy but not quite crunchy. Absently, I reached to pick one up—

A blur of motion slammed into me, solid as a Humvee. I hit the floor hip-first, so hard my teeth jarred against my lip. My attacker fell with me. His fingers dug into my shoulder, his elbow jabbing my side. I shoved at him as I squirmed onto my back, and found myself staring into Davey's startled eyes.

At least, they should have been Davey's eyes. They were in his face, right where they were supposed to be. But Davey's eyes were a muddy hazel: not quite brown, not quite gray. The ones I was looking into now gleamed so light they were almost yellow. I flashed back to the beast-thing's face, the golden animal eyes peering out amid a man's features, and flinched.

Davey released my shoulder. I jerked away, and he dropped back onto his butt, off of me. The taste of blood prickled across my tongue. My breath was raw in my throat, as if I'd just run a mile.

"What the fuck was that?" I snapped.

I knew even as I asked the question that I was screwing up. I should keep cool, not show how freaked out I was. But I *was* freaked, and the words burst out.

Davey's hands flexed. He looked back toward the bathroom and then at me again.

"I— You were taking my bacon. I saw you, and suddenly we were on the floor. I didn't mean to." He glanced down at himself with a bewildered expression. "I didn't know I *could* do that. Whoa."

In the time he was talking, I recovered my wits. It wasn't his fault. He hadn't been in control, uneasy as that made me feel.

I bumped his arm with my fist and got up, like it wasn't a big deal after all. "Well, next time you get possessive about your breakfast, try talking it out first, all right?"

Davey sat there frowning for a few seconds longer. He

hauled himself to his feet.

"You know, the last couple days… Sometimes I've felt totally okay, but sometimes it's like I'm not totally in my head."

I swallowed. "You probably shouldn't've been smoking up last night. Some weird interaction with the meds, of course it'll throw you for a loop." But I didn't believe it was just that, not even slightly. "If there's something else going on, we'll figure it out," I added. "We already got you mostly healed up."

Davey's face cleared. "Yeah. Right. I guess it was kind of dumb going for the pot already." He laughed and grabbed a piece of bacon out of the pan.

I went over to the fridge. By the time I'd dug out a couple slices of leftover pizza, the pan was empty. Davey's hand went for the open package. He lifted a wobbly raw strip, dropped it straight into his mouth, and reached for another.

My stomach lurched. "Davey."

"Sorry, man." He gulped down the second strip and nudged the package toward me. "I feel like I haven't eaten in days. You want some?"

"Nah," I said, fighting to keep my voice even. "I'm good with the pizza."

To my relief, he sealed up the package and tossed it back into the fridge. "You know," I said, "it usually tastes better cooked."

The look he gave me was puzzled. "Well, yeah."

He hadn't even noticed what he was doing. He probably wouldn't believe me if I told him.

Yesterday, I'd let myself think he was pretty much back to normal. But none of this was normal at all. What if he lashed out at his dad? Mr. Reeve might kill him—literally. I'd seen how pissed he could get when Davey said one word he took as an argument.

"Hey," I said. "I think you should take it easy here at least a couple more days. You're obviously not totally yourself yet. You don't want to screw up your recovery."

"But my dad."

I shrugged. "I'll make up a new story. It's all under control. Maybe you should stay out of school a couple more days too. I can take care of your assignments a little longer. Better to avoid a repeat of Monday's puke performance."

"Yeah." He flushed. "Crap. I almost forgot."

"So let's not remind everyone. You chill out, we'll make sure you're one hundred percent, then you head back to the front lines."

"It's not like I really want to hang out in class anyway."

"We couldn't be friends if you did." I grinned, feeling like I'd averted a crisis. But only temporarily, and I wasn't even sure what kind of crisis it was.

The gravel rattled against the jeep as Jena pulled into the otherwise empty lot in front of a ramshackle building. The shingles along the edge of the roof were warped, and the mottled gray siding looked like it'd been yellow once upon a time. A wooden sign announcing the place as the Repository of the Unknown dangled above the doorway from two rusty chains.

"Here we are." Jena made a face. "I can't believe we're

doing this."

"Jena," I said, and waited until she met my gaze. "If you think I'm being ridiculous, you have to tell me. But I spent all yesterday after I got back from Reuben's looking for a medical condition that fits all Davey's symptoms, and there wasn't anything that covers even half of them. And we already know it wasn't anything a blood or urine test will pick up."

She sighed. "I couldn't find anything either. And my dad wasn't any help."

"Do you really think it's possible some unnatural *thing* out there bit Davey and infected him with whatever it is? Or are you just humoring me?"

A little laugh jolted out of her. "I wouldn't drive across the state just to avoid telling you you've gone bonkers. I've been thinking about it a lot and... I don't think it's *imp*ossible."

I let out my breath. An uncomfortable weight settled on my gut. "Then this is what we're left with. If Davey needs some weird supernatural cure, we've got to figure out what that is sooner rather than later."

"Right." She shoved open her door, and I followed suit.

The drone of an air conditioning unit filled the dim space we stepped into. Beyond the spindly wooden entry desk, glass display cases scattered the scarred floorboards. A yellowed page of calligraphy hung next to a mounted head of what I'd have thought was a regular possum. A clay statue with a grimacing face loomed over a row of jars holding twisted forms in clear liquid.

A dank, tangy smell like lemon cleaner that'd gone bad

tingled into my nose. Were we going to get any actual answers here, or was this just a conspiracy fanatic's paradise?

My doubts burrowed deeper when a woman emerged from the depths of the room. Her posture was slouched and a multitude of box braids swayed around her pinched face, violet and crimson threads woven through the blonde strands. The colors matched her baggy patchwork blazer. Her hands were shoved deep in two of its at least a dozen pockets. The collar shifted with her strides, revealing a sinewy red snake tattoo that wound around her neck.

It wasn't hard to believe she ran this place. She came to a stop on the other side of the desk and said in a breathy voice, "Welcome to the Respository of the Unknown! Entrance is five dollars each."

Okay, if she was as close as we could get to an expert, maybe I was bonkers after all.

Jena nudged me. We were here now.

I summoned some enthusiasm along with my cash. "Did you put this collection together? It looks pretty amazing."

"I did. This museum represents many years of work." Her gaze narrowed. "Please be careful of the artefacts. They should be treated with proper respect."

I held up my hands. "No problem. Actually, we mostly wanted to talk with you. We're working on a school project on how supernatural ideas intersect with reality, and I was hoping we could get an authority on the subject to weigh in."

"Of course," she said, brightening a little. "I'm happy to help. Here, take my business card so you can properly source me."

The textured ivory card she handed me identified her as Claire Nichols, Ph.D., anthropologist of the supernatural. I hadn't known they gave doctorates in that subject, but sure.

We meandered past the desk. "We're mostly interested in human transformations," I said. "You know: vampires, werewolves, zombies, that kind of thing." Not that the beast I'd seen had exactly looked like any of those. Not that anything *here* looked remotely connected to it.

"You must be familiar with the classic stories. Vampires sleeping in coffins, werewolves transforming under the full moon?" Dr. Nichols pointed to a preserved human hand—large and hairy. "A church in France had this for centuries, supposedly cut from a wolf-man. And Chinese sorcerers wrote up this incantation to raise the dead." She indicated a tattered scroll.

"What about modern-day accounts?" Jena asked. "Or are there any of those?"

"Oh, yes, I keep track of modern encounters as well. I could bring out some of the albums..." She paused, her gaze flicking over us. "I'm not sure all of the material is appropriate for kids."

I restrained myself from rolling my eyes. "We're both eighteen. I can show you I.D. if you want." My real one, even.

"Well, I guess it's fine then."

She ducked into a back room, and Jena leaned closer to me. "Do you think we should tell her?"

"I don't know," I murmured. "I get the impression she might see Davey as a research specimen rather than a person."

Dr. Nichols emerged carrying a few old-fashioned

photo albums, which she set on top of one of the lower display cases. Her voice became even more animated as she flipped one open. "This one has my most recent findings. The accounts are always from victims or witnesses of attacks."

She motioned to clippings and computer print-outs of articles and photographs: A young woman with deep gouges slashed across her face. A close up of bloody fang marks on a pale neck. An elderly man whose torso appeared to have been wrenched right in half, only the intestines connecting the segments. My gut lurched. *That* all looked awfully real.

"In each of these cases, people claimed the attacker was a monster, either conventional or one they couldn't name," she went on. "The creatures themselves haven't been caught to verify, obviously. Even when someone tries to take a photograph, they're always blurry."

The memory of the beast-thing charging off into the shadows swam up in my head. "The things move too fast?" I suggested.

Dr. Nichols made a humming noise. "People often report unnatural speed and strength, yes. It's also that the attacks generally happen at night or in secluded areas, where visibility is difficult and there are few people, if anyone, around to intervene. Even skilled professionals find it hard to react effectively to an unexpectedly animalistic attack from a fellow human being."

Her hand stilled over a page that showed two men in military uniforms sprawled in a pool of blood, one's head tipped back as the gaping slit on his throat formed a second mouth. A rifle that looked as if it'd been bent in half lay beside his limp hand.

The air conditioning's chill pierced right through me. Fuck, that was brutal.

Jena's lips had gone pale and tight, but being Jena, she kept on track. "You said it's always victims and witnesses... Doesn't anyone ever report they're worried *they're* turning into a monster like that, or that someone they know is?"

Dr. Nichols chuckled, her neck tattoo twitching, and my back tensed.

"The killers aren't in any hurry to brag," she said. "We do see reports from people afraid they're in process sometimes."

"So how do those people get help?" I asked. "Are there cures or treatments or whatever?" With all the research she'd been doing, she *had* to know something useful.

She flicked her braids over her shoulder. "Well, you have the traditional approaches. Garlic to fend of vampirism, wolfsbane for werewolves, iron for faerie creatures, and so on. But realistically, you're going to be talking psychological interventions."

Jena's forehead furrowed. "Psych interventions?"

"Of course. Obviously none of those people are *actually* turning into monsters. Human beings can pull off bizarre feats or horrible acts without any obvious reason, and then people turn to paranormal explanations as a way to cope or to cover up the truth." Dr. Nichols twittered and closed the album.

Wait, what? This time her laugh hit me with a jab to the gut. "But when there are *that* many people reporting things —" I started.

She shook her head. "Stories of supernatural creatures

take root in our collective consciousness because we're fascinated by the inexplicable. Facts wouldn't haunt us the same way. Besides, a lot of the time the situation is such a mess you can't discern the facts in the first place, at least not enough that they would reassure the victims."

I stared at her for a second before I caught myself. My heart had plummeted. Even *she* didn't believe in any of this? Was it all just a fun little pastime then, gawking at people's messed-up corposes and snickering at how ridiculous their stories were?

It was a good thing we hadn't mentioned Davey. She'd probably have laughed in our faces. And then sent us all off to the looney bin.

"So you don't think there could be any truth to those stories at all?" Jena said hesitantly.

"Truth is subjective. But do I think there are monsters stalking us in the night? That would be a stretch." Dr. Nichols paused, and her tone turned cajoling. "Why am I starting to think you two have a story?"

Every nerve in my body balked. I made myself chuckle. "No way. I wish we did!"

The creature I'd seen hadn't been imaginary, and neither were Davey's symptoms. But maybe I should have known we were never going to convince anyone of that, not when I could hardly accept it.

Well, so what? We could still get what we'd come for.

I kept my voice breezy. "Anyway, for our project, would you mind going over the theoretical supernatural cures? The common ones *and* the rare ones. We want to be thorough."

8

So it turns out you can order wolfsbane on the internet, I texted to Jena as I ambled into the school. *Holy water too.*

I'm pretty sure you can buy ANYTHING on the internet, she wrote back. *How long will it take to get here?*

A few days. I paid for express. The stuff I can get locally I'll grab after school.

I hit send when I spotted Vicky in the hall. Between roadtrips and writing papers for two, I hadn't had much time for her lately. But her face lit up when she saw me. I owed her.

"Hey, beautiful." I tugged her in for a kiss. "What do you say we get out of this place for lunch, just the two of us? Maybe we can do something tonight too—I'll just want to check in on Davey first. He seemed kind of out of it again on the weekend."

"Really?" Her eyes widened with concern. "He looked fine when I saw him today."

I froze. "You saw him—here?"

"Sure. He was just heading in when I got here. I actually

thought he looked better than he normally does. More energetic or something."

I stepped away from her. "Well, in that case, I'd better catch him before class. There's something I need to ask him about. See you at lunch!"

I jogged to the hall where Davey had his locker. He was crouched down in front of it, fishing out one of his binders. He glanced up the second I saw him, as if he'd felt my gaze.

Vicky was right. He looked better than the usual Davey. His hair was rumpled, but in a way that appeared windblown rather than ungroomed. His muscles flexed as he straightened up—muscles I didn't remember existing in his scrawny arms. Those awful eyes tracked my approach, the yellowish tint to the irises making them almost seem to glow.

Two weeks ago I could have given him the eyebrow-raised, 'what the hell do you think you're doing?' expression I had on right now, and he'd have hunched his shoulders and dropped his gaze. Instead, he stood there calmly until I stopped a few feet away. Then his eyes twitched sideways, but only for a second.

"Hey," he said.

"Hey. I thought you were going to chill at Reuben's today," I said, leaving out the unnecessary, *like I told you to*.

"I've been feeling great since Saturday morning. You have no idea how boring it gets hanging with Reuben all day. It didn't seem fair to leave you doing all my work when I'm fine."

"Did you go back home then?"

"Nope." His mouth curled into a half smile more sly than anything I'd seen on Davey's face before. "No reason to put up with that asshole, right? Reuben said I can keep sleeping at his place until it's New York time, as long as I help him and Crystal shift their product now and then. So I called my dad last night and told him I'm out of there for good."

I could tell I was gaping at him, but I couldn't stop. "Just like that?"

The smile faltered. His voice would have sounded like regular old Davey again if it hadn't been for the words coming out of his mouth. "It wasn't that hard, you know, after I worked up the guts to do it."

I should have been happy for him. After all that time putting up with his dad's crap—the yelling, the put-downs, the bruises that by tacit agreement we never talked about— he'd finally freed himself.

Except I couldn't believe the Davey I knew, the Davey I'd grown up with, had summoned even half the nerve to tell his dad off out of thin air. Whatever had given him that boldness, it was the same thing that was sharpening his fingernails and drawing him to raw meat. The same thing that might turn him into a thoughtless, crazed thing like the beast that had attacked him. The bloody images from Dr. Nichols's album flashed behind my eyes.

He'd freed himself from his dad, but maybe because he was being taken over by something even worse.

I swung my bag around to pull out a folder. We'd find a cure that worked. Whatever that thing was, it wasn't stealing my best friend.

"I guess you can hand in your own assignments then." I passed him the folder. "History, critical thinking paper.

English essay. I made sure not to sound too smart, so they'll believe you actually wrote them."

I had to force my jokey grin, but Davey smiled back at me as he took the folders.

"Thanks," he said. "From here on, I'll be carrying my own weight."

"It wasn't a big deal," I said, but he shook his head.

"Sure it was. I'm going to pay you back for everything you did for me, Max. I promise."

I was a block from home that afternoon, pharmacy store purchases stashed in my backpack, when my phone rang. I snapped to alertness at the sound of Reuben's voice.

"Hey, Max! You have to watch this, man. Freakin' amazing."

"What's going on, Rube?"

"Can't explain it. You gotta see for yourself. I'm shitting myself, seriously. Davey's a freakin' superhero."

My stomach sank. What the hell was Davey doing now? "Okay, I'll be over in twenty," I said, and hung up.

I'd assumed I'd have a little more time to decide how to approach Davey next. I picked up my pace. There were a couple of things I could try without much prep, but I needed to stop by the house first.

I didn't see the figure sitting on the porch bench until I was halfway up the steps and he stood up. My heart flipped over before I recognized him.

I put on a smile, resisting the urge to grit my teeth. "Hi, Mr. Reeve. Surprise visit?"

Davey's dad didn't return the smile. He stalked across

the porch and glowered down at me, something he could only do because I was still on the steps. His striped dress shirt suggested he'd come from the office, but he hadn't shaved that morning. The shadow on his jaw was patched with gray, unlike the rest of his light brown hair.

Davey's hair used to be the same color. It *was* way darker now.

Mr. Reeve clapped his hands. "You know where my son is. And you're going to tell me, right now."

He thought so, did he? I drew my eyebrows together in innocent confusion. "He should've gotten home on the weekend. I saw him in school today."

"He's told me that he's staying at a friend's house," Mr. Reeve said. "I know your parents wouldn't put up with that, but it's got to be someone from your crowd. So who is it?"

"I don't know, honestly. If that's true, he hasn't told me."

Davey's dad let out a sharp huff. Then he came at me, so suddenly I stumbled backing down the steps. He grabbed the front of my shirt and yanked me to a halt, his knuckles jabbing my neck. His breath hit my face, hot and pickley smelling.

"Do you really think I'm going to believe that?" he demanded, his voice low. "I know the whole pull-the-wool-over-his-eyes routine. It's not going to work, you little shit. So stop dicking around and cough up a name and an address for me."

Holy fuck, Davey's dad had finally completely lost his marbles. I swallowed hard, my throat pinching at the pressure of his fingers.

"Or what?" I asked quietly. "Are you going to take a swing at me, Mr. Reeve? That's what used to work on Davey, isn't it? Except I'm shouting distance from my parents' house and in plain view of an entire street, and *I'm* not going to take it quietly."

His chest heaved, and his eyes narrowed further, but after a moment he let go of my shirt and eased back. I exhaled. How the hell had Davey managed to survive living with this guy twenty-four-seven? One way or another, he was tougher than anyone—including himself—gave him credit for.

"I'm his father," Mr. Reeve said. "I'm supposed to look after him."

Before, I never would have provoked him. But Davey had escaped; I didn't have to play nice for his benefit anymore.

"I guess he figured out you weren't doing such a great job of that," I said. "Good for him."

I dodged around Mr. Reeve and reached the door before he'd so much as turned around. I glanced back as I fished out my keys. His face had flushed red.

"You—" he started.

"Sorry." I twisted the key in the lock. "I've got a ton of homework to tackle. Have a good afternoon, Mr. Reeve."

I shut the door between us.

Inside, strains of violin and flute vibrated through the air. Ash was sitting on the living room couch, swaying with the melody, her eyes closed and her lips moving silently.

I raised my voice over the music. "Ash."

My sister's eyes popped open, and her mouth snapped

shut. Smiling crookedly, she leaned forward to turn down the volume on the stereo receiver.

"Sorry," she said.

My heart was pounding from my encounter with Davey's dad. I still had to get ready for my trip to Reuben's. "Why're you hanging out down here?" I said as I headed for the dining room cabinet. Ash trailed after me.

Upstairs, something thumped against the floor. Mom's voice filtered down. "I stood by you every step of the way. I've given everything I have. You should respect that!"

Ash winced and pointed upward. That answered my question. "What are you doing?" she said.

"Just grabbing a couple things." I tugged open one of the drawers and started pawing through. "What's this fight about?"

"I don't know. They were already in the middle of it when I got here. Probably the same old."

Text messages Dad had forgotten to delete, suspicious charges on the credit card bill, or simply gossip that had gotten around. Sometimes I thought Dad must want to get caught, that it was part of the thrill.

He was talking too low for me to hear more than a murmur of his voice, but he always made the same sorts of excuses. *I'm not the kind of man who can be tied down, Liz. You know I never have been. I've got to follow my moods where they take me. It doesn't mean anything. You're still my one true muse.*

Imagining it made me want to gag.

When the first drawer failed me, I moved to the next. "You could just take off."

Ash sighed. "Tonya's supposed to be coming over after detention so we can do this stupid science project. I don't want to look like a dork hanging around out front, and I won't hear the door in the backyard."

"Well, it'll be over soon. Always is." There: the box containing Mom's grandmother's antique silver cutlery. I jiggled open the box.

Ash looked at me sideways. "How can you just not care? You really don't, do you?"

I shrugged, shoving a butter knife into my back pocket. Then I tugged open my backpack. "Why should I?" I said. "It's got nothing to do with me. And they're obviously okay with this whole scenario, or they wouldn't play through it so often. It's just what gets them off."

As if to prove my statement, a different sort of thump carried through the ceiling, along with the rattle of the brass headboard. Mom squealed. I grimaced. I might not *care*, but hearing one's parents go at it is manifestly gross.

Ash hugged herself. "It bothers *me*. I hate hearing them fight. I know it'd be better if I didn't let it get to me, but it still does."

"Hey." I paused to squeeze her shoulder. "You've just got to keep working at it. You're still getting over that whole heart-on-your-sleeve thing. But you're doing really good."

"Yeah," she said. The word hung in the air, like there was more she wanted to say, but instead she drifted back to sink onto the couch. After a moment, her frown crept into a smile. "Emmett was trying to make up with me today. I told him to piss off. Like I'm so desperate for a guy I'd settle for him."

"Thatta girl." I dug out the circular mirror and the little bottle of witch hazel I'd bought. That was a start. I wasn't making it to Reuben's in twenty minutes anyway—I could make a quick detour on the way.

Common knowledge told me vampires hate garlic and don't show up in mirrors. Dr. Nichols had mentioned a cure for werewolfism involving striking the person on the forehead three times with a knife, and of course everyone knew about silver bullets, so I figured I might as well combine the two. The witch hazel, if I got the chance to use it, was supposedly a general curse breaker. I walked up to Reuben's front door carrying the equipment I'd brought from home and a pizza box: extra meat, extra garlic.

The door was unlocked, as usual. I pushed inside to the sound of something solid smacking into skin. Down in the basement, Reuben cheered.

"Yeah, man! That was the best one yet."

"Hey," I called down. "I brought pizza."

"Awesome!" Reuben yelled back. "Come down and check this out, and then we'll eat."

I found them in the bedroom. Reuben was setting an empty beer bottle on the steel shelving unit against the wall. Davey stood by the door. He was breathing hard, as if he'd just dashed up and down the stairs a few times, but he was grinning.

Reuben grabbed a ratty broom from the floor and jumped onto the mess of sheets on the bed. He bobbed there a couple of times, smiling even wider than Davey.

"What are you on, man?" I said.

He shook his head and chuckled. "Totally clean right now. This is the real deal. You ready?"

The last was to Davey, who nodded and flexed his hands.

"Here we go!"

Reuben whipped out the broom like a baseball bat. The bristled end connected with the beer bottle, and it dropped toward the concrete floor. I winced in anticipation of shattering glass—and somehow Davey was there, snatching the bottle up and tossing it onto the bed. He leapt to the other side of the room, so fast I swear he started to blur, just as Reuben swept a seashell-encrusted jewelry box off the dresser. Davey caught the box, chucked it on the bed, and shot back to the shelving unit where Reuben had sent a ceramic bowl toppling off. Reuben laughed like a little kid given free rein in a toy store.

"Rube!" I shouted as he aimed the broom at a tall, lit candle I'd only just noticed at the back of the dresser. He whacked it and spun around to hit the globe on the top of the shelving unit. The flame flared as the candle fell. I blinked, and it was teetering in Davey's hand as he dashed back to catch the globe in the curve of his other arm. He stood there gasping, his face flushed, still grinning. Reuben whooped and raised his arms in the air.

"I've gotta start taking some of those meds, if that's what they do for you." He bounced to the end of the bed and stepped off. "Have you ever seen anything like that, Max?"

I dragged in a breath, the air sharp in my throat. Of course I hadn't. A human being wasn't supposed to be able to move that fast. I thought of the beast-thing darting away through the trees, and a sour taste crept through my mouth. I rested my hand on the side of the now-empty shelving unit. The cool metal steadied me.

"Nope. Pretty freaking amazing, like you said."

Davey rolled the globe onto the bed with the other things he'd caught and blew out the candle. "I guess I don't have to worry about being last anymore, Max," he said as he set it back on the dresser.

His tone made my back stiffen. Without thinking, I let my hand slide to the back of the shelving unit, tested its weight, and pushed.

It was so tall and heavy I'm not sure I expected it to move at all. But it did. With a creak, it tipped forward and plummeted toward the bed.

Davey's head snapped around, and he sprang onto the bed. The metal rungs smacked straight into his hands. Grimacing, he shoved the shelves upright. They thumped back against the wall. He stood there on the mattress, rubbing his palms on the hips of his khaki shorts and looking down at me.

"Not bad," I said. "I wondered if you could manage it without the whole set-up." I kept my voice cool, but my pulse was thudding. If he could handle steel like that, what could he do to a person?

"No problem at all," Davey said. The excitement in his eyes had dimmed, replaced by a harder shine. "You want to try now, Max?"

"Nah, you can be the King of Catching Falling Objects. I'd rather have pizza."

"Hell yeah," Reuben said. "I'm starving."

We all trooped upstairs—Reuben in the lead, me in the middle, the back of my neck creeping with the feeling of Davey's gaze on me. We dug into the pizza, and he gulped down four slices without a hint of discomfort. Beast: 1, popular mythology: 0.

I followed him into the kitchen to grab a drink, taking out the mirror and setting it on the counter while I pretended to search my pockets for something. He glanced over, and his face wavered in the glass. Well, I hadn't really figured he was vampirish.

That left the silver knife. In other words, the hard part.

A few days ago, I might have simply asked him to let me try. But the sense that the guy before me was not quite Davey amplified with every movement. The twitch of his thumb popping the cap off the beer. The sardonic curve to his lips as he lifted the bottle to his mouth.

As soon as he knew what I intended to do, he could stop me, if whatever was *inside* my best friend wanted him to stop me. The element of surprise might make the difference between driving it out of him and failure. If I moved fast enough, I could probably get in three light taps on his forehead before he realized what I was doing.

I eased my hand to my back pocket as Davey leaned against the counter. Dr. Nichols had said another, at least temporary, cure for werewolfism could be saying the victim's name three times. Might as well throw that in too. Maybe the silver and the knife and the name all in combination would be the ticket, if there was something powerful about threes.

My fingers curled around the knife's handle. I slipped it out, holding it against my wrist to hide it. Then I reached as if to open the cupboard behind Davey's head.

At the last second, I jerked my arm toward him. The blunt edge of the blade dinged the skin above his left eyebrow.

"Davey—"

His hand shot out and clamped around my wrist before I could tap him even the second time. He wrenched my arm to the side.

"Davey, Davey," I finished lamely. At least I'd gotten one part of it done.

Davey was staring at me as if I were a total stranger who'd appeared in his best friend's place. "What are you *doing*?"

I chuckled, like it was nothing, like the tendons in my wrist didn't feel as if they'd snap if he squeezed any tighter. Cross name-three-times off the list.

"Just goofing around, man. Take a joke?"

His grip relaxed. He lowered my hand so he could see what I was holding and studied the knife.

"Is that silver?"

"I don't know. Could be, I guess."

His gaze slid back to my face. I braced myself for anger and suspicion, but what I got was worse.

Years ago, I'd been at Davey's house when he'd shown his dad the fifth-grade history project he'd done on ancient Egypt, the sketches he'd worked on for hours, that had earned him his first ever A. His dad had glanced at the posterboard, snorted, and said only, *It must have been your lucky day.*

Davey had looked at him the way he was looking at me

right now, startled and wounded.

Betrayed.

"What are you doing, Max?" he said quietly.

I opened my mouth, and the vulnerability washed out of his face like a wave sweeping by, leaving only cool, gleaming sand in its wake. He broke into a laugh.

"You're one crazy guy." Still snickering, he dropped my arm and sauntered back to the living room.

I stood there for a moment, gathering my composure. An uncomfortable certainty had settled over me like a cold fog.

Davey had guessed what I was doing, but the thing inside him didn't care. The part that did care—the part that was still the real Davey—he liked the speed and the strength and the cocky new attitude. Of course he did.

He didn't want me to change him back.

9

It's not like me to get spacey. I am on; I am with it; I am fully in tune with my surroundings at all times. But the next morning I found myself standing in front of my locker with no memory of anything between walking out the front door of my house and arriving there. I shook my head to clear it, and a soft voice beside me said, "Max?"

I glanced around my locker door. Sofia stood there with her arms crossed awkwardly in front of her.

She looked so *needy* that my gut clenched. At the uneasy sensation, my jaw clenched too. We'd barely spent five minutes total together. She had eyes—she knew I had a girlfriend. Did she really think a little fooling around was the start of some grand romance?

I turned away. "Yeah?"

"I was just thinking," she said, hesitantly, "my sister... She's been away at college, but she's coming home this weekend. She's having a big party Saturday night. It should be pretty wild. She said I could invite a bunch of people if I wanted."

"And you want to invite me."

She pulled herself up a little straighter. "Yeah. I think we'd have a lot of fun."

I raised my head, and my gaze caught on a figure at the far end of the hall. Dark hair, sharp chin, a flash of bright eyes aimed my way.

A second later he merged into the bodies milling around the stairwell, and I wasn't totally sure it'd been Davey. Even if it had been, of course he'd be at school again today. But my stomach listed as if the floor had just tipped.

"Max?" Sofia said.

I snapped my attention back to her. "You should be inviting your friends," I said. "I'm not one of them."

She smiled. "I wasn't thinking of you as my *friend*."

"I'm not your anything. There is no 'we' here."

"I know. I mean, I wasn't trying to—"

I hefted my bag over my shoulder and shoved my locker door shut. "Drop it, all right? I'm not in the mood for this right now."

I'd say her lower lip wobbled, but it was more like her entire face. She blinked a couple of times, her cheeks flushing. Then she turned and walked away.

I watched her go, the queasiness in my stomach sharpening. Not smooth at all, Max.

But maybe this was for the best. The state Davey was in these days, pushing Sofia his way no longer sounded like a good idea. She'd have been more than enough for the real Davey; beast-Davey might eat her alive.

Vicky came up beside me, slipping her fingers around my elbow. "What did she want?"

"She was wondering if I knew where Ash is," I said. "Have you seen Davey around?"

She shook her head. "He *is* okay now, right?"

"Oh yeah. He's great. Those meds Reuben picked up really did the trick."

There were a lot of anti-supernatural strategies I hadn't tried yet. One of them had to work. No matter how much Davey might be enjoying this metamorphosis right now, he couldn't be thinking it all the way through.

Davey only sauntered into the cafeteria when I was halfway through my lunch. As if to confirm my earlier thought about Sofia, a cute brunette who looked like a freshman was gabbing away with him. A couple of her friends ambled over, and suddenly he was chatting them all up. From their smiles, there was actual flirting going on.

I tried not to stare, but my gaze kept drifting back. For Davey, keeping his cool around a bunch of pretty girls was more incredible than the super-speed he'd shown off yesterday.

Any enthusiasm I'd had for my food evaporated. I shifted in my seat and glanced across the caf toward the table where Jena and Joss and their literary mag/art club gang was hanging out.

I'd texted Jena last night after I'd gotten back from Reuben's, but the only response I'd gotten was *Emergency situation?* and when I'd admitted it wasn't, *Not a good time. We'll talk at school tomorrow.*

Well, it was tomorrow now. I made myself scarf down the rest of my lunch and got up to squeeze around the tables to her corner. When I reached her, I touched her shoulder and leaned close.

"Got a minute to talk?"

Instead of ignoring me like usual, Joss glanced over and frowned. He didn't like me invading their group, maybe? I offered him my brightest smile as Jena shrugged off my hand and stood up. We stepped closer to the wall where we'd be less likely to be overheard. Joss's gaze followed us, approaching a glare now.

"What's up with your manpanion?" I asked. "He's giving me the death stare."

Jena made a face that looked like she was trying not to laugh and trying not to grimace at the same time.

"I told him. About you and me, that time at Tyler's aunt's chalet?"

I just about swallowed my tongue. "You *what*?"

It wasn't that I took issue with Joss knowing I'd hooked up with Jena once upon a time. No, after the few seconds that idea took to sink in, I kind of liked it, and the fact that it clearly bothered him. But Jena and I had spent so long acting like the hook-up had never happened that having her bring it up out of the blue knocked all my other thoughts off kilter.

The event itself had been pretty out of the blue. Over Christmas holidays our junior year, Tyler's aunt had given him free run of this posh four-bedroom ski chalet she owned near Bayse, so a bunch of us had gone up to ring in the new year. I hadn't been seeing anyone right then, but I hadn't minded. There'd been lots of girls who might be interested coming along.

Somehow after all the drinking and dancing and

streaking through the snow, at three a.m. Jena and I were the last two awake in the living room. We polished off a fifth of a bottle of coconut rum, which was the only thing halfway decent left, as we cackled at some old British comedy show on the TV. When the episode ended, Jena got up and wavered on her feet.

"Crap," she said. "I don't remember were I put my bag." And started giggling again.

"Scavenger hunt!" I said, which wasn't particularly funny but got her giggling even harder.

We picked our way around the sleeping bodies and swayed down the hall, trying doors as we went. We finally found her duffel in the second floor loft, which was still empty because apparently everyone else had been too drunk or too high to attempt the stairs. Jena gave a cry of victory when she spotted it and threw her arms around me.

We'd hugged before, but this time was different. She tipped her head forward so her lips brushed the bare skin by the collar of my shirt, and all I could think was I needed to feel that mouth against mine. So I teased my fingers into her hair and kissed her. And she kissed me back. And I wondered why the hell I'd gone all these years without ever trying this with her before.

I kissed her again and she slid her hands up under my shirt, and it felt so good it never occurred to me to stop.

It felt good until I woke up the next morning and opened my eyes to see her lying across from me on the bed. My head was thumping from last night's alcohol, but the first thought that popped into it was, *This is what I'd like to wake up to every day until I die.*

Then Jena opened her eyes to look into mine and said, "Well, that was kind of unexpected," with a tightness in her voice that made me tighten up inside too. Why was I getting mush-brained?

I sat up, and Jena slid out of bed to grab her sweater. She had a stiff little smile on, and her eyes hadn't left me for a second.

"Just the booze, right?" she said. "These things happen."

"Yeah," I said. "But hey, I wouldn't mind it happening again."

I grinned at her, but her smile didn't budge. She laughed, and that was stiff too. "Oh, no, I've seen what you're like. I'd like to be able to stay friends with you, if that's all right."

It had startled me how much, in that instant, it wasn't all right. How much I wanted to leap off the bed and beg her to give it a chance. Which was so ridiculous I didn't let myself keep thinking.

"Of course," I said. "I was kidding."

And until that moment in the cafeteria, neither of us had mentioned it since.

Jena looked at her feet and then back at me. "It just came up. I wasn't going to lie to him. He got a little weirded out about it, but it'll be fine. It's not like it meant anything."

"Right," I said, recovering my equilibrium. "Of course not."

"So what's up with Davey?"

I filled her in on Reuben's game and the failure of my attempted cures, and then nodded in Davey's direction. He had five girls clustered around him now—this one laughing, that one gazing at him through her eyelashes—and he was soaking the attention in with yesterday's sly half smile.

"Look at him now. Have you ever seen him talking with even one girl who looked like that without his face going red and his eyes getting all twitchy? He used to be hopeless."

"It is kind of weird," Jena said. "Though not really a bad thing."

At that moment, Ash walked by Davey's little harem. He must have said her name, because she glanced over and waved hello before rejoining her friends. My body tensed. I'd almost forgotten his sort-of confession.

"My best friend is turning into a monster," I said. "I'm pretty sure that's the definition of bad. You didn't see the thing that attacked him, Jena. There was hardly anything human about it."

"I know. I'm sorry." She rubbed her mouth. "The knife thing could still work, right? Maybe that's why he stopped you."

"The problem is how to do it *without* him stopping me."

Joss swooped in on Jena and slid his arm around her shoulders. I'd been so distracted by Davey's unDaveyness that I hadn't noticed him getting up.

"Still working out your 'werewolf problem'?" he asked, raising his eyebrows at me like I was a five-year-old babbling about the monster under my bed. A flush of heat spread up from my neck. I looked at Jena.

"You told him about *this*?"

It was worse than the other thing. The other thing was long over, and it'd only made Joss jealous. This was happening right now, and it gave him an excuse to keep thinking I was an idiot.

"He came over when I was in the middle of looking things up," Jena said, leaving unspoken what she'd said earlier: *I wasn't going to lie to him.* No, of course she couldn't have lied to Lover Boy to save me some face and to keep Davey's problems private, the way they should be. Who else might Joss tell, for a laugh?

"You do realize there've been multiple studies trying to prove the existence of the supernatural," Joss said, "and even the few that initially appeared successful have been discredited?"

"You do realize I don't give a shit what you think?" I snapped back without thinking. I took a breath and said more calmly to Jena, "I just wanted to brainstorm ways for trying out the other stuff Dr. Nichols told us. Think about it and let me know if you come up with any ideas." And then, because I had the feeling anything else I said would only make things worse, I headed for the doorway. It was almost time for class anyway.

I'd just stepped into the hall when someone jostled me. I looked over, and Davey grinned back at me. For a second, it felt like old times. Except I'd have been the one jostling Davey.

"Hey, man," I said. "I saw you working those freshmen. Nicely done."

His grin stretched thinner. "Guess I'm not so hopeless after all, huh?"

"I wouldn't say *hopeless*..."

But I had. To Jena, five minutes ago.

Davey had been on the other side of the cafeteria, with

hundreds of chattering people between him and me. There was no way he could have heard.

But then, there was no way he should have been able to catch that shelving unit yesterday either.

Those bright eyes were watching me. What else had I said? Or Jena? How long had Davey's ears been that good?

I forced out a laugh. "You've got to stop pulling new superpowers out of your ass. It's freakish."

"Or, you know, you could try not talking shit for five minutes here and there," Davey replied.

"Getting a little thin-skinned?"

"Nope. Just hearing things more clearly now. You'd better watch your mouth, Max." He poked me with his elbow, but there was an edge in his voice.

That was the first time I'd ever been happy to arrive at Mr. Peck's chemistry classroom.

⁜

The Pecker, as he'd been "affectionately" known for longer than I'd been around, was by far the jerkiest teacher in school. Rumor had it he'd failed to get the university position he wanted and had settled for teaching high school out of desperation. He certainly reacted to every instance of teenage stupidity as if it were a personal affront. But I'd rather have listened to him for a whole hour than continue my conversation with Davey a minute longer.

Since the Pecker had assigned seats instead of letting us pick, I was able to escape to the other side of the room, leaving my best friend at a safe distance. A few other kids were already sitting around the lab tables, but my partner hadn't shown up yet. I tossed my bag onto the table. Davey perched on his pedestal chair, his gaze unusually intense as he watched our classmates trickle through the doorway.

How far buried was the real Davey now? I wasn't sure I'd felt him in there at all. But he'd been within reach last night—I'd seen him. I just wished I knew how to pull him back out.

Well, even if she had blabbed to Joss, Jena wouldn't let me down. She'd come up with something, and I'd stew on it some more too. Maybe I could try the knife thing again if Davey was asleep?

I went through the motions of setting up the day's lab while my mind kept whirring away. I was just thinking how strangely quiet the Pecker was being when he barked out a name.

"David!"

My pulse hiccupped as Mr. Peck stalked to Davey's table. Where before Davey would have cowered or flinched, today he only gave a reptilian blink. Mr. Peck didn't seem to notice anything was odd.

"What on earth is this?" He gestured to the equipment on the table. The mousy girl who was Davey's partner cringed in her seat. Davey cocked his head.

"The apparatus for preparing acetic acid, like we're supposed to be setting up," he said.

The Pecker clicked his tongue against the back of his teeth. "Then perhaps you can explain to me why the sodium acetate is in the funnel and the acid in the flask.

Davey looked at his set up, at the instructions, and at the set up again. His confident expression had faded into confusion. In that moment, he looked like the Davey I knew.

"Do you realize what will happen if you switch the substances in this experiment?" Mr. Peck asked.

Davey shook his head.

"Absolutely nothing! Quick, there are a couple of extra sets. You'll need to start over."

As Mousy Girl started taking apart their original

apparatus, Davey headed to the front table to pick up another tray. Mr. Peck didn't even wait until he got back to start in on him some more.

"Perhaps after taking the week off you've forgotten how to read basic instructions. Twice as careful this time, please, if you can manage it."

"I was sick," Davey muttered, setting the tray on his table.

"Hmmm," the Pecker said, as if he didn't believe it.

Davey raised his eyes. "And everyone makes mistakes."

There was a challenge in his voice. Everyone heard it. The murmurs around the other tables halted; heads turned. I shifted forward, resting my feet on the floor, as if I'd really be able to intervene if things got bad. *No, Davey.*

Mr. Peck's eyes had narrowed. "Yes, but the ones with any brains learn from them and don't keep making them."

"So you're basically calling me a moron?" Davey said.

Even the Pecker looked a little taken aback to hear it put so baldly, but he recovered quickly. "I wouldn't need to if you didn't act like one. Now—"

It happened so quickly I hardly saw it. As Mr. Peck spoke, he jabbed his forefinger toward Davey, and Davey reacted in a split-second. He lunged forward, teeth bared, hands shooting out, and then the Pecker was stumbling backward. His face had blanched white. I couldn't tell whether Davey had actually shoved him or just scared him, but the expression he turned on Davey a moment later was murderous.

I had leapt to my feet, but Davey didn't need my help. He lowered his arms and smiled almost sweetly at Mr. Peck.

"No problem, sir. I'll head down to the office."

Before the Pecker had managed a word, Davey had picked up his backpack and sauntered out of the room, leaving the rest of us staring.

"I heard he broke two of the Pecker's ribs!" Reuben crowed. "He had to spend all night in the hospital or something."

"I'm sure Davey wouldn't have pushed him that hard," Vicky said. She'd insisted on coming along to Reuben's place to check on Davey after his first day in exile—since naturally the principal had suspended him after the Pecker incident.

"And if he had, he would've been more than suspended," I added. But Mr. Peck hadn't shown up for his classes today, which had started the rumor mill buzzing twice as loud.

"Oh, man." Reuben bobbed around on the sidewalk, more dancing than walking. "I wish I'd seen it. Slammin' the guy right in the chest!"

"Yeah. Brilliant." I could still picture the way Davey had smiled at Mr. Peck afterward. Even out here with the sun baking down on us, it gave me a chill.

I was pretty sure his reaction hadn't been some random burst of anger. He'd been planning to find an excuse to hurt Mr. Peck all along.

I tensed as we walked up to Reuben's door. Davey had seemed almost calm when I'd stopped there briefly yesterday evening, but withdrawn. A couple minutes after I'd shown up, he'd yawned, said he was wiped, and headed down to the futon. I didn't know what to expect today.

"Hey, Davey, enjoying the sweet life?" Reuben called as

we came in. No one answered. The fan stood silent by the half-open window, the still air thick with accumulated heat. The living room and kitchen were empty, and so was the laundry room. Crystal emerged from the bedroom, pulling a ratty robe around her.

"Have you seen Davey?" Reuben asked her.

She shook her head. "I was sleeping until five minutes ago."

We trooped back upstairs. "You don't think he would've gone home, do you?" Vicky said.

"Like his dad wasn't pissed off enough before the suspension? Not unless he was looking for trouble." Which, I supposed, was possible. I dragged in a breath. "He probably just went for a walk or something."

"I bet he'll come around soon," Reuben said. "We can hang until then."

He turned on the TV and flipped through the channels. After a few minutes, Crystal returned from her shower, rubbing her spiky black hair with a towel. She perched on the arm of the couch next to Reuben. Then she stiffened.

"Did you let Jon and Tyrion out again?"

"Huh?" Reuben said.

She picked up the gerbil cage. "They're not in here. Reuben, I told you to leave them alone when I'm not around. You remember how long it took to get them out of the walls last time."

"I haven't touched the cage since then," Reuben said, sounding petulant. "You must've forgotten to close it."

"Well, then the door would still be open, wouldn't it?"

Vicky got to her feet. "Let's start looking. Finding them

is the important thing, right?"

Crystal and Reuben stomped down to the basement, still bickering, and Vicky started lifting the couch cushions. I wandered into the kitchen. "Here, gerbil gerbil gerbil," I said into the cupboard under the sink. Nothing was down there but dish soap and mildew.

As I stood up, a shadow shifted in the alley outside the kitchen window. I stopped and peered out.

A neighbor's oak tree leaned over the fence that separated their patio from the cracked concrete slab where Crystal parked her Vespa. A figure stood in the shade it cast, his face turned away, brown hair and gray clothes blending into the pavement. I wouldn't have noticed him if he hadn't moved. But now that I had, it was unmistakably Davey. Something in my chest twisted.

I eased open the back door, but it squealed like a dying pig. Davey glanced back, showing a flicker of pale face. He'd turned away again by the time I'd stepped out. The heat there was thinner but sharper. A faint breeze tickled past me, raising the hairs on my arms.

"What're you doing out here, Davey?" I said. "Reuben's wanting to congratulate you. You scared the Pecker so bad he didn't even show up today."

He gave a chuckle: a short, thick sound. "I needed a little space."

I took another step toward him, and my gaze caught on a small red smear shining wet on the concrete by the edge of the oak's shadow. Another few droplets speckled the ground where the shade turned them black.

"Are you okay?" I asked.

"Oh yeah," he said, so convincingly I started to relax. "It had to happen," he went on. "I saw them cramped in that dinky little cage, and I knew they needed to be out under the blue sky. It was torture, keeping them locked up."

The twisting feeling inside me tightened. "You took Crystal's gerbils out."

Davey kept going as if I hadn't spoken, his tone distant. "It's funny. I really only meant to set them free. But when they were out here, darting around on the ground, instinct kicked in, just like that. Like a fucking miracle."

"An instinct to do what, Davey?"

He looked at me then. A dribble of red stained the corner of his lips. His eyes were pure yellow, like sunlight reflecting off gold, and the pupils had narrowed, ever so slightly oval now. When he opened his mouth, his teeth were streaked crimson.

"It only took two bites," he said. "First the head, then the body. I had to spit out most of the fur, but the bones were nice and crunchy."

He paused, and I thought I saw a flash of fear in his eyes. Or maybe it was horror. This wasn't about speed or strength or getting revenge on bullying teachers anymore.

My stomach churned. "Davey," I said, "I can try to help. If you—"

He shook his head. His shoulders quivered, and his expression hardened. When he spoke, it was as if he hadn't heard me. "You should try it some time, Max. I bet it'd be right up your alley."

I kept my voice steady and made myself hold his gaze. "Sure. Why don't you come in and wash your face off, and you can explain all this to Reuben."

He considered me, inscrutable. Like maybe he was contemplating trying to bite *my* head off. I shifted my weight.

"Come on, Davey. Let's go inside."

"Because you said so, Max?" He sucked a smudge of blood off his thumb. "No, I don't think so."

He stalked away into the alley. I stood frozen, watching the top of his head disappear behind the fences. No plan came to me, no words that would make this workable. Only a single question sinking heavy into my gut.

After this, what came next?

Silence filled my bedroom when I finished telling the whole story, starting with Davey's attack the night of the party and ending with our talk in the alley. After Davey had taken off, I'd dragged Reuben and Vicky to my place and called Jena for backup. She, of course, had brought Joss. Ash had come home while I was letting them in.

Vicky cringed where she was perched on the bed next to Ash and Reuben. "So Davey... You think he really did *eat* them?"

"That's what he said. And there was blood out there. From the way he talked, he hadn't planned to, but..." My stomach knotted at the memory. "Whatever's happening to him, he doesn't have total control anymore. And it's getting worse, fast. So if we're going to help him, we've got to get on with it."

Reuben shook his head. "I don't know, man."

"I get that it sounds ridiculous," I said. "But Jena knows how bad Davey was hurt when we first got to him. Reuben, you've seen how quick he can move now. Vicky, he's talked with you more in the last week than he has the last three months put together. And dozens of people saw him take on Mr. Peck."

Vicky shot a glance at Jena, who was sitting on my computer chair, Joss behind her with a hand on her shoulder. "Why didn't you tell me any of this before?"

"I didn't want you to think I was crazy."

She bit her lip. "I know you wouldn't make something like that up. And… Davey has been acting pretty different. But he never seemed like he'd hurt anyone."

"Shit, I can't tell Crystal my friend *ate* her gerbils!" Reuben said.

"You don't have to. Let her think they ran off." I spread my hands. "We *have* to remember that none of this stuff is really Davey. Something's taking him over, changing him. But he's still in there." That fleeting horror on his face in the alley. "We've got to bring him back."

"Do you think he's going to turn into some kind of monster, like you saw at the lake?" Ash said quietly.

Joss rolled his eyes, but I ignored him. "I don't know. But I'd rather we stopped it before we have to find out."

Before Davey graduated from gerbils to something bigger. I remembered the blood stains on his teeth, the gore in Dr. Nichols's photos, and swallowed hard. Who knew if the reports she'd shown us were even from a beast like the one that had attacked Davey, or truly supernatural creatures at all? But I didn't want to take that chance.

Jena leaned forward. "It was a full moon, the night of the party. Maybe he won't totally transform until the next one. Some of the mythology says the curse isn't permanent until the final transformation happens."

"How long do we have, if that's right?" Vicky asked, her face still pale but her voice determined.

"Eighteen days."

"Not so bad." Reuben rubbed his hands together. "More than two weeks. No problem."

"Of course you have a problem," Joss broke in. "He belongs in a hospital. A mental one, from the sounds of it. And even if there is some beast out there that 'infected' him, you have no idea what it is. You don't have a hope of 'curing' him unless you know what he's sick with."

Reuben laughed. "So what? We go find Mr. Beast and ask him what's up?"

"Maybe we could." Ash glanced up at me. "You said it looked at least partly human. And that was during the full moon. Maybe it's walking around like a normal person right now. Maybe we could talk to it."

"It might even want to help," Vicky said. "It must be miserable, living like that. If it helps us fix Davey, we could try to cure it too."

"Or maybe you'll find out it was really some homeless guy, not a beast," Joss muttered.

Sure, whatever. I could see everyone else's uncertainty receding at the thought of something concrete to do. This was why I'd wanted to get everyone together—now we had a plan that hadn't occurred to me on my own.

"Okay," I said. "That's worth a try. So we go out to the lake. But we've got to be careful, in case it isn't all that human even now. It jumped Davey without any obvious provocation. Seeing the whole group of us scared it off last time, and we'll go slowly and be ready to back off, but I think we should have some way of defending ourselves."

Vicky paused. "My mom has a gun. A pistol, for self-defense. I could borrow it, just in case."

Jena turned to Joss. "Your dad has a couple of rifles, doesn't he?"

"You're really going along with this?" he said.

"You didn't see him that night."

"Well, you don't know how to shoot. If you're going off to chase some maniac, I'll come along with the rifle."

"We're not going out there wanting to shoot something," I put in. "We've got to be careful—anyone could be walking around in the woods. The guns will be just for if one of us is in danger."

"Of course," Vicky said.

I straightened up. "So are we all in?"

Around the room, one by one, my girlfriend, my friends, and my sister nodded their heads. Joss stood still, his mouth tight, but he'd already said he would follow Jena.

"Okay," I said. "Then let's go now. I don't want to find out what Davey's going to do tomorrow if I can finish this tonight."

As everyone else headed downstairs, I pulled Ash aside.

"You're not coming," I said.

Her face fell. "What?" she said. "But it was my idea!"

"Ash, that thing almost killed Davey. What kind of idiot would drag his little sister along to go looking for it?"

"Everyone else is going."

"I'd go alone if I didn't know how suicidal that might

be," I said. "But just five of us was enough to overwhelm it before. I've got to look out for you."

She glared at the floor and sucked in her lower lip. "You think I won't be able to handle it. You think I'll wimp out."

"Ash—"

She shook her head and backed away. "No, it's okay. I'm not sure I wouldn't either."

She vanished into her room, tugging the door shut behind her. But the bitterness in her voice stuck with me. She had to know I would've wanted to protect her no matter how tough she'd gotten. Frowning, I stepped toward her door to knock.

"What's the hold up, Max?" Reuben called from downstairs. "Jena says we've got to go or it'll get dark."

I let my hand fall. I could sort things out with Ash later. This we had to do as soon as possible.

"Coming." I hurried down the stairs and grabbed the car key out of the dish on the hall table. "Mom?"

"Your dad took off with her on the motorcycle," Vicky said. "It was kind of cute."

It was a kind of pathetic exhibition of his masculinity, but it suited our purposes. "I guess I don't have to ask then."

We headed for Vicky's place first. She came back out holding her purse furtively at her side. "I told my mom I forgot my house keys," she said, her cheeks flushed. Stealth missions looked good on her. "She doesn't even know I went into her bedroom and took it."

I high-fived her and drove on toward Joss's humble abode. Which turned out to be not so humble. He directed me to the new development on the edge of town, where rows of nearly identical houses in pastel brick stood on sprawling lawns. I should have known it took a lot of money to afford that level of pretension.

I parked outside the house he indicated and waited for him to get out. But he just sat there in the back seat like we were asking him to storm an enemy base camp rather than walk into his own home.

"I shouldn't be encouraging this," he said. "It's completely irrational. There's no monster out there."

"Just because you haven't experienced something yourself doesn't mean it can't exist," I pointed out. "Do you really think Jena would buy into this stuff if she hadn't seen enough to know it was real?"

His gaze flicked toward his girlfriend and then back to me with untempered disdain. He thought she was humoring me as a friend, or worse, that I had enough sway over her to convince her of something she'd never have considered otherwise. He'd been dating her for over a year and he still didn't know she was so much smarter than that. My hand tightened on the steering wheel.

"Look," I said, "either you come along or you don't. It's no skin off my back either way. If you can't bring yourself to believe this thing might exist, why don't you take off so we don't have to bother acknowledging *your* existence?"

Joss's eyes narrowed, but it was Jena who spoke. "Max, shut up."

She nudged Joss, and he finally opened the door. They got out together. I watched them conferring on the sidewalk in the rearview mirror. Their voices were too low to hear. The last words she'd said to me stung. He'd been acting like a prick—why shouldn't I call him on it?

After a minute, Jena came to the passenger window. I braced myself for the news that the two of them were bowing out, already trying to calculate whether we should risk it with only three of us and Vicky's pistol, but instead she gave us a half-smile and said, "He'll be back in a minute."

"Wow!" Reuben said behind me. "Monster hunting. Crazy." His feet shuffled restlessly against the floor. How long had it been since he'd popped his last pill? But I'd rather deal with a Reuben in slight withdrawal than a Reuben hopped up on who-knew-what.

Eventually Joss emerged from the garage, carrying a hunting rifle under his arm. Jena ducked back into the car and he followed. He laid the rifle across their laps, the trigger end under his hand.

"All right," he said. "Let's get this over with."

This drive to the lake was very different from the one I'd taken with Davey, Vicky, and the others a week and a half ago. I only edged a little over the speed limit, and I think we all eyed the fields and the forest as we zoomed by, as if we might spot the beastly figure lingering near the road.

The clearing by the lake was empty. A few bikes leaned against a picnic bench on the western edge. A boyish laugh filtered through the trees from that direction as we got out of the car. Probably a bunch of kids out exploring the wilderness the way Davey and I, and sometimes Reuben or Jena, used to do. We were heading east, so that was fine.

Vicky retrieved the pistol from her purse. She held the gun gingerly.

"Do you know how to use it?" I asked.

She nodded. "My mom insisted we take a lesson after she bought it. She didn't want us to have an accident." She looked down at it, curling her fingers around the grip a little more firmly. "Hopefully I won't have to think about shooting anything."

"It might not be here anymore," I said, as disheartened as it made me to admit that. "I never heard about any ripped-up animals before. It must move around a lot, I'd guess, so no one has a chance to notice it."

"And if it is here, we don't know that it'll try to hurt us."

"We've just got to be ready in case it does." Jena glanced at me, and I knew she was remembering the same thing I was: the bloody mess of Davey's chest and shoulder after the beast had savaged him.

I waited for Joss to argue, but maybe he was so convinced that we wouldn't find anything dangerous that he couldn't be bothered to. He flanked Jena, and Reuben fell into step at my left between me and Vicky. I led the way into the woods toward the spot I thought I'd found Davey and his attacker that night.

Twigs snapped under our shoes, and pebbles rattled against each other in our wake. We were never going to take the beast by surprise, that was for sure. I didn't spot the exact place Davey had fallen, but it wasn't as if the beast would be hanging out there waiting for us. We tramped closer to the dips and crevices that mottled the cliff's gray face. Most of the caves were shallow, but there were a few that snaked farther back into the hill, like the one Davey had gotten stuck in all those years ago.

All I could see when I peered into one was shadows, but

stepping any farther inside struck me as supremely unwise. "Let's keep walking along the cliff," I said. "Check out all the caves. Stop if you see anything move."

Sunlight wavered over us as the breeze stirred the leaves overhead. The shadows inside the caves expanded and contracted as if they were breathing. Vicky squealed and her pistol hand flinched up, but it was only a badger springing out of the crevice she'd peeked into. It scrambled on up the cliff.

"Hey!" Reuben called a few minutes later. He leaned into a narrow opening before I could stop him and pulled back looking sheepish. "Never mind. Just a weird-looking patch of moss."

Joss sighed and shifted the rifle under his arm. "How long are we going to keep this up for?"

"Now that we're out here, we might as well go to the end of the cliff," Jena said.

Sweat trickled down my back. Below the treetops, the air was still and warm even in the shade. I dragged in a breath. My nose filled with smells dry and earthy and green —and a hint of sourness that faded almost as quickly as I caught it.

I stopped, turning my head, and took a couple steps forward. There it was again, that funky old-gym-clothes stink I'd first noticed when we found the cow and smelled again when I tackled the beast on Davey.

My pulse sped up. Motioning for the others to stay with me, I eased along the cliff.

It was here, somewhere close. I rose up on my tiptoes to look into one of the higher caves. Nothing but lichen-spotted rock. The stench had gotten stronger. Jena crinkled her nose and glanced at me. I nodded, my chest tight.

The next opening was too small to fit anything bigger than a fox. The one after held only a tuft of dry grass and a bare wall a couple feet in. Above us, the line of the cliff was dipping lower as the hill sloped toward the ground. But the smell hadn't faded.

Maybe it wasn't coming from the caves after all. I let my gaze sweep over the forest around us, scanning the brush and the lower branches. Who said the beast couldn't climb?

A pine tree had sprouted up right next to the cliff face. As I sidestepped it, a slice of darkness behind it caught my eye. I glanced into the half-hidden crevice and froze.

Just beyond the last smattering of sun, two large catlike eyes reflected the light back at me.

As my heartbeat hammered in my ears, part of my mind insisted it *was* just a cat. A tiger escaped from some zoo, or a cougar straying from its usual habitat. But my eyes were adjusting to the darkness. A pale face formed around the eyes: dirty but hairless, lips curled back over crookedly pointed teeth, a heap of stringy dark hair blending into the deeper shadows. Knobby fingers dug into the rough stone floor like claws. Hunched shoulders heaved with a breath. Knees shrouded in fraying fabric bent at the creature's sides, as if it were poised to spring.

I stared into those inhuman eyes not for an instant like before, but for full seconds ticking away with the thudding of my pulse. My skin went cold and my bladder twinged. Every hair on my body stood on end.

The thing in the cave wasn't human. It wasn't an animal.

It was something completely other, alien, unknown—something my mind balked at even trying to name. But it knew exactly what I was. Here we were with our bravado and our guns, and all it had to do was look at me for me to nearly piss my pants.

We were so stupid. We could never have been prepared for this. It was going to rip each and every one of us apart, and there was nothing I could do.

"Fuck," someone said. It might even have been me. But it was enough to pull me out of the long, dark well I'd been falling into inside the beast's eyes. I blinked. Reuben was standing beside me, leaning forward for a closer view. Jena had gone rigid at my right. Vicky eased forward next to Reuben. Her lips parted, the color draining from her face. The leaves above us shifted, letting the sunlight stream down and making the shadows inside the cave deepen.

"What?" Joss said with the same skeptical tone he'd used all afternoon, too far away to see. Jena reached back to grab his arm, and the beast-thing crouched lower. A growl rasped from its throat.

I swallowed. My mouth felt parched, but somebody had to do this. "Hey," I said in more of a croak than a voice. "Can you talk? We just want to… ask a couple questions."

The beast just kept staring at us, its narrow pupils darting from face to face, the growl reverberating in its chest. A string of drool swung from the corner of its lips.

Without warning, it threw itself forward.

I flinched to the side, my shoulder bumping Jena's. The beast rammed into Reuben and knocked him to the ground. Vicky shrieked. Joss's rifle clicked as he released the safety, but the thing was already leaping away. It bounded off through the underbrush. I spared a second to glance at Reuben, who was struggling to his feet unmauled, and then I threw myself after it.

"Come on!" I said. "If it gets away…"

If it got away, we were never going to figure out what it was, or what was happening to Davey.

I sprinted through the trees. Behind me, Reuben was telling someone else, "No, go on. I'm okay. Holy shit!" Footsteps crackled across the forest floor after me.

The beast was making for the far end of the woods. Its loping, ape-like strides, dropping from two feet to speed itself along with its hands, should have been ungainly, but somehow it was pulling ahead.

"Over here!" Jena yelled. She ran past me, her feet flying along a narrow path that was probably normally used by deer. I veered after her. As soon as my shoes hit the firmer ground, I lurched forward with a fresh burst of speed. The beast wavered between the trees to our right, but now I thought we might actually be gaining on it.

Then it broke from the forest altogether.

We stumbled after it onto the fallow field that lay on the other side of the trees. Up ahead, the dark water of the river that fed from the lake streamed east, flecked with white foam. The beast bolted across the pale grass. It might as well have been putting miles between us with every step.

My lungs stabbed with each breath I took, but I kept running. The thing had to stop at the water. Could it swim? If we could corner it there…

"It's heading for the bridge," Jena shouted. In the

distance, a wooden bridge arced across the river. On the other side of the water, a short span of field bled into another stretch of forest—one I'd never explored.

If the beast reached those woods, it would have completely vanished by the time we'd caught up. We'd never find it. And I doubted it would ever come back here, not after being chased like this. I ducked my head, ignoring the ache in my calves, but I was losing steam.

Jena drew to a halt. As much as I hated to, I forced myself to slow down. Maybe if we took a moment to think, we'd find a better option than trying to outrun it.

"Stop!" Vicky cried after the thing as she reached us. She stumbled, her breath rasping. A choked sob burst from her throat. "You have to stop!"

The beast was racing along the river now, a few seconds from the foot of the bridge. It didn't so much as glance back.

"*Stop!*"

Vicky raised her arm. A shot crackled through the air.

The beast's body jerked. It swayed back and forth, and crumpled, tipping over the edge of the bank to tumble into the water.

Vicky gave a little moan. The gun slipped from her fingers and thumped onto the grass. She covered her mouth with her hands.

I gripped her shoulder for a second before I yanked myself out of my shock. "Come on," I said to Jena. We jogged to the bridge.

Our feet thumped over the worn boards. I stared out over the course of the river. The water twisted and rippled as it raced away from us, slivers of light blue sky reflecting off the deeper indigo.

There was no sign, in the river or along the bank, of the thing we'd been chasing.

The current could have carried it out of sight in the time it'd taken us to reach the bridge, if it'd been so badly injured it couldn't swim to shore. Or if it'd been dead. I remembered the way its body had spasmed as the bullet hit it, and my throat tightened.

"Maybe it's hiding underneath." I hurried off the bridge before Jena had a chance to respond. I didn't need her to tell me how unlikely that was. In the fleeting moment as I leaned over to peer into the bridge's shadow, it was possible. I wanted desperately to see those alien eyes gleaming back at me, and just as desperately I wanted to never have to look into them again.

It was my second wish that came true. There wasn't even room for a beast-sized creature to sit against the underside of the bridge. The narrow ridges of stones lining the sides of the river were mossy but uninhabited. I straightened up.

Vicky was walking over to us, biting her lip. Her face was sallow. She'd picked up the pistol, but she held it by the muzzle, as if she were afraid of what might happen if her fingers got too close to the trigger.

Only the three of us had emerged from the forest. Joss must have stayed back with Reuben. I guessed running after crazed beasts was not his style.

Jena sat down at the foot of the bridge and ran her hands over her hair. As Vicky reached us, I made myself say what we both knew was true.

"It's gone."

Vicky swallowed audibly and looked down the river. "Do you think I killed it?"

"Hard to tell. What were you thinking, Vicky? Why did you shoot it?"

"I don't know." Her head drooped. I put my arm around her, and she sank into me. "I didn't mean to, not really. I just wanted it to stop running. It was going to get away, and then how were we going to help Davey? And all of a sudden I was pulling the trigger. I didn't want to *kill* it. I think I thought if I hit it in the leg or something, it'd have to stop. It'd have to listen to us…"

That wasn't a completely stupid idea. It might even have worked, if she'd been a good enough shot to aim across that distance at a moving target.

She shivered against my side. "I'm sorry."

"If it makes you feel any better," Jena said, with a smile so tight all the humor was wrung out of it, "the 'expert' at the museum did say that, according to some of the legends, you have to kill the monster to cure its victims. So shooting it might have been exactly what we needed to do for Davey."

"I still didn't want to—" Vicky sucked in a ragged breath.

"There's no way we can change what's already happened," I said. "Come on. We'd better go make sure Reuben hasn't gotten himself into even more trouble."

We found Reuben back by the cliff side with Joss, who was trying to explain to my friend that he'd imagined the glowing eyes and jagged teeth because he'd been expecting to see them. Apparently Lover Boy hadn't gotten enough of a look at the beast when it had jumped out of the cave to reconsider his skepticism.

"It was some filthy homeless guy who needed a haircut," he was saying. "Gone kind of wacko, sure, but nothing *supernatural.*"

I didn't bother to argue. Reuben was unscathed except for a couple of shallow scratches on his arm, so we headed right back to the car. Joss took a break from his psychoanalysis to shoot a pointed look my way.

"I heard a gunshot."

I shrugged, my hand tensing around Vicky's. I had no idea how he'd react if he knew the truth, but I was sure it wouldn't be good.

"I was pissed that we'd let it get away," I said. "Vicky let me try firing at a tree to blow off some steam."

Joss shook his head. "Playing around like that's dangerous, you know."

His condescension blew right past me. We'd lost the beast. How were we going to save Davey now?

By the end of the day, I'd realized we had a much more basic problem: how were we going to *find* Davey?

I texted him in the car and got no response. When I called, his phone went straight to voicemail. I left a message and called three more times over the next hour, and then I stopped because it was getting pathetic. Before hitting the sack that night, I checked in with Reuben, who reported that Davey still hadn't shown up at his place.

He wasn't at school in the morning, of course, because of the suspension, but I casually dropped his name in at least a dozen conversations that day, watching for a hint that he'd imposed on someone else in our crowd. No one had so much as seen him.

I couldn't imagine Davey going back home to hole up, at least not with his dad there. As soon as I thought of that, images rose up in my head of all the various horrible fates Mr. Reeve might have met in the last twenty-four hours. He'd done a lot worse to Davey than the gerbils had.

I called the Reeves' landline that evening and was unexpectedly relieved to hear Mr. Reeve's gruff voice on the other end saying, "Hello?"

"Oh, sorry, wrong number," I said, and hung up.

On the weekend, Vicky, Jena, Reuben, and I took a stroll through town, checking some of Davey's favorite hangouts. When our search turned up nothing, we trudged back down the main street. Our shadows made sharp splotches on the sidewalk in the blaze of the noon sun.

"Do you think he left town?" Vicky bit her lip: something she'd been doing so much the skin was starting to crack. The angry pink stood out against her face, which was wan because she hadn't slept so great the last few days. "Could he be that embarrassed about the gerbil thing? It's not like we don't know he never would've done that if he wasn't… sick."

"I don't think he's *gone*," I said. "Where would he go? He's got no money. God knows where his mom is these days, and his closest family otherwise is his grandparents all the way down in Florida."

"His stuff's still at my place too," Reuben said. "Wallet, ID, all that."

Jena frowned. "He's got to be around, then. It's so warm, he could be sleeping anywhere outside and not be all that uncomfortable."

"He's got to eat too," I said. "He used to be a real chicken about shoplifting, but I guess he's got to be stealing food."

"Or dumpster diving." Vicky shuddered.

Reuben grinned. "Or he's catching squirrels."

He said it like a joke, but my stomach turned. Of all the possibilities, that one actually sounded the most likely.

"That doesn't help us find him."

"Maybe we could file a missing persons report," Reuben said. "Get the police tracking him down. That'd do it."

"I don't think so," I muttered. "Let's leave the cops out of this."

Jena swiped her hand through the perspiration on her forehead. "Why don't we search some more of the parks? But let's stop and grab something to drink first."

We ducked into a convenience store. Vicky and Reuben drifted ahead toward the fridges at the back. Jena touched my arm.

"You know, Reuben might have a point. If Davey's missing much longer—"

I shook my head. "No way. The cops can't even find what's right in front of them, so if he doesn't *want* to be found? Yeah, right. It'll just make him more wary of talking to us."

She arched her eyebrow in question, and I grimaced.

"Look, don't ever tell him I told you this," I said, and paused. The memory made my chest tighten even now. "There was one time when we were eight, I was talking to him on the phone and his dad got into a rage, and the next thing I knew he'd dropped the phone and... I knew from the sounds his dad was hurting him. I freaked out and called the police."

"Of course," Jena said, her eyes wide.

"Yeah, well, I guess Davey didn't have any obvious marks, and his dad made out it was a big mistake. Davey was always too scared to speak up, so they shrugged and walked away. Mr. Reeve had him on lockdown for practically a year after that. I don't know if I'd *ever* have seen him again outside of school if his dad knew who made the call. And who do you think they'd turn Davey over to now? He's a minor for two more months. So, no, I'm not in a hurry to try my luck again."

Jena opened her mouth, but right then Vicky dashed over to us. She grabbed my elbow, her fingers digging in, and nodded to the TV mounted in the corner. "*Look.*"

On the screen, one of the county news reporters stood in front of a small pond, a solemn expression fixed on her normally perky face. I stepped closer to make out the audio.

"The body was found in the water here, not far from Arlington city limits, at the edge of this bunch of reeds. While it had clearly been in the water for some time, Channel Six has learned that the victim had also suffered a bullet wound in the back. An autopsy is being performed to determine the cause of death. In the meantime, police are searching for any relatives of the victim, who was carrying no ID, and anyone who might have information about his activities in the last several days. Their artist has created an image of what he would have looked like alive."

An image filled the screen: a young man, maybe in his late twenties, with shaggy, dark brown hair and blue-gray eyes, a narrow forehead and a soft chin. The only part of him that looked familiar was the straight, wide nose. My back stiffened.

Vicky's voice came out pleading. "That can't be... He can't be *it*, can he?"

"Well," I said slowly, "if it is, he definitely didn't look like that when we saw him."

"In most of the stories I've looked up," Jena murmured, "when a supernatural creature is killed, the body shifts back into its previous human form."

Reuben ambled over, carrying a bottle of grape soda. "What's so exciting over here?"

The clerk shifted at the counter on the other side of the store. The back of my neck prickled. "Let's get going."

We made it a few steps down the sidewalk before Vicky bent forward, dropping her face into her hands. "I didn't mean to kill him," she mumbled. "I really didn't. I was just trying to help Davey."

Jena rubbed her mouth. Her jaw had clenched, and her voice came out strained. "Maybe you did. Maybe now that it —he—that thing is dead, Davey will go back to his normal self too. And maybe it would be happy to be out of the misery it must have been in, living like that. Like a monster."

"Or maybe I killed someone we should have been trying to help."

I set my hand on Vicky's back with a soothing stroke of my thumb, but my mind was spinning.

If the beast was still inside Davey, we'd seen how this could end. The face on the TV had looked as normal as he used to. Somehow that guy had warped into the thing that had crouched in a cave and lunged at us like a rabid animal.

"Wait," Reuben said in a rare moment of clarity, "if you're saying that was the guy who messed Davey up... who messed *him* up?"

Jena and I exchanged a glance. "I guess there isn't any way of knowing," I said. Our "expert" hadn't believed anything like it existed at all. "There can't be *that* many of those things out there, or we'd hear about it."

Vicky choked back a sob. I squeezed her shoulder. "Hey. You saw how it came at us. I don't think there was any helping that guy, not anymore."

She wiped at her eyes and drew up her chin. "Maybe not. But then we *really* have to help Davey."

I was heading to the caf to grab lunch on Monday when my phone vibrated in my pocket. I didn't recognize the number.

I brought the phone to my ear. "Hey."

"Max?"

The voice at the other end was soft and wavering—and definitely female. I realized I'd been hoping it'd be Davey. Damn it. All our searching on the weekend hadn't turned him up.

"Yeah?" I said. "You'll have to talk loud. I'm in the hall."

"I need you to come to my house," the girl said. I couldn't place her voice, though it was vaguely familiar. "Right away. Please."

I ducked into an empty classroom as she drew in a shaky breath, and for some reason that sound hooked my memory. "Sofia? Why are you calling me?"

"It's important. I need you to come over."

Was this some amateur attempt at a seduction? "My girlfriend's waiting for me in the caf," I said pointedly. "If you need to say something important, just tell me now."

"No," she said. "You have to come to my house. Just for a few minutes. I need to see you. Please."

We barely knew each other, and the last time we'd talked I'd told her to take a hike. I hadn't even given her my number—she must have begged it off Ash. What did she think she was doing?

I obviously hadn't cut her off firmly enough. Keeping her hanging wasn't doing any of us any good. In private, I could be brutally clear, and we could just end this. It wasn't as if the Davey I'd pictured swooping in to comfort her even existed for more than a few seconds at a time these days.

My chest clenched. "I promise I won't tell anyone," Sofia started again. "Just this once, I—"

"All right," I said. "Give me the address."

As I headed out onto the street, an uneasy feeling crept under my skin. I hadn't known Sofia well, but I thought I knew her type. And that was the type to get moony over guys she hardly knew, sure, but not outright obsessive. She'd sounded almost *afraid* of the idea that I might not come.

Overhead, gray clouds were congealing in the sky. The humid air pressed down with the weight of rain to come.

I stopped at the split-level bungalow that Sofia had directed me to. The driveway was empty, but at this time of day, her parents ought to be at work. I hopped up the steps and peeked through the screen door. The inner door stood open.

"Sofia?"

No one answered.

A prickle ran across my back. I rapped my fist against the screen door. "Hey, Sofia, I came. Stop kidding around."

Maybe she hadn't expected me to get here so fast, and she'd gone into the backyard or something? I opened the door and stepped inside.

"Sofia?" I padded farther in. The air conditioning

hummed, and the sweat on my arms and back chilled. I passed a living room with a leather sofa set and a kitchen where dirty breakfast dishes scattered the granite counter. At the other end of the house, the backyard's muted sunlight slanted through a sliding glass door. I hurried down the few steps to the lower level family room.

To the right of the stairs, a door stood ajar. I only meant to glance in as I walked past. But my gaze halted on the girlish wallpaper and the figure lying on the bed's pink duvet. I turned toward the doorway.

I could only see a sliver of her side: a socked foot tilted to the left, an arm turned upward, a hand with fingers slightly curled like a flower unfurling its petals. A curve of pale jaw and cheek, a splash of dark hair.

"Sofia!" I pushed the door open, expecting her to stir. At my first full glimpse of the bed, an icy wave of nausea rushed through me, so swift my balance tilted. I stood there, clutching the doorknob as if I needed it to hold me up, and stared.

She was staring too. Her eyes, wide as always, gazed blankly at the ceiling. Her face was not just pale but white, the same color as the bed frame. Her shirt was white too— what was left of it. It had been torn in half down the middle, exposing her chest. Her chest where the flesh gaped open from collarbone to belly like an anatomical diagram gone wrong, revealing the tips of ribs and red muscle, ragged ends of arteries leaking blood into the yawning hollow. She looked as if someone had torn her open and ripped out her heart.

As my pulse hammered in my ears, it occurred to me that somebody probably had.

13

"Davey," I said, too quietly. My voice was hoarse. "Davey!"

I let go of the knob and strode to the back door in time with the deafening thud of my heart. My legs wobbled under me.

I didn't want to think it. I didn't want to *believe* it. But four days ago he'd been eating gerbils. Murder was a logical progression, in the warped sort of logic I was left with when allowing for beast-things and supernatural transformations. What were the chances that some blood-lusting sicko had come into town and started wreaking havoc at the exact same time Davey was turning into a monster?

Obviously Vicky killing the thing that'd attacked him hadn't fixed anything.

The view through the glass revealed nothing but a patio set and an apple tree shaking in the growing wind. The sliding door was unlocked. He could have slipped out as I was coming, scaled the fence, and run off to wherever he'd been hiding. The way he could move now, it would have only taken him a second.

I wandered back to Sofia's bedroom, unable to suppress a sharp inhale at the sight of her body, even though I knew what to expect this time. My stomach twisted. Blood was blossoming across the pink duvet beneath her now.

I'd talked to her ten minutes ago. Ten minutes ago, she'd still been alive.

Swallowing my nausea, I glanced over the shelves, the desk, the dresser, but everything was clean and neat. There was no sign she'd struggled. No sign anyone but her had been in the room. As if she could have done that to herself. I inhaled again, closing my eyes as I tried to steady myself. A metallic tang hung in the cool air.

Why had Davey picked Sofia? Had he even *known* her, other than as one of the many faces at my parties? He hadn't seemed to recognize her name when I'd said it last week.

And why hadn't she told me she thought she was in danger when she'd called? I hadn't misheard her—she'd been terrified.

I dropped down onto the carpet and slid my hands behind my neck. Racing thoughts collided in my head until the only question that really mattered shivered apart from the others.

What the hell was I going to do now?

Sofia was beyond help. But if I just left, her parents would find her, call the police, and my fingerprints would be on the doors, the railing by the stairs, maybe other things I hadn't thought about touching. A neighbor might have seen me go in. And Sofia's phone would show her last call was to me. As much as I wanted to walk out and wipe the whole thing from my brain, that would only make it look as if I were responsible. As if I were the one who'd…

An image of Davey leaning over her, bloody-fingered, flashed through my mind. I clamped my mouth shut against the heave of my gut.

It hadn't really been him. It was the beast, growing inside him like a parasite. That was the real murderer. That was what we had to destroy.

I stood up, turning my back to the bed, and pulled out my phone.

Around the time last period would have been ending, Ash came walking up the street toward Sofia's house. She was alone, her messenger bag slung over her shoulder, slim arms crossed over her burgundy T-shirt. Police officers and related personnel were still coming and going through the front door. Ash hesitated, her eyes growing round.

It took her a moment to find me, sitting on the bottom step outside the house, squeezed to the side so the officials had plenty of room to go by. They hadn't made me move, I think because after seeing what was inside they figured just about anyone would need to sit down.

One of the officers stepped away from his car to stop Ash as she crept closer, but after a few words he let her go by. She came to a halt in front of me. I hauled myself to my feet. My legs prickled where the nerves had started falling asleep, and my mouth itched for a cigarette, even though I hardly ever bothered with them. I wanted to do something with my hands and my lips that wasn't pointing or talking.

"It's true?" Ash said. "She's really…"

I nodded, and she closed her eyes. Her eyelids looked at

me like a second pair, blank and purple. Her forehead creased. "And you found her."

"She called me at the beginning of lunch," I said. "Wanted to bounce a couple of birthday present ideas for you off me. Then there was a weird noise, and she hung up all of a sudden. I got worried and came over."

It was my story for the record: the one I'd told each of the three officers who'd asked. The one I was going to have to tell again, in greater detail, when they finally stopped taking photographs and samples and brought me down to the station for my official statement. The truth would have sounded way too complicated and wasn't exactly what I'd want Vicky to read about in the newspaper. And the parts about Davey...

I didn't know for sure. And I couldn't point the finger at the real beast without accusing him as well. It wasn't like the cops would believe my story enough to see a difference between the two. Every time I considered it, the image rose up of Davey's body jerking in a hail of gunfire like the beast by the river, and my gut knotted. *No.*

"They'll probably want to ask you a few questions later," I said when Ash stayed quiet. "Anything you might have heard or seen that was suspicious. Since you were her friend."

"Yeah." Her breath hitched. When she opened her eyes again, they were shiny with tears. "But why would somebody hurt her? It doesn't make sense."

I touched her arm, and she swiped at her cheeks. "I'm sorry," she said. "It's so crazy. I couldn't believe it when people started talking about it. That's why I had to come."

She looked toward the house. "Is she still in there?"

"They took her out about a half hour ago," I said. "You wouldn't have wanted to see her, Ash. It was bad."

"But, if she was okay when she called you, and then when you got here… It must have been pretty fast, right?"

That depended on how long Davey toyed with Sofia before she'd decided to call me. If that had even been her decision. The way she'd begged me to come, so insistently but so vaguely... I was starting to wonder if Davey had told her to summon me without letting me know why. Why else would she have called *me*?

The physical pain, at least, would have been brief. "I don't think she was suffering very long," I said.

Ash hugged herself. "Okay. That's good."

One of the officers I'd talked to earlier came over and cleared her throat. "It's time to take you in, Mr. Weston," she said. "We'd have to do this with anyone who was first on the scene. It should only take an hour or two."

"Sure," I said. "Can you give me a sec with my sister?"

I put a slight emphasis on the last words, and the officer obviously caught the connection to my earlier story—dead girl's friend. She dipped her head and crossed the sidewalk to wait by her car.

"Listen, Ash," I said, leaning close as if I was comforting her. "I know you're upset, but this is really, really important. I just don't want you mentioning it to anyone else, not yet, okay?"

"What?" she said.

Saying it felt like a betrayal. But I had to, for her.

"If you see Davey, you stay far away from him. Don't

talk to him. Don't let him in the house if he comes by. You got it?"

Her expression twitched into a frown. "You don't think —"

"I don't know for sure," I said. "But you're going to be careful anyway."

I hugged her quickly and walked over to the police car. The last look I had of Sofia's house was with Ash standing out front, her startled eyes following me as the police whisked me away.

"There you are," Mom said when Dad and I came in the door a little after seven. The 'rents had been called to the station for Ash's interview, and Dad had stuck around to wait for mine to finish. "They finished talking to Ash an hour ago; I was wondering what was taking so long with you."

"I found the body," I said. "I guess that takes a lot more questions."

Mom patted my arm in what I supposed was meant to be a soothing gesture. "You must be worn out. I can't imagine how awful it was, having to see something like that. Are you all right?"

"I've been better." My stomach still hadn't settled. And every now and then it lurched with the image of Sofia's body flashing through my mind.

Mom drifted over to the liquor cabinet to grab the bottle of absinthe, Dad's usual drink of choice, and a glass. "Do you know if they have any leads? I won't feel secure until they've arrested someone."

"I doubt they would've told me if they did."

Dad dropped onto the sofa and shook his head. "I never would have believed something that horrific could happen in this town. I can't remember the last time there was any kind of murder here. Goes to show you can't take anything for granted."

"I'm sure they'll catch whoever did it soon," Mom said as she poured his drink. "We'll all take extra care of ourselves until then. Not quite so many late nights?"

"You can think that way," Dad said. "But sometimes it's best to look the darkness in the face, not to shy away. It's the ugliness in life that makes us see the beautiful parts more vividly." He raised the glass, as if proposing a toast to the empty air in front of him.

I wondered if he'd still talk like that if he'd been the one who'd come across Sofia's ruined body. But I had more concrete problems to deal with.

Thunder rolled in the distance as I stepped into the backyard. The air smelled electric, but the clouds were holding tight. I walked to the chain link fence at the back of the lawn and peered between the trees on the other side. Nothing moved in the ravine except the leaves shaking in the wind.

If Davey were going to hide anywhere, it'd be here. We'd practically grown up in the ravine. He'd escaped from his dad into it so many times, it might have felt like a second home. The bunch of us had walked through on the weekend, but it was worth another try.

My fingers curled around the top of the fence. I hauled myself up, swung one leg over, and hopped down on the other side.

The trail that led from our yard down to the main path along the creek was overgrown. Heading down the slope, I pushed aside the branches of new saplings and the grasping edges of bushes. Even though it hadn't rained yet, the patches of grass felt slick under my feet.

In the bottom of the gully, the creek burbled along through the muddy ground beside the main path. Bugs skimmed across its surface. A few raindrops pattered against the leaves overhead and then halted.

My skin crawled. I'd always seen the ravine as a sort of playground before, like a huge natural jungle gym. Right then, with the sunlight blotted out above and the air thick and humid around me, the underbrush was murky, the shadows shifty, nothing as clear or solid as I wanted it to be.

A shoe scraped bark behind me. I turned, my back stiffening. I'd spent the last four days looking for Davey, but suddenly I wasn't so sure I wanted to see him.

He stood on a log a few feet off the path, his thumbs hooked in the belt loops of his jeans, his shoulders straight and head cocked. In the dim light, his hair was almost black. His eyes gleamed golden-yellow as they fixed on me. His lips curled into a smirk.

It looked too much like him. I wanted to see a monster wearing a Davey mask, but everything about him still felt like *him*, just tweaked like the color of his hair. I didn't want to think of Davey when I remembered the things the beast had done.

"Hey, Max," he said. It sounded like him too: his voice, putting on a new, amused drawl.

"Davey." His clothes looked clean, his hair unmussed,

not what I'd have expected if he'd been living here the last few days. "It's been a while. Where've you been hiding?"

He shrugged, but his smile widened. He bobbed on his feet. "Here and there. Nowhere special. Not like you."

"Special?" I said stupidly, and my mind darted back to my first glimpse of Sofia opened up on her bed. I shoved the image away.

The beast was trying to mess with me. I couldn't let him.

"How was the police station?" Davey asked. "Did you have some interesting stories to tell them?"

"What, you mean you couldn't hear everything I said through the walls?"

"I'm not Superman. Yet. And I'm curious."

I swallowed thickly. He was talking about it so casually, as if we were discussing some prank and not a girl who'd died.

"They asked me about you a little, you know. They'd heard from someone about the incident with Mr. Peck. Was there something else I should have told them, Davey?"

"So you didn't." He didn't sound surprised. "Well, it wouldn't have made much difference anyway."

"You're not worried about what they'd do to you if they come after you?"

"Nah. It might be fun to see them *try* to stop me."

A different memory darted through my mind: Dr. Nichols's photo of the soldiers, a neck gouged out, a broken rifle. My voice came out with a rasp. "What would *you* do to them?"

Davey shrugged. "Why don't you set them on me and find out? It's up to you, Max. You seem a little upset, though.

I thought this was what you wanted."

"Wanted?" The image of Sofia's body resurfaced, and this time it lingered even when I shook my head. "Why the hell— Why would I—"

"Get inside her and break open her heart." His eyes turned intent. "Pretty fucking cold, sure, but that's how you roll."

I *felt* cold then, from the inside out, as if I'd just chugged a bottle of ice water. Bile rose in my throat. I was staring at him, and at the same time I'd fallen back through my memory to the only other moment I'd felt like this: watching Ash raise her tear-streaked face, the nail scissors dropping from her fingers, the little lines of blood dribbling down the inside of her arm.

It was fear. Sharp, undiluted fear.

"I saw you talking to her," Davey went on. "I saw her and I knew exactly how it could go. I could already feel it, perfect, in my hands."

"I was doing it for you," I said. "I was setting her up for *you*. It wasn't even really going to hurt her."

Davey held my gaze. Could I reach the real him somewhere behind the golden sheen of those eyes?

"I had her," he said. His mouth twitched, and the slow sneering smile crept across his face again. "Not a bad meal."

Every organ inside me clenched. I had to suck in a breath before I could speak. "Davey, you know I never would have wanted *that*. You've got to—"

"It doesn't matter," Davey interrupted. "We're doing things my way now, Max. And I can do so much more than I ever could before."

He paused. His hands balled into fists at his sides. "You know what I'd really like to find out?" he said quietly. An odd tremor crept into his voice. "I keep thinking about it. How would Ash taste?"

I froze, and he stepped backward off the log.

"Wait!" I said, and the clouds finally cracked open. Rain poured down so densely the gods might as well have tipped a gigantic bucket over onto our heads. I lunged after Davey, and my shoes skidded in the mud.

My arms windmilled, but it wasn't enough. I toppled onto my ass. The impact jolted up my spine. Wincing, I scrambled back onto my feet. Davey had vanished amid the rain, leaving me soaked to the skin and shivering for completely different reasons.

It was past one when Ash's bedroom door clicked shut. I closed the game I'd only vaguely been paying attention to on my phone and leaned back in my desk chair, the tension seeping out of me. After dinner, a few of Ash's friends had come by wanting her to hang out. For once in my life I'd wanted Mom to be a real mom and tell her no, but she'd seemed to think Ash needed company in the face of the tragedy and just said not to be home too late.

Davey's last words ran through my head again. *You know what I'd really like to find out? How would Ash taste?*

I got up and checked the locks on the front and back doors. Back in my bedroom, I set my pillow at the opposite end of the bed from usual and lay down with my head by the wall between my room and my sister's.

In the morning, Ash swished into the kitchen in an all-black ensemble, from her off-the-shoulder top to her fishnet tights. Her eyeliner looked heavier than usual, more party-night than school-day.

"Kind of dark," I said, and then understood. "Mourning

clothes?"

She nodded as she peered into the fridge. "I feel like I should do something… and I don't know what else I can do." She closed her eyes for a second, her face tight, and I wondered if she'd gotten much more sleep than I had last night.

The words hovered in the back of my throat: *Don't go out there. Don't take the risk. Stay home.* But home wasn't safe either. Sofia had been killed in her own bed. At least at school I'd be able to keep an eye on Ash, some of the time.

Now, in the daylight, it was hard to imagine Davey hurting her. Sofia almost made sense. I'd brought his attention to her by accident. If I hadn't…

My hands balled on the countertop. How could I have known? But Davey had *liked* Ash.

Of course, that was before the beast had taken him over. Who knew how much control the real Davey had left?

"Not hungry?" Ash asked. I realized I'd been staring at the waffles the toaster had ejected for me for at least a minute without seeing them.

"Thinking," I said. "You remember what I told you yesterday, right? About—"

Had Davey heard me tell her to stay away from him? I could see the beast in him taking that as a challenge. With that sharper hearing of his, he wouldn't have needed to be very close. He might be able to hear us talking right through the walls.

"—about being careful," I finished lamely. "You'll look after yourself?"

"Of course." Ash frowned, but she didn't say anything

else. She poked at her half-finished bowl of cereal, picked it up, and dumped what was left in the trash. Her footsteps pattered up the stairs. I sat down at the table and rested my forehead against the knuckles of my clasped hands.

I was losing it. *That* was what the beast wanted. Maybe he wasn't after Ash at all; maybe he'd only wanted me to think so, because he'd known how much it'd shake me up. I had to think this through. Davey was in there, no matter how far the beast had squashed him down. We needed to get him out.

When Ash came back down, I walked out into the hall as if I'd just happened to be ready to go at the same time she was. We headed out for school together, Ash gripping the strap of her messenger bag tightly by her side. The first two blocks passed in silence. She kicked at a pebble.

"So that thing on Wednesday, that didn't fix anything."

It took me a second to figure out what she was talking about. "When we all went out to the lake? No. The situation… If anything, it's worse."

She nodded, and I realized we were on exactly the same page. She'd heard my account of Davey's new super-hearing. I gave her a pained smile, but a little of the weight in my chest lifted. Maybe Ash would be okay even on her own.

It was just the rest of the town we had to worry about.

I went through the motions when I got to school— opening up my locker, finding the books for my morning classes—while my mind worked away. Our expedition on Wednesday had ended badly, true, but it had also been the first time I'd felt like we were close to solving anything. And that had happened because I'd let everyone in and we'd worked it out together.

The beast wasn't just my problem. It was all of ours. I had to remember that. And it *was* ours. The cops in this town hadn't even managed to deal with Davey's dad, so what the hell could we expect them to do about a literal monster? I still didn't want to put Davey in the line of fire... and I didn't want the beast tearing apart the entire police force, either. At least he'd been willing to talk to me.

First we needed to find out where Davey was spending most of his time. We couldn't accomplish anything if we didn't even know where—

My legs locked up as I stepped into the English classroom. I almost tripped over my own feet. I caught my balance with my hand on the closest desk and grinned apologetically at the girl sitting there, but I couldn't manage to put any warmth into it. Too much of my attention was focused on the desk one row over and two seats back.

The desk where Davey was sitting.

He glanced up and nodded to me as I walked by to my own seat, with a crook in his smile that disappeared when I blinked. The golden sheen in his eyes glinted. Then he was tossing some remark to the girl in front of me in a low teasing voice that made her laugh and blush. I sat down and got out *Othello*, my heart thudding.

Davey's suspension was over. He had every right to be here. Every right, I guessed, to be flirting with the girl he'd almost puked on two weeks ago. Was he going to rip out her heart too?

She wasn't actually looking like she'd mind.

The pen I'd taken out wavered in my fingers. I set it

down with a snap.

"Hey, Hannah," I said casually. "Why's it you've never come to one of my parties?"

Her gaze slid over to me, and her cheeks went a little pinker. "I don't think you ever invited me."

I made a dismissive sound and stretched my arms in a way that subtly displayed the results of my morning push-ups. "No invitation required. The more the merrier. I thought everyone knew that. The next one I'll make sure you hear about ahead of time, okay?"

"Cool," she said. And then, without hesitating, she turned back to Davey. He winked at me before making a comment about her bracelet that required him to fondle her wrist while she giggled.

Okay, so we'd found Davey. Now what were we going to do with him?

I reached for my phone and started texting.

Fifteen minutes before final bell, I asked to go to the bathroom, rewarded Ms. Duffy for her grudging "All right" with my most charming smile, and headed off with my bag in tow as if I usually brought it with me when I needed to piss. I didn't stop walking until I reached the edge of the school lawn. Jena was already waiting there.

"Is the covert approach necessary, or are you just doing it for fun?" she asked.

Her tone sounded light, but her eyes were serious, the corners of her mouth drawn as if she didn't have the energy to smile. My gut tightened. I had to keep Jena on my side.

"Well, we know he's been listening in when we've talked

at least once," I said. "And nothing's going to work if he already knows what we're planning. By the time he leaves class, we'll be long enough gone he won't know where we are. We never hang out at your place anymore. I don't think he'll look there, not right away."

She was still watching me. "You think he did it. That girl yesterday. You think he... killed her."

"Don't you?" I hadn't told anyone about my conversation with Davey in the ravine yet, because the thought of officially labeling him a murderer, saying the words out loud, made my stomach churn even more than the memory of Sofia's body did. "We know it wasn't the thing that attacked him."

"I guess there could be others, though, couldn't there? I just— It's *Davey*. Even if he's different now, the idea that he could do something like that... It seems crazy."

"Yeah."

Reuben and Vicky slipped out of the school. Reuben rambled over like his usual carefree self, but Vicky's head was drooping, her hair starting to straggle out of her ponytail. I suspected she was still thinking about the footage we'd seen on the news. I twined my arm with hers when she caught up, and the four of us set off across the street.

"Joss is going to drive over when school's officially out," Jena said. "But that'll look normal enough."

"I thought he didn't believe in any of this," Vicky murmured. "Did he change his mind?"

Jena shrugged. "I'm not sure. It's not that he's trying to be mean about it, you know. He just finds it hard to accept that anything so out there could be true and, well, he's honest about how he feels. But when I mentioned you were all coming over, he wanted to be there."

"The guy is a real downer." Reuben tipped his head to the side, cracking his neck. Vicky winced.

I leaned closer to her. "How are you doing?"

"I'll be okay," she said, sounding not okay at all. Her voice wavered. "I just— There are so many horrible things happening at once. It must be worse for you. Finding Ash's friend... The police came around and talked to me this morning. They wanted to know if I thought there was anything going on with you and her, like *you* might have done it. How ridiculous is that?"

So despite their friendly enough send-off yesterday, the cops had their eye on me. I guessed I couldn't blame them for that. "They have to follow up on all their leads. But it's good to know you don't see me as a murdering type."

She let out a cute little snort, and I finally saw a hint of a smile.

We reached Jena's house around the time the rest of school would have been getting out. I hadn't realized how long it'd been since I'd last come around. The once-asphalt parking pad was repaved with interlocking stones, and the porch railing had been painted blue.

It felt like walking up to a stranger's house. How could that have happened? Since Jena and I had first started hanging out in elementary school, I'd dropped by here at least once every week or two.

Until Joss. Joss had happened.

We trooped downstairs to the big entertainment room Jena's parents had converted the basement into. That, at least, looked the same. A wall of built-in shelves, lined with books and framed photos and sports trophies Jena's older brother hadn't bothered to take with him when he'd moved out years ago, surrounded the widescreen TV. The smell of the spicy-cedar potpourri Jena's mom liked lingered in the air.

I sank into one of the corduroy armchairs while the others settled on the couch. "So Davey is back at school. And still not the normal Davey, so obviously what happened by the lake last week didn't cure him."

Vicky winced and looked at her tightly clasped hands. "I just want to know," she said quietly. "Are we assuming he's the one who went after that girl yesterday? I mean, I never would've thought Davey would hurt someone. Not at all. Definitely not like that."

"Yeah," Reuben said. "That was fucked up."

"It wasn't *Davey*," I said. "We have to stop thinking like that. Davey wouldn't push a teacher or eat a gerbil either. Whatever that thing infected him with, it's taking him over, and that's what would've killed that girl. That's what we've got to get rid of. We need to get the real Davey back before he's forced into doing something even worse."

Vicky nodded.

"Do you really think we can take him on?" Reuben said.

"I think we've got a chance at getting through to him. To try the cures and see if something works. It's a better chance than—"

The squeak of the door opening upstairs interrupted me. "We're down here," Jena called to Joss. He stalked down to the basement and eased himself into the chair by the other end of the sofa, his knee touching Jena's.

"So you're going to tell the police about this, aren't you?" he said without so much as a hello.

We all stared at him. I tipped my head. "Tell the police about what, exactly?"

"About your friend no longer being in his right mind. That's what this big secret meeting is about, right? You know he murdered that girl. You have to go to the police."

"We don't know," Vicky protested.

"And what would you suggest we tell them even if we did?" I said. "*You* think we're crazy for believing what's happening to him—why would the police listen?"

Reuben chuckled. "Even if they listened, do you think they could catch him?"

"Maybe I don't think he's carrying some supernatural curse, but that doesn't mean I can't tell something's wrong with him," Joss said. "What do you think *you* can do that professionals can't?"

Believe that what was happening really was supernatural, obviously. Wasn't Joss the one who'd said there was no hope of curing somebody if you didn't know their disease? But there didn't seem to be any point in bringing that up.

Jena set her hand over his. "I know what you're saying. And you're right, in theory. But what if it wasn't him? We can't go ruining his life because he's been acting weird."

I wondered if she would have felt the same way if she knew that Davey had all but admitted his guilt to me.

"And if we try to, he won't trust us at all afterward," I said. "We'll lose any chance of helping him. He doesn't deserve that. He doesn't deserve any of this. And Rube's right —the cops don't stand a chance against something that fast, that strong." That vicious. "If we don't find a way to deal with what's really happening in time, *more* people might die."

Joss let out a huff of breath. "What about the murder we do know about? That body they found that came out of the river down by Arlington? You shot him. I knew something sounded off with your story about the gun."

I'd forgotten I'd told Joss I was the one who'd fired Vicky's pistol. "It wasn't a man," I said. "You didn't see it."

"I don't think you really did either." He stood up. "I didn't figure you'd want to admit it, but someone has to do the right thing. I just wanted to give you the chance first."

"Joss!" Jena started.

Vicky interrupted her. "It wasn't Max," she said, her voice ragged. "It was me. I was the one who shot it. Him."

An emotion that looked suspiciously like disappointment flickered across Joss's face. I gritted my teeth. Of course he'd wanted to blame me. He hesitated now, looking at Vicky. I reached across the arm of the sofa and squeezed her shoulder. She leaned into my touch. A quiver passed through her body.

"It was an accident," she said. "I only wanted to… to slow it down. And Max is right. You have no idea what you're talking about. It wasn't human. And Davey won't be either soon, if we don't stop arguing about this stuff and start figuring out how to help him!"

She raised her eyes as she said the last sentence, with a challenge in them.

"Why do the police need to know about what happened

by the lake?" Reuben said with honest confusion. "That guy, or whatever it was, is dead already. How is getting Vicky in trouble going to make anything better?"

"Personal responsibility!" Joss tossed up his hands. "You all— You don't care about that at all, do you? What if that guy had family who want to know what happened to him? Maybe you're the psychos here."

Jena got up and grabbed his arm. "Joss," she said before he could keep ranting, "stop shouting at my friends. We're going to talk for a minute, just the two of us."

His mouth snapped shut. He hesitated and then, frowning, followed her up the stairs.

"Do you think he's right?" Vicky asked shakily. "Maybe I should tell the police. It was my fault."

"Don't let him get to you," I said. "Not even Jena thinks you should. Look what that thing did to Davey. How many other people do you think it hurt, or even killed, since it's been like that? If you hadn't shot it, it would've gotten away to do more damage."

"It would've been better if we could have talked to it. Maybe we could've saved Davey by now if we had. I never should have shot at it."

"Maybe. But it didn't look to me like it *could* talk. You know you didn't mean to kill it, Vicky. And if you tell anyone, it'll be on your record. You'll screw up your college plans, and any time you apply for a job... For what? For a beast that would've killed *you* if it'd had the chance?"

She exhaled. "I know. I just feel so awful."

"Wish I'd been there," Reuben said, his leg jittering. "I would've shot it. Kapow! Wouldn't have bothered me."

The sad thing was, it probably wouldn't have.

I rubbed Vicky's shoulder. "Remember what you said a couple minutes ago. We've got to move past all this and focus on Davey. If Jena was right about the full moon thing—"

"—we've only got two weeks left," Jena finished for me. She'd come back down the stairs alone. The edges of her eyes looked a little red. "I'm sorry, Vicky. I didn't know he was going to… I thought he was trying to understand. You don't have to worry. I got him to see that he needs to leave things alone. And that it probably wouldn't help if he stayed right now."

Even with Joss gone, tension hung in the room like yesterday's rain clouds. I leaned forward in the chair. "Good. Then we can get to the important stuff. All the supplies I ordered have arrived. We've got wolfsbane and holy water and the rest to work with."

Jena nodded. "From what Dr. Nichols said, there are a lot of different approaches… I guess we try everything? Even the knife thing you couldn't get past him the other day, Max—we should give that another shot."

"Good luck getting anything past Davey these days." Reuben chuckled.

"That's the real problem," I said. "*Maybe* we could trick him into eating or drinking something—I'm not even sure about that—but how are we going to pull off any of the other cures?"

"What if he was sleeping?" Vicky said.

I rubbed my wrist, where three thin lines of scabs reminded me of how quickly Davey could wake up. "I don't think he sleeps very deeply anymore. And besides, we don't know *where* he's been sleeping."

"That's a natural sleep." Jena glanced at Reuben. "You remember when we had to take him to the hospital because of those pills—he was pretty much in a coma."

Reuben's eyes lit up. "I can totally get sleeping pills."

"We'd still have to trick him into taking them," I said. "We won't be able to get away with much at school."

"Throw a party, man!" Reuben said. "My place, Friday night. It'll be perfect."

Vicky frowned. "Do you think he'd come?"

My first instinct was to say no, but on second thought, it didn't seem like such a bad idea. "The beast side of him is getting cocky. If we ask him to come, he probably will so he doesn't look like he's worried. So he can prove *he* can do whatever he wants."

"Are we going to be able to get through everything in one night?" Jena asked. "Some of the possibilities—dunking him in fresh water and all that—we'd have to take him outside town."

"We can try."

"If we need to hold on to him longer," Reuben put in, "I'll lock him in the basement. He might be strong, but that lock's the only good thing in the house."

"Where will you and Crystal sleep?" Vicky said.

He shrugged. "Couch. Floor. I don't care. We'll get Davey fixed up, and then it won't matter."

At least if he were locked in Reuben's basement, he wouldn't be able to go around cutting open Ash or anyone else. But Reuben was sitting there grinning, as if this were a big game. As if the beast couldn't just as easily rip into him. He still didn't get how real this was.

Jena's brow knit as if she'd noticed the same thing. "Are you sure you're okay with this, Reuben? We don't know what he'll do if we can't cure him before he wakes up."

"Not a problem," Reuben said. "Gotta do my part."

Well, it was his home, if he wanted to risk it like he risked just about everything else in his life on a daily basis. And we didn't have a lot of other options. Jena still looked worried, but I ignored the knot in my stomach and smiled.

"Okay," I said. "Let's party."

15

Being a man of my word, I leaned over my desk to tap Hannah on the back with my pen the next morning. "Party," I said when she glanced back. "Friday night at Reuben's. Now you're officially invited."

Davey was watching from his seat across from her. I didn't so much as glance his way. The feeling had started creeping up on me that he'd be more likely to come if he thought I didn't want him there. For whatever reason, the beast inside him enjoyed messing with me.

The cure prep fell mostly on me and Jena. I didn't trust Reuben to handle the supplies with care, and when we started talking wolfsbane potions and silver knives, Vicky balked.

"It's silly," she said, when I was walking her home. "I know we're doing this to help him. But preparing all this stuff behind his back, it feels mean somehow. Like we're planning to hurt him. It makes me all..." She shivered. "I wish we could just ask him to let us try the cures instead of sneaking around on him."

"I know," I said, even though it did sound silly, especially from a girl who'd *shot* a living creature on Davey's behalf a week ago. Sometimes Vicky's bleeding heart got a bit soppy. "Jena and I can take care of the rest. You just try to relax. In a few days we're going to get the real Davey back, and there won't be anything to worry about anymore."

"I really hope so," she said.

I didn't tell her how much I did too.

The night before the party, Jena came over to my place for dinner. After Dad slunk back to his studio and Mom retired upstairs, we took over the kitchen.

"This stuff is poisonous if you have more than a little bit," Jena said, holding up one of the capsules that supposedly contained some form of wolfsbane. "I guess we start with one pill. Maybe dissolve it in a bottle of water and give that to him when he wakes up as his only drink? I wonder if he'd be able to taste that there's something in it."

I filled a glass at the sink. "Here, I'll try it."

She dropped the capsule into the water, and we waited as it dissolved. It left a little cloud in the bottom of the glass, but with a quick stir, that disappeared. I took a sip.

"Tastes pretty normal to me." But how long would it take Davey to drink whatever water we left for him, if nothing we tried while he was unconscious worked? The beast would probably hold him back until he was dying of thirst. That would take days. "Are you sure we can't make him drink some while he's out?"

"We'd be just as likely to choke him as cure him that way," Jena said. "But we can try putting a bit in his mouth. And we need to make some sort of paste out of a bunch of these pills. I guess mash them up with a little water? Since Dr. Nichols said some sources talk about rubbing it on the person."

"Wolfsbane massage!" I said. "Lovely."

She cracked a smile. A strand of hair drifted across her face, and without thinking, I reached out and brushed it aside. My fingers grazed her cheek. Then she was getting up, going to the cupboard, and I was touching empty air.

"Would your parents mind if we borrowed a bowl or something?" she asked.

"There's about a hundred of those reusable sandwich containers in the back over there." I pointed. "No one will miss one."

She grabbed a container and a spoon, and sat down again. Her expression was completely intent as she poured a couple dozen wolfsbane capsules into the container. Like nothing in the world mattered more.

"You know, I couldn't have done all this without you," I said. "If you hadn't been here, I probably *would* have thought I was insane."

"No, you wouldn't have. Anyway, thank me when something we try works." She frowned at the powder forming under the press of the spoon. "I hope this is enough. Maybe you should've ordered two bottles."

"We could mix it with Vaseline or something instead of water. There'll be more to spread around that way, right?"

She kicked me lightly under the table. "There, now you're making yourself useful."

I knew the question was stupid before I asked it, but I couldn't stop myself. "Is Joss coming tomorrow?"

Jena's mouth tightened. "That doesn't seem like a good idea, does it?"

"So you don't tell him absolutely everything."

"He'd freak. And he hasn't asked, I think because he knows that." She sighed. "Look, I know you don't like him. But if we weren't in this crazy situation, he wouldn't have given you any reason not to. Remember that, okay? Maybe I haven't made it clear enough, but I do like him. A lot. So if we're going to stay friends, you'll have to find a way to get along with him."

"Yeah, yeah," I said, looking away. I could think of several reasons to dislike Joss that had nothing to do with supernatural beasts. His pretentious clothes, his haughtiness, his condescending attitude. The fact that he owned an admittedly kind of awesome car, and I had to borrow Mom's. But mostly, right then, I hated him for making Jena say those words, for having whatever it was she liked about him enough to threaten our friendship. Part of me wanted to walk right over to his house and hit him until I'd pummeled it all out of him.

He didn't deserve her. Why the hell had she picked him?

When it could have been me.

"Max?" Jena said.

I glanced up. My thoughts scrambled as if someone had taken an electric beater to them. She was looking at me with those deep blue eyes of hers—looking concerned. That wasn't how I wanted her to look at me.

I said, brilliantly, "What?"

"I thought I'd lost you for a second there." She smiled,

and my heart literally pattered. Why did I have to be tongue-tied for the first time in my life at this particular moment?

"Nope, still here," I said. "Just wondering if a few of those pills would cure the jerk in Joss."

She rolled her eyes and pushed back her chair. I wanted her to come over and lean so close I could feel her breath. I wanted her to look at me like she had that New Year's after the first time I'd kissed her. I wanted her to say, "I like you, Max. A lot."

"I think we're good to go," she said. "I'll pick up some Vaseline on the way home."

I walked her to the door, made some joke I don't remember, and watched her disappear down the street in the twilight. And I realized it boiled down to something much simpler than any of those things. Like a secret code telegraphed ages ago, to which I'd suddenly stumbled on the key.

I wanted *her*.

I turned to go back inside and noticed a piece of paper sticking out of our mailbox: a flyer for some window-cleaning service. It was fluttering in the breeze. I grabbed it automatically as I headed in. Then I caught a glimpse of the picture inked on the other side, and my pulse stuttered.

The drawing was done in Davey's distinctive style. A figure stood in the middle of the page with his hands raised, smiling at the viewer. He wore the same sort of crown Davey had placed on my head in the doodle he'd drawn for Vicky, but it was clearly Davey himself this time. The eyes had slit pupils and two little fang tips poked from the corners of his grin, and he'd sketched in one of his favorite shirts—the

Spider-Man one with the black sleeves and the spider logo on the front. The one he hadn't worn out of the house since I'd told him two years ago it was way to kiddy for a self-respecting teenager to be seen in.

Lines of motion arced over his head, broken by vaguely oval shapes. I stared at them for a second in the brighter light of the hall before my brain caught up.

Hearts. He'd sent me a drawing of himself juggling bloody hearts.

I crumpled the paper and stuffed it into the garbage can. But the image kept dancing behind my eyes as I lay down for the night with my head set close to Ash's wall.

The crowd at Reuben's house that Friday was pretty much the same bunch who'd come out to the lake the night this whole mess got started. Music was blasting and people were squeezing in and out of the living room and kitchen, spilling onto the parking space out back. Reuben had locked the basement door to remind himself not to let anyone go wandering down.

I hadn't been sure whether I'd rather have Ash there with me or at home with Mom and Dad, but she'd heard Reuben talking about the party that morning and invited herself. She was dancing with her friends in the living room now—that tight, undulating kind of dancing everyone does when there's hardly room to breathe—swigging from a beer and laughing a little too hard. Her makeup was painted especially thick to cover the dark smudges under her eyes. Our gazes met across the room once, and she gave me a lopsided smile that looked more sad than anything.

A week ago, Sofia would have been there dancing with them.

One of the guys said something in Ash's ear, and she put her coy smirk back on. Like that was the only face she knew how to wear. It didn't seem right.

The night was a little cooler for once, but with us all packed into that small space, the apartment was sweltering. When Vicky came over with a couple of rum and cokes on ice, I held my glass to my forehead for a second before taking a drink.

Her eyes twitched as she glanced around the room. "He isn't here yet, is he?"

I shook my head. I hadn't moved out of sight of the door since I'd arrived.

The party had been going strong for more than an hour. Maybe Davey had figured us out. Or maybe he just couldn't be bothered.

Eleven more days. I swallowed, and the drink went down cold.

Fuck it. Why was I standing around here waiting for him? He'd either come or he wouldn't. Staring at the door wasn't going to make it happen.

I set down my cup and grabbed Vicky by the waist. "Come on, let's dance."

She hesitated, exhaled, and smiled at me. We eased partway into the crowd. I pulled her close to me so her hips met mine. She swayed, running her hand down the front of my shirt. I bent to kiss the edge of her jaw.

The dance should have been electric. It should have started the slow burn that sparked hotter each time my skin brushed hers, until there wasn't anything in either of our heads except finding the nearest private room. That was what I wanted. But even as the music pounded louder, I couldn't lose myself in the feel of her.

It wasn't just Vicky and me. Jena was there in the back of my mind.

Halfway into the second song, the atmosphere shifted. A current of tension wove through the room. I looked up, and Davey was standing just inside the door, his mouth slanted at an angle somewhere between bored and satisfied.

Seeing him killed the last of any desire I'd had to keep dancing. "Thirsty," I said to Vicky. She nodded and moved off to join a couple of her friends. I edged my way back to my abandoned rum and coke. The sip I took left my mouth sour and sticky.

"Rube really packed the place," Davey said over the din, picking up the glass that had been Vicky's. He tossed back half of it in one go and grimaced. "God, I hate rum."

In that second he sounded so much like his normal self, I started to relax automatically. "You hate everything. Killjoy."

His eyes darted over to meet mine with a flash of yellow-gold, correcting my momentary lapse. Not Davey, not really.

"I thought *you* hated partying here in the summer." He slid his gaze back to the crowd. "'Like shoving everyone into an oven.' Did you decide the place has some benefits after all?"

His voice was so even I couldn't read it. Was he just taking a dig, or digging for ulterior motives?

"Reuben insisted," I said, watching Davey's expression.

"You know how he is when he gets stuck on some idea."

"That never stopped you from bowling right over him before. You must be going soft, Max."

He was still peering into the mass of dancers. I couldn't see her right then, but I was suddenly sure his gaze was fixed on Ash. My hands clenched. "I guess the police finally tracked you down?" He'd been called to the office during English class earlier that week.

Davey didn't appear fazed by the question. "Yep. We had a nice chat. I showed how contrite I was about that misunderstanding with Mr. Peck and offered to help their investigation in any way I could." The edge of a smirk curled his lips.

Before I could think of what to say next, Vicky broke through the crowd beside us.

"You made it!" she said to Davey. "You haven't been around much all week—I was getting worried about you."

His cockiness faded; his voice gentled. He tipped his head to the side almost shyly. "I've been getting by. I'm not sure I'm totally over that bug I had."

I could have laughed. What a load of bullshit. But it wasn't all that funny, because I could see Vicky buying into his act exactly the way the cops must have. "Do you have any of those herbal pills I brought you left?" she asked. "I can get you some more if you think they'd help."

"Nah," he said. The soft modulation of his tone had an almost hypnotic quality to it. "Those were great, but I think the best thing is just taking it easy. I didn't want to miss tonight, though."

"Hey, this *is* taking it easy." Vicky motioned toward the

kitchen. "Come on, I'll show you where Reuben stashed the best booze."

At least she'd remembered the plan. I raised my glass. "See you around."

Davey shot me one last little smirk before he let Vicky lead him away. He was playing her like a fiddle, and he didn't mind that I knew. I took another gulp of my rum and coke.

Well, he wouldn't be laughing in an hour or two. The beast in him thought he had us all under his thumb, obviously. The last person he'd suspect of pulling a fast one on him was Reuben.

I started to edge along the wall toward the kitchen. The drink would come from Rube, but I wanted to keep an eye on things, make sure he didn't screw up. Who knew how many chemicals the guy had in his system already?

I was halfway there when Jena emerged through the kitchen doorway, her cheeks a little pink, her hair windblown. She must have gone out back for a bit. She caught me looking and nodded.

I'd hardly talked to her since we'd set up the place, pushing the couch and chairs against the walls to make room for dancing and stashing our anti-beast supplies in the back of the cabinet under the sink. When she headed toward me, my heart pattered giddily the way it had yesterday night. I tossed back the last of my drink.

She had to stand with her toes practically touching mine for me to hear her. She'd gotten more dressed up than she usually did for these things: a silky dark green blouse that would have slid off her shoulder at a touch. But the eyebrow arch she gave me was familiar Jena.

"So the party's going well."

"Seems like." I gestured to her empty hands. "Staying dry tonight?"

"For now. I don't totally trust anything Reuben's already opened."

"Well, I can't blame you there."

I should have continued on to the kitchen like I'd planned for that very reason, but she smiled at me. The sparks I'd been missing before leapt under my skin.

This was stupid. Out of all the girls in town, why did I have to be hung up on the one who'd already decided she wasn't interested?

Or had she? I'd never really given it a shot. Why the hell was Max Weston sitting around waiting for what he wanted to come to *him*? That wasn't how this worked. All I had to do was pretend she was one of those other girls, lean in, and—

"I like this shirt." I tapped the short sleeve and let my finger trail down the side of her arm as I lowered my hand, almost as if by accident. Jena turned her face toward mine, and it would have been so easy to close those last few inches between us. For a second, the way her gaze held mine, I was sure she was thinking it too.

I caught a flicker of blond hair from the corner of my eye and raised my head. Vicky was hurrying toward us, her eyes wide and worried. The moment fizzled. I stepped back, running my hand through my hair.

"What's up?" I said when she reached us.

She twisted her hands in front of her. "I think Reuben made a mistake."

16

A chill washed over me. "What do you mean?"

"He—" Vicky paused, glancing back at the kitchen. I motioned her closer so she could murmur into my ear. "He poured the two drinks like we planned. I didn't see him slip in the pill, so I doubt Davey noticed. But then Davey pointed at something out back, and Reuben put the cups down for a second to look, and after they started drinking, he sounded even more out of it than usual. He just told me he thinks he picked up the wrong one."

"Did Davey hear?"

"I don't know," she said, her voice wobbling. "He'd stepped out of the room."

Jena hadn't heard most of the conversation, but she must have gotten the gist. I jerked my head toward the kitchen, and we hurried over. If this was just Reuben's stupidity, we could still salvage the situation. As long as I got to him before he started blabbing about his mistake directly to Davey.

Neither of them was in the kitchen now. I pushed past a

couple of sophomores standing by the sink and peered out the window. In the hazy light, I couldn't make out anyone who looked like Reuben or Davey. Rube hadn't tried to lure him down to the basement anyway, had he? I wouldn't put it past him.

Vicky and Jena followed me back to the front of the apartment, all of us scanning the crowd as we went. The basement door was still locked. I raised my eyebrows in question at the girls, and they both shook their heads. Vicky bit her lip.

That was when I noticed a couple of guys by the living room window, poking at the glass. Gaping at something outside.

I bolted for the front door, stomping on more than one set of toes along the way and not particularly caring, and yanked it open.

Down by the corner, Davey was dashing back and forth across the sidewalk. Reuben chased after him at a lopsided run. He stumbled, laughing so hard he sounded as if he were choking.

"Rube!" I yelled. Davey waved and ducked around the corner, and Reuben staggered after him.

Vicky had come up behind me. "What's he doing?"

"I don't know, but it's definitely not anything he *should* be doing."

I hurried down the front steps and jogged up the street. Reuben's laughter carried between the houses. As long as he kept that up, I wouldn't lose them completely.

I reached the corner just in time to see Reuben disappearing around another bend up ahead. They were following the route we'd have taken if we were heading to Davey's house. Why would Davey want to lead Rube there?

"Where are they going?" Jena asked, catching up with me. Vicky joined us a moment later, her cheeks flushed.

"I don't know," I said. "But maybe we can cut them off."

I veered down a different road. It was almost midnight, nothing but a sliver of moon in the sky, and the streets were empty and quiet except for Reuben. His laugher rose and fell in fits and starts from one street over.

I could tell when I drew ahead of them. We were only a few blocks from Davey's house now. I pushed myself to a run, hoping the noise Reuben was making would drown out the thump of my shoes hitting the pavement.

Unless Davey *wanted* me to follow.

I hesitated as I came up on his street. Jena and Vicky slowed behind me. Davey and Reuben would have to pass us to get to his house, but the sense that Davey—or rather, the beast—had orchestrated this little detour nagged at me. Was that what I was now: a dog he tugged around by its leash? What would he do if we turned around and just walked back to the party?

Jena was breathing hard. "Are they here?"

Reuben let out another burst of giggles from the next street down. "Just about," I said.

"What are we going to do?" Vicky asked.

Well, I couldn't suggest turning back now. "We get Reuben and haul him back to the party where he's supposed to be."

I stepped around the corner. It took a second for my eyes to find Reuben in the dim light. He wasn't heading toward us as I'd expected. Just down the street from us, a low yellow fence stood beside the entrance to the ravine. Reuben was bounding past it into the deeper darkness beneath the trees.

My pulse lurched. I threw myself after him, as if I could possibly run fast enough to catch him before the shadows swallowed him completely.

Reuben's chortling echoed out to me at the edge of the ravine, but I couldn't make out even a hint of movement in the darkness. The space beyond the first line of trees was so solidly black it might as well have been a wall. His laughter wavered into the distance. I had to guess Davey was in there too, leading him farther.

I dragged in a breath. The cool night air prickled in my lungs. Jena fished out her phone and turned on the flashlight. A thin beam of light split the darkness ahead of me.

"Do you think we should go after them?" she said. The glow gleamed off the nervous whites of her eyes. What a deranged world this had become, where we were afraid of Davey of all people.

"We've come this far," I said. I reached for my own phone, but Jena shook her head.

"We don't want all our batteries to end up drained."

"Right."

Vicky reached for my hand, and the three of us plunged into the ravine together.

We hustled along the path as it wound down into the shallow gully. The smell of mud and decaying wood saturated the air. Somewhere to our left, the water of the creek burbled over its stony bed. Jena stubbed her toe on a fallen branch and cursed softly, and I realized something had changed.

"I can't hear Rube anymore."

We halted. Vicky's fingers tensed around mine. The sounds of the ravine were all around us, but Reuben's laughter had faded away completely.

"I don't think he could have walked very far off the path in that condition," Jena said. "As long as we keep following it, we should find him."

A breeze trickled after us on our way to the stream. Jena's light quivered as she held it for Vicky and me to follow the mossy boards that led across the water. Something skittered through the underbrush, and Vicky flinched.

I scanned the ground for footprints heading off into the deeper forest. "They might've gone right out the other end. We're already almost halfway—"

Vicky shrieked. Her hand squeezed mine so tightly I thought my fingers would break, and the light tumbled to the ground. Jena scrambled after her phone with a rasp of breath. As she snatched it up, a footstep crunched toward us. The light caught on a figure to the right of the path, dark-haired and pale-faced.

A crooked smile twisted Davey's mouth. "Feeling a little jumpy?"

Vicky let out a gasping sort of laugh. "Surprised. I wasn't expecting to see someone so close."

"Where's Reuben?" I said.

Davey shifted his weight from one foot to the other. "What have I done with him, do you mean, Max?"

"Of course not." Vicky released my hand to take a step

toward him. "We know you guys were only goofing around. We're just worried about Reuben. He was so out of it."

"So sweet." Davey was still looking at me. "That's a good thing for you, isn't it?"

"We just want to help," Vicky said. "I know things have been kind of weird lately. Why don't you show us which way Reuben went, and then we can all go back to his place?"

Davey raised his eyebrows. "And so understanding. And we know how good she is at sharing too, don't we, Max? Especially when it comes to you. Hey, these days even dead girls are getting a piece."

Vicky's gaze darted to me.

"Just tell us where Reuben is," I said.

"Oh, he's around."

"Is he okay?" Jena broke in.

Davey grinned. "Well, he's pretty high, but he likes it that way, doesn't he?" He started to turn. "Guess I'll leave you to it."

"Davey!" I lunged at him before I even knew I was going to do it, which is maybe why he didn't seem to know either. He jumped back, a second too late. I'd already grabbed his arm. "You've got to—"

He kicked me, his heel slamming into my thigh. Blunt pain shot up through my hip.

I stumbled, and my grip loosened. Davey twisted his arm away with a snap. The underbrush rustled in his wake as he vanished into the trees.

I steadied myself against the closest tree as the ache spread through my leg. Yeah, he was strong now. Vicky touched my shoulder.

"I'm okay," I said. "I just need a sec." I dragged in a little air and pulled myself away from the tree, keeping my weight on my other leg.

She opened her mouth, paused, and said, "What did he mean, that stuff about sharing? Was he talking about Ash's friend?"

"Who knows?" I said. "The guy's insane. The important thing is we still have to find Reuben."

Jena shone her light over the bushes that surrounded us. "Davey said he was around. Reuben! Can you hear me?"

No one answered. I closed my eyes, trying to shut out everything else: the pressure of Vicky's uncertain gaze still on me, the dwindling pain in my thigh. He'd said something else. *He's around. He's pretty high...*

My gut knotted. I let Jena call Reuben's name one more time. Then I grabbed my own phone and tapped on the light.

This wasn't necessarily the right spot. Reuben could be anywhere in the ravine. But this was where Davey had stopped us, and I was pretty sure he wanted us to know.

I braced myself and aimed the light upward.

At first it revealed only fractured shadows as the beam cut across the leafy branches overhead. I turned, aiming it in a circle around us. Halfway through the rotation, Vicky gasped. My body went still. My eyes focused on a gray oblong object hovering about ten feet above our heads.

The sole of a running shoe.

My stomach dropped. I took a step back to reposition the light. It crept over the second shoe, the jeans covering the dangling legs, the striped wifebeater Reuben had been wearing. "Reub—" Vicky started, but her voice died before she finished his name.

Just above his shoulders, Reuben's body merged with the tree. His neck was wedged into a narrow fork between two branches. The distant shape of his head listed at an angle no living person could have survived. I thought I could make out the edge of his lips, curled upward in his stupid, goofy smile. A shudder passed through me.

Pretty high. Just the way he liked. Oh, Rube.

Someone's breath hitched. Vicky turned and bowed over to upheave her dinner at the base of the nearest tree. She gagged and spit between sobs.

Jena's fingers wrapped around my tensed hand and lowered it so the light pointed down at the path. In the dim glow that reflected back at her, her face was sallow. Her lips pressed into a tight line.

"It's our fault." Vicky's voice quavered. "We told him to give Davey the drink. I didn't know— I didn't think—"

Jena's light dimmed and blinked out. Vicky shut up. Jena glanced up at the tree that held Reuben and then at me.

"Let's get out of here while we can still find our way," I said with a rasp in my throat. "We can't do anything for him now."

By the time we made it to the street, Vicky had stopped crying. Her shoulders shivered as the breeze crept past us. I put my arm around her, and she let me, but her body stayed rigid. Our feet drifted back toward Reuben's house, dragging on the pavement.

A couple times I opened my mouth, only to find I didn't have anything to say. There were too many thoughts in my head, crowding each other out before I could make sense of any of them.

Why Reuben? Was Vicky right—had Davey realized the trick, gotten pissed off, and wanted to hurt him for it? He hadn't seemed angry. But then, what did I know about the beast inside him? I'd thought we had everything planned out so fucking well…

"Hey," Jena said. I raised my head. A slender figure stood on the sidewalk a half a block ahead of us, wavering on three-inch heels. Ash turned at the sound of our steps. She brushed her hair back with a pale hand, her black-rimmed eyes relieved, and hurried toward us.

"There you are! I saw you guys run out, so I came after you, but by the time I made it to the door you were gone." Her gaze caught Vicky's face, and her voice lowered. "What happened?"

"You've been wandering around out here alone?" I said before anyone could answer. The memory of Sofia's body, open and bleeding, flashed through my mind. It'd be so much easier to slice through a girl on a dark, empty street. "What the hell were you thinking, Ash?"

She blinked, startled. "I was worried. I wanted to make sure you were okay."

"Well, it was stupid. You have no idea— People are dying, Ash. I can't follow you around every second making sure you're safe. You're supposed to be looking after yourself."

"I didn't mean to—"

"Then don't fucking *do it*!"

Her lips pursed, and she drew in a shaky breath. The frustration, anger, whatever it was that had welled up inside me ebbed until only an aching hollowness remained. Jena was staring at me, Vicky at the ground.

"Come on," I said. "Let's get back to the house."

As if we were that much safer in there.

I paused by Reuben's front door, looking through the window into the living room. Music and light radiated through the glass. Everyone was dancing and drinking and shouting into each other's ears like they'd been doing when we left. Like the guy who'd been hosting this party wasn't dangling from a tree half a mile away. My throat tightened.

It wouldn't make any difference to them when Reuben

didn't come back. They'd keep partying until they wore themselves out and either tottered home or fell asleep in a corner, without ever noticing.

"Is Crystal here?" Jena asked.

Right. Crystal. I rubbed the spot between my eyes. My head was starting to pound. "She had to leave for work at ten, won't be home until something like seven in the morning."

"So what are we going to do?" Vicky whispered. "We just left him…"

"It's not like anything worse can happen to him," I snapped, and immediately regretted it. She pulled away from me, her eyes tearing up again.

"We can let the police know," Jena said. "It's going to sound crazy, but we'll figure something out."

"Anonymously," I said. "Leave them a tip. There's no way we can explain what really happened that they'll believe. And I don't think they'll be too happy to hear I found two bodies in less than a week."

Understanding crossed her face. The cops already had me on their radar; this incident would send their suspicions into overdrive.

"What are we going to tell them about Davey?" Vicky asked.

Ash's gaze skipped between our faces. "What did Davey do? Where were you? What happened?"

"You don't want to know." I kicked the concrete step. "What *can* we tell them about Davey? Our friend's turning into a homicidal monster? It's not going to sound any less insane than it did three days ago."

"But he did it," Jena said quietly. "He killed Reuben.

And Ash's friend too—I don't think we can say we don't know that now."

"*He* didn't do it!" I said. "That thing isn't Davey. *We* fucked up. We're the ones who know what's going on, we were supposed to be helping him, and instead we screwed it all up and he's still out there. And we haven't even tried most of the things that might make him better."

"Max—"

I cut off her protest with a shake of my head. "Think about Davey, the real Davey, the one who'd get tongue-tied talking to you and draw pictures just to make people laugh. If we give up now, he's gone. No one else is going to try to get him back. We might as well have killed him."

Vicky winced. There was a moment of silence. Then Jena said, "If it saves someone else's life…"

As if I hadn't thought about that. As if I didn't know he could come after any of the rest of us next.

"And what do you think will happen if we send the police after him? Even if he *lets* them catch him and take him in, he'll act like he has no idea why anyone would accuse him. They've already talked to him, and he brushed them right off. There's no proof he did anything. Our story sounds crazy. They're not going to be able to lock him up. And when he gets out of there…"

"What?" Ash said.

I grimaced. "If we assume he did this to Reuben because Reuben was trying to put a pill in his drink, then what's he going to do to the people who sent the cops after him? Bringing the police into this isn't going to save anyone. Not Davey, not us, not whoever the beast in him might go after if it decides it's safer to leave town."

Vicky looked down at her hands. The hands that had shot another beast less than ten days ago. They trembled. "Max is right. We can't abandon him. We've got to figure out another way to help him."

"How?" Ash said. The word hung in the air. I was suddenly aware of all the open space around us, the shadows where a stealthy figure might conceal himself.

"This isn't a good place to decide that," I said. "We'll sleep on it and see what we've got in the morning. Okay?"

After a second's hesitation, the others nodded. I glanced through the window again and swallowed thickly. Poor clueless Reuben.

"I'll get the stuff we brought," Jena said, "and call the police from a payphone on the way home."

"None of us should go anywhere on our own from now on," I said. "The beast only hurt Sofia and Reuben after they were alone. Like Dr. Nichols said: no witnesses, no one to intervene."

She nodded. "I'll call Joss. He'll pick me up."

She went inside and closed the door behind her. I glanced at Vicky. "I'm walking you home." And then at Ash. "And you're coming with me."

My sister opened her mouth as if to argue, but sighed instead. "Let me tell my friends I'm taking off, at least."

While she ducked inside, Vicky finally turned to me. "Do you really think Davey is still in there?"

"Where else would he be? I've seen him, Vick. Just for a moment now and then, but... He's not all gone."

She bit her lip. "He must hate what it's making him do."

Did he? Or was the beast so tangled up in him now he didn't know the difference? I pictured the real Davey, the way I'd told Jena to, but in every memory I called up, he cocked his head and smirked at me the way he had when I'd asked him about Sofia.

Ash popped out of the house. "Okay, let's get out of here."

As we walked, Vicky asked Ash about her sophomore classes, and Ash asked Vicky about her post-grad plans, and neither of them said a word to me. I guessed Ash was smarting from the way I'd talked to her when I'd found out she'd left the party.

Outside her house, Vicky offered me her cheek when I bent to kiss her. "I want to talk to you tomorrow," she said.

"Are you still worrying about what Davey said?" I asked. "You know he's just trying to make everyone upset."

"I know. But I'm wondering why he picked that way. I'm not saying you did anything, I just need to think a little."

"Vick..."

"Tomorrow." She went inside.

Then it was just me and Ash. Her shoes hit the sidewalk with lonely sounding clunks next to my softer sneakers. She turned her back on me when we went into the house. I followed her up the stairs.

"Ash," I said. She paused with her bedroom door partly open. "I wasn't saying those things to be mean. I just don't want anything to happen to you. But I was harsh. I'm sorry, okay?"

She rubbed her eyes. "I know. I'm not mad at you. Wandering around by myself like that *was* stupid. I don't want you to have to worry about me."

"Well," I said lightly, "be smarter next time and I won't have to."

"Yeah," she said, but she smiled with only half of her mouth. The door closed behind her, and her music switched on, the melody muffled as it wormed its way through the wall.

I went into my room and flopped onto the bed, not bothering to take off my clothes. My head hurt, my mouth tasted like dirty socks, and my stomach was a massive knot. All those questions about what we were going to do tomorrow whirled in my head. But what lingered behind my eyes for the many minutes before sleep dragged me under was the image of Reuben's shoes floating in the darkness above my head.

I woke up in the darkness with my belt digging into my side. As I shifted, Ash's voice filtered through the wall. Sleep-talking, I thought hazily, burrowing my face into the pillow. It sounded like quite the conversation.

I'd almost drifted off again when her voice stopped, and another one answered.

I flinched into full awareness. My heart thudded so loud that for a second I couldn't hear anything else. Squirming upright, I leaned close to the wall.

Ash was speaking again, too quietly for me to make out words. I had to have imagined it. But I stayed there, my ear an inch from the plaster, waiting.

For a few seconds, there was nothing. I rested my head against the wall. And a voice spoke on the other side, too low to be Ash's.

A guy's voice.

My legs tangled in the sheet. I kicked it off and blundered into the hall. At my push, Ash's door flew open.

Two heads turned toward me. Ash's snapped around, her eyes wide and her freckles standing out on her cheeks, which were drained of color. She was sitting cross-legged on her bed, her blanket wrapped around her torso, hiding everything below her collarbone except one bare foot. Her bare arms were folded over the blanket, holding it in place.

Davey's head swiveled slowly, as if my arrival wasn't a surprise, only a curiosity. He stood propped against Ash's desk, in the same T-shirt and cargo pants he'd worn to the party.

The clothes he'd murdered Reuben in.

His hands rested on the edge of the desk, empty. I was so little threat to him he didn't even uncross his ankles.

Beyond him, Ash's window gaped open. A stubble of screen ran around the edge of the frame. The rest lay on the floor beneath in a neat square. I could have believed he'd cut it with his fingernails. That he'd jumped all the way from the back fence onto the window ledge. Just another lesson in not underestimating him.

Vicky's question came back to me. *Do you really think he's still in there?* I met Davey's eyes, searching for a glimpse of my best friend, for the guy who'd murmured about Ash as he fell asleep. An image of his hands snapping Reuben's neck flitted through my mind, and my stomach turned.

If we did get the real Davey back, how was he going to get over what the beast had made him become?

"Davey," I said, "you know you don't want to hurt her."

"Of course I know that," he said, sounding amused. He glanced at Ash. "Have I said anything about hurting you?"

She raised her chin and shook her head. But despite the defiant set of her mouth, her fingers were whitening where they clutched the blanket.

Davey saw it too. "You're still scared. You don't have to be."

"You hurt Sofia," she said. "And Reuben."

"That's different," he said, as calmly as if he was talking about tossing a bottle in the trash. "That needed to happen. Your friend was doing everything she could to get herself eviscerated. And Reuben, well, he's been nothing more than a waste of space for at least a couple years now. Right, Max?"

My jaw clenched. "Are you going to say I wanted him dead too? He might have been a screw-up, but he still had a right to live." And who knew what Reuben could have ended up accomplishing or whether he could have pulled himself out of that drugged-up haze, if he'd had the rest of his life to do it?

"No," Davey said. "But you didn't have much use for him anymore either. Anyway, he enjoyed himself. I didn't exactly drag him out of the party. All you have to do is give people what they want. After watching you for so long, I don't know why I never realized how easy that is."

He turned back to Ash. "But you're smarter than them, aren't you? You're strong. And you want to be stronger. It's so easy, Ash. I promise."

"No," Ash said, but she hesitated first.

"What are you talking about?" I demanded.

They both ignored me. Ash was staring at Davey now. He pushed himself off the desk and took a step closer.

"None of them would ·matter anymore. Even *he* wouldn't matter." He jabbed his finger at me. "You can't imagine what it's like. All you have to do is think of what you want, and then you take it, because there's no one who can stop you."

He raised his hand to her, and it clicked. No, he didn't want to hurt her. He was here to take Ash in a completely different way.

I moved to her side. "And then what? If you keep this up, how long do you think you've got before you end up like that thing by the lake, snarling and slavering and living in the dirt? Why don't you tell her about that part, Davey? Is that what you want to happen to her? Is that what you want to happen to *you*?"

His gaze flickered, and his stance slackened, just slightly. For a second, I thought he was listening.

"You can't imagine it," he repeated, his voice softer now. "Maybe it doesn't have to turn out that way."

If that was the real Davey speaking, he didn't stick around any longer than it took to say those words. Those yellow-gold eyes snapped back to Ash. "I know you want this. If you didn't, you would've started screaming the second I came in."

He shot forward, faster than I'd ever seen him move before, and snatched her arm. I threw myself at him. Ash squeaked and flinched back, and I collided with Davey with the full force of my weight. He twisted, and I stumbled around him. My shoulder banged the wall. I swung at him again, and he wove out of range with a chuckle. Then he whipped around and vaulted out the window.

His feet hit the ground with a thump so faint I wouldn't have heard it if I hadn't expected a sound. I charged to the window, but I couldn't exactly go leaping after him, not unless I wanted to break both my legs.

Behind me, Ash let out a whimper. I turned, and my mouth went dry. Her chin trembled as she looked up at me, cradling her arm. In the middle of her forearm, on the underside where the skin was palest, blood dribbled from a round, mottled wound. From the place where Davey had bitten her.

18

I opened the front door when I heard the thud of Jena's old bike dropping onto the lawn. I guessed she hadn't been sleeping too well either. She'd picked up her phone on the third ring and gotten here in under twenty minutes.

"We washed the bite as thoroughly as we could," I murmured as I ushered her past the dark living room. With Dad's white noise machine thrumming away and the bathroom between their room and Ash's, my parents hadn't stirred through the entire incident, and I didn't want to change that. "Did you bring the wolfsbane stuff?"

"I brought everything." She shifted the straps of the bag off her shoulder and into her hands.

She tugged out the plastic container as we came into the kitchen. Ash straightened up at the table. Her face was drawn, her eyelids heavy. I wondered how much sleep she'd gotten before Davey interrupted.

"It might sting," Jena said, pulling off the lid. The paste she'd made with the powdered pills and Vaseline coated the bottom of the container.

Ash eyed it and lay her arm on the table. "That's okay."

The wound still looked raw: a circle of teeth marks with two darker, deeper punctures near the top. Davey was growing fangs. As Jena dabbed the paste on, those spots started to ooze fresh blood. Pain darted across Ash's face. Her mouth flattened, her expression going carefully blank.

She tucked her arm back against her body when Jena was finished. "Is that all it would take?" she asked, her tone detached, as if she were talking about a stranger instead of herself. "One bite and I'll be like him?"

"We don't know," Jena said. "When Davey got attacked… The beast tore him up really bad."

I took a sterile pad and a roll of gauze from the first aid kit, and started to bandage the wound. "And he might not have all the same powers yet, right? The next full moon's still more than a week away. That should make a difference."

"If it even works that way." Jena dropped into one of the other chairs and rubbed her forehead. "We'll just have to wait and see what happens."

"We should figure it out pretty quickly," I said. "Davey started healing in no time. If you don't, you're fine."

"But you don't know for sure." Ash's arm tensed under my fingers as I tied off the gauze. "You don't know if it always works the same way or not."

Neither of us replied right away, which must have been answer enough. She pushed back her chair. "I'm going back to bed."

"I'll get out my sleeping bag and camp out on the floor," I said, but she was already shaking her head.

"Why would he come back? He did what he wanted to

do."

I followed her upstairs, Jena trailing behind us. "What if he decides one bite might not be enough?" I lowered my voice as we reached the hall. "I can't let you—"

She spun around. Even under her breath, her tone was sharp. "What could you do anyway? You were there the first time, and you couldn't stop him then, could you?"

The words hit me like a sucker punch. It took a few seconds before I could force any sound out of my mouth. "I tried."

"I know," she said before I could go on. "You've got to let me deal my own way, okay? I already locked the window. I doubt he can cut through glass."

I wouldn't have put it past him, not anymore. We considered each other for a moment. How had my little sister gotten tougher than me? I exhaled.

"If you need anything…"

"I know," she said, and vanished into her bedroom.

I stalked into mine, thinking I'd camp out by her door instead, but as I crouched down by my bed to pull my sleeping bag out from under it, it occurred to me that it'd be tricky to explain that to Mom and Dad, and besides, I could probably hear just as well through my wall. I straightened up, walked to the window, and walked back to the bed. My feet wouldn't stop moving. My hands clenched and opened.

"Damn it. God fucking damn it!"

Jena was standing in the doorway. "It isn't your fault," she said.

"It is! You heard her. It's true. I was standing right there, two feet away from him, and I still couldn't move fast enough to stop him. I couldn't do anything." I'd been too slow. Just like when we'd chased after Reuben. Just like when I'd answered Sofia's terrified call.

"We'll figure this out."

"And if we can't? Are we going to shoot Davey too, like Vicky did with the thing that got him? How about Ash? Aim a rifle at her, *pow*, problem solved!"

"Max."

"There's got to be something, right? They don't make problems that have no fucking solution. That's not how things work. They can't just—"

"*Max.*"

The urgency in her voice curbed my tirade. I meant to turn toward her, but somehow she was already in front of me, one arm sliding around my waist, the other against my back, wrapping me in her embrace.

All the other words I'd wanted to shout melted away. I tipped my head forward, resting my cheek against the side of her head. Her hair smelled smoky from the party and like that silly potpourri in her basement. She hugged me even closer, her breath warm against my neck. I wanted to sink right into her, away from the horrors of the last few weeks, but at the same time an ache formed in my chest.

"So this is what it takes," I murmured into her hair.

"Hmmm?"

"To get you like this. I have to be freaking right out of my head to get a hug."

Jena snorted. "I didn't know you were so in need of hugs before."

"Well, you wouldn't, would you?" I pointed out. "It took

this whole mess for you to even start giving me the time of day again. You've been one AWOL friend the last year."

"Hmph," she said. "You missed me so much?"

I could have made another off-the-cuff remark to keep it a joke, but when I opened my mouth, whatever I'd been going to say caught in my throat. I swallowed and let the truth slip out.

"Yeah, I did."

Jena went still against me. Then she pulled back, just enough to meet my eyes. "What are you doing?" she asked softly.

Not half the things I wanted to be doing with her when she looked at me like that, that was for sure. "I'm telling you I've missed you."

She held my gaze for a long moment. Her eyes were sleepy, languid. So freaking beautiful. I hadn't seen it before, and I'd made myself not see it after, but ignoring it was impossible when she was standing so close, her arms still around me, her fingers curled into my shirt. I lifted my hand to touch her cheek.

She let go and stepped back. "No. I can't."

That... was not the response I'd been going for. "Can't what?"

"This." She gestured around her. "You. Do you—do you even think, Max? About Vicky? About that girl Davey killed, the one he talked about, whatever you did with her? All the others, however many it's been? You have no idea—" She stopped and shook her head. "No. I'm sorry this happened to Ash, and I promise we'll figure something out. I'll leave the bag of supplies with you in case you need to try something else. And I'll text you in the morning."

I went after her into the hall, but something—pride? Frustration? Plain old common sense?—prevented me from following her down the stairs. She ducked out the front door without once looking back. I needed to go down and turn the deadbolt behind her. I told myself to, but my body had locked itself in place. Only my fingers moved, tensing around the railing.

The floor creaked. Mom emerged from the bathroom. She paused and looked down the stairs the way Jena had gone. Then she gave me a small, sad smile. It was such an unfamiliar expression on her face that I couldn't tell if she was awake or only sleepwalking.

"Didn't go the way you imagined, did it?" she said. "I don't think anything ever does."

"Mom?" I said.

"We do our best." She nodded to herself, her gaze drifting away, and headed to her bedroom. "We do the best we can with what we have."

I didn't sleep any more that night. I lay under the sheets and pressed my head into the pillow and listened to Ash's wall. When the sun had been up for an hour, I decided that was enough waiting and got out of bed.

I knocked on Ash's door. "Come in," she said.

She was already dressed. The bandage had wrinkled as she slept. She rubbed her hand over it.

"I haven't checked it yet." She laughed awkwardly. "I almost don't want to."

"Ash," I said. "It's going to be okay."

"Even if the bite does change me, I wouldn't have to do what he does, right? The other beast-thing, you said it was eating cows. It's not like I'd have to hurt anyone."

"You're not going to hurt anyone because you're going to be okay," I said firmly.

She pressed her lips together and held out her arm. "Here. You do it."

I detached the end of the gauze and slowly unwrapped it, careful for places it might have stuck to her skin. But no blood had seeped from under the pad. I started to peel back the pad itself, and she winced.

"Maybe we should leave it on for now," I said.

"We have to see, don't we?"

I eased back the edge closest to her face, so she could see without me peeling it off completely. Dark scabs dotted the places Davey's teeth had broken her skin. The movement of the pad had broken one, and a bead of blood was welling up there.

I let out the breath I'd been holding. "It looks normal. See, I told you."

She kept eyeing the spot as I rewrapped the bandage. "Do you think it was the wolfsbane that stopped it from taking or the moon not being full? Or is it because he would have had to bite me more?"

"I haven't got a clue," I said. "Let's just not let him bite you again, and it won't matter."

The corner of her mouth twitched. She lowered her arm. "A bunch of us are hanging out at Beth's tonight. I'm still going."

Part of me wanted to lock her up in her room until all of

this was over, but I suspected that strategy would be ineffective anyway. What the beast in Davey wanted, he seemed to have gotten awfully good at getting.

"Can you get someone to pick you up and drop you off?" I said. "And stay with the big group at the house? As long as you're not alone, I don't think he'll bother you. So *I* won't bug you if I know you'll always be with someone else. Fair?"

"Yeah." She ducked her head. "I can do that."

"And… here." Since I was still wearing my clothes from last night, the pockets of my jeans held all my usual paraphernalia. I pulled out my Swiss Army knife, flicked the blade open and closed, and offered it to her. "It's not a lot, but at least it's something. If it comes down to that."

Her fingers closed around the knife, and she brought it to her lap. "Thanks."

I still didn't feel like I'd done enough. "Look, I'm sorry I couldn't stop him last night. I should've been able to. I'll be more prepared if he tries anything again. I'm going to make sure you're okay, Ash."

Her mouth slanted, and her eyes suddenly appeared to be focused on something far away.

"I know you want to, Max," she said. "But maybe that should be my job."

She squeezed my arm, flipped her hair back over her shoulders, and went out, I guessed to grab some breakfast downstairs.

I sat down on my sister's bed. Her room looked almost entirely Ash now: black plush blanket and indigo sheets, candid photos of her friends taped all over the stark white walls, a string of blue Christmas lights framing the mirror over her desk.

But there were still hints of the girl everyone had called Ashley. The poster of her favorite singer, whose concert she'd gotten to attend with the school choir when she was twelve, hung in the corner by her closet. And her bedside table still held a framed photo of her and Gabrielle, her junior high best friend, perched on the school steps and laughing. A couple weeks ago, I'd have wondered if I could convince her to put those away and set the past completely behind.

This was what I'd wanted. I'd wanted her to be strong, to be able to look after herself. But I thought again of her lopsided smile last night as she'd tried to pretend Sofia shouldn't have been at that party with her, and my stomach twisted.

I got up and walked over to her window. My gaze fixed on the trees at the far end of the backyard. On the ravine, where Davey might be lurking right now.

My hands balled. I marched back to my room, where the bag of supernatural repellents was waiting.

19

Joss's honk blared through the living room window. I scanned the yards on either side of the street as Ash and I went out, as if Davey might be skulking somewhere I could see.

The carpooling had been Jena's suggestion, to make sure none of us could be caught alone going to or from school. She waved to us from the passenger seat, smiling exactly the same way at me as at Ash. Joss looked straight ahead in stoic silence.

Since Jena had left Saturday morning, she hadn't said a thing about those last few minutes we'd spent together. Hadn't given the slightest hint that she remembered them. While just seeing her made my chest clench up.

But then, I couldn't exactly blame her if she had other things on her mind right now.

We slid into the back, where Vicky was already waiting. As Joss hit the gas, I leaned over and kissed her.

The spark was gone. When I'd called her Saturday afternoon and the sound of her voice hadn't made me feel anything more than if I'd been talking to her mom, I'd almost broken up with her right then. I had no interest in stringing her along. But then she'd said something about Reuben with a quaver in her voice, and I couldn't do it.

She was already so torn up about the shooting and what had happened to Reuben. If she wasn't with us, who would she talk to? Who would protect her if Davey decided to go after her next? I couldn't ditch her in the middle of this.

So I'd said some mush about how she was the only girl I wanted and we couldn't let what was happening split us up. It helped, of course, that Davey had made himself look batshit crazy.

Jena glanced back. "How're you doing, Ash?"

Ash touched the wide Band-Aid that had replaced the gauze on her arm. "Healing up normally," she said. "Thanks for coming that night."

If Joss didn't know what they were talking about, he was wise enough for once not to ask.

At school, we piled out of the car and walked to the entrance as a group. I hung back as the others went in, which was the only reason I spotted Davey before he saw me.

He was standing in the shadow of the stairwell on the other side of the doors, shooting the breeze with a girl so waifish she hardly looked old enough to have graduated from elementary school. Obviously his taste in women hadn't changed. Every now and then he glanced casually toward the entrance. When Ash breezed past the doors, the glance turned into a stare. His glinting eyes followed her until she vanished down the hall.

He looked like a wolf sighting a prime deer.

There was no point in talking to him. All that would come out of his mouth was the same bullshit he'd been spouting since he'd become more beast than Davey. I knew that. But when his gaze slid back and collided with mine, glaring at him through the window, my legs balked. I wasn't going to run off like some scared puppy.

I felt for the bottle I'd slipped into the outer pocket of my backpack. It had been some sort of salad dressing spritzer until I'd nabbed it from the fridge, emptied it, and refilled it with a mixture of holy water and dissolved wolfsbane capsules. I let my hand rest on it with my fingers hooked around the nozzle.

Davey pushed past the door and sauntered over to me, smirking. "Ash is looking fine today."

"She is fine," I said. "Completely fine. It didn't work. You can't change her."

He looked back the way she'd gone, his expression suddenly thoughtful. Was some part of him relieved, way down deep?

Then he aimed that smirk my way again. "Maybe I just need to give it another shot."

My grip tightened on the spritz bottle inadvertently, and Davey caught the movement. He cocked his head and raised his eyebrow at me. "Whatcha got in the bag, Max?"

I didn't want the bottle out of my reach, but I didn't want him messing with it either. I eased my hand out and tucked my bag farther behind me. "What do you think? Books, papers. Are you going to steal my lunch money now?"

"No," he said. "But I think I'll take a look at whatever

you're trying to hide from me."

He snatched at the bag, and I tried to push him off. He shoved back, laughing. His elbow rammed my ribs as he caught my arm and twisted. I squirmed away and put my back against the brick wall beside the doors. My breath was coming hard.

How many times had we done this, the other way around? Me grabbing some note Davey had been writing, a sandwich I'd wanted a bite out of. A jerk of his wrist, a bump to the shoulder, and it'd been mine, easy as that.

Now he was cuffing my ear with enough force to make my head spin, still grinning as if this were all in good fun. I stomped on his foot and heaved him backward with my hands. He just rocked lightly and sidestepped to reach for my backpack again. It felt like we'd stepped into a warped house of mirrors that had shrunk me and inflated him.

He was going to get the bag. Now or a few seconds from now—it didn't make much difference. The one thing he wouldn't expect was for me to give it to him.

I dodged and whipped the bag around in front of me. The full weight of three textbooks thumped Davey in the gut. At the same time I jammed my hand into the pocket. My finger found the trigger, and I yanked the bottle out. I squeezed once, twice—

Davey caught my wrist and yanked my hand away from his face. My bones ground together, the pain making me hiss. My fingers released. He caught the spritz bottle before it had dropped an inch.

I hadn't missed. Davey wiped at the mist of droplets that had splattered his face and studied the bottle. He chuckled.

"What the hell is this, Max? I'm not the Wicked Witch of the West."

"No?" I said. "What are you then?"

He ignored the question, raising the bottle to eye level. Then he unscrewed the top and sniffed the contents. His expression stilled for a second. His fingers tensed. With a flick of his hand, he tipped it to his lips and took a gulp. He paused as if considering the taste and smacked his lips.

"Ah. Excellent vintage." He handed the bottle back to me.

As if I had any use for it now. I contemplated emptying the rest over his head to see if a thorough soaking would do it, but I suspected I was far more likely to end up getting the shower myself if I tried.

He was still pressing the bottle into my hand, his gaze locked with mine. "I don't know what I am," he said. "But this isn't a storybook. There are no magic potions. I'm *real*."

Somewhere in the depths of his eyes, I saw a flash of an emotion I recognized. A hint of the Davey who'd clutched his college acceptance letter in his hands like a rescue line and said, *I'm going to get out of this town. I really fucking am.* Maybe he was even more tangled up with the beast than I'd thought.

Maybe whatever was left of Davey in there didn't want to give this power up, even now.

"It must be nice," I said. "Being that strong, that fast. Picking up on people's feelings, knowing how to use them. But it's not going to last, Davey. Somewhere in there you know that. You're going to become that thing in the woods. You're becoming a monster."

His smile softened, but somehow it looked just as cruel. "Then I guess I'd better enjoy it while I can, don't you think? It's my turn to have the fun, Max. You're all going to keep jumping when I snap my fingers. I'm not stopping, not for anything."

"I just want to hear what he'll say," Vicky said. "Maybe it was an accident somehow. I still can't believe Davey would *want* to hurt anyone."

She dropped a few of Reuben's sleeping pills into her can of Pepsi, coughing to cover the sound. Jena was standing between us and Davey to block his view. We'd come up with our new plan over the weekend, but we'd missed our chance yesterday when he'd taken off with a few of the other guys to Mickey Ds. Today he'd staked out a spot in the midst of some of the seniors from our usual crowd and his new freshmen groupies.

"It's safer to leave him alone until we figure out what to do," I said. Since we'd already discussed each step of the plan through texts and emails, we didn't have to worry about Davey overhearing. In fact, we were counting on it. This little dialogue was our cover story.

Vicky stirred the pop with a straw. At her nod, Jena stepped back. Her jaw was tight, but she kept her voice even. "I promised Joss I'd sit with him. I'll let you know if I think of anything."

Vicky picked up the Pepsi and sipped. We didn't think a tiny bit of the meds would affect her too much, and it'd make it look like it really was her drink, if Davey noticed. Her hand trembled as she set it down. "You'll see," she said to me, still following our loose script. "I'll be totally safe."

I watched as she headed for Davey's table, my pulse picking up to a heavy, heady thump. I'd wanted to be the one to do the switch—I hated sending Vicky in there—but I knew better than anyone that Davey would be twice as suspicious of me. Despite her nerves, she'd insisted he'd listen to her. So I simply wasn't going to let her out of my sight, not for one second, not until we had him.

My big job was going to be after, hauling Davey out of here. Jena had gotten Joss to lend her his spare car key and "forgotten" to give it back, so we were counting on being able to throw the unconscious Davey in the back of the Mini and driving him someplace we could try the other cures. And then we'd have to figure out what to do with him if none of them had worked when he woke up.

Vicky sidled up beside Davey. She gestured as she said something to him and set her can of pop on the table a few inches from his. Lucky for us, his taste for blood didn't appear to have interfered with his Pepsi addiction.

Davey glanced at her drink, but I didn't see any hint of suspicion in his face. He said something back to Vicky and smiled that gentle smile he used on her these days.

Three tables over, Jena motioned to someone in her group. One of Joss's friends slid over his phone. Jena started poking at the buttons.

Even though I was expecting it, the sudden blare of music made me flinch in my seat. Jena had found the perfect song, some heavy metal thrasher that wailed out of the phone's speakers so loudly they crackled. She waved her hands, obviously apologizing, as someone else fiddled with the volume control. Davey and most of the people at his table startled and glanced over.

While his head was turned, Vicky executed the maneuver we'd practiced on the dining room table for a good three hours Sunday afternoon—the same move Davey had probably pulled on Reuben at the party. She nudged her drink forward and swiped his, tugging it to the spot where hers had been before. When Davey looked back, she was standing exactly the same. She laughed at something he said and lifted the can that had been his to take a sip.

Under the table, I texted Jena: *Mission complete.*

Vicky chatted with Davey a minute longer before returning, carrying the can. She'd kept her hand on it the entire time to make sure she held on to the right one. She sat down across from me, and her shoulders slumped. I reached out to grasp her arm.

"We'll see," I said.

I don't think either of us had much appetite, but I dug into my burger as eagerly as I could, trying not to look Davey's way. Once, when I couldn't help it, I saw the Pepsi in his hand, and the tension inside me unclenched a little.

There'd been no screw-ups this time. He didn't have a clue.

With that light in his eyes and that grin on his face, the way he elbowed the guy beside him and winked at one of the girls, he looked pretty freaking happy.

Could the real Davey possibly be enjoying this—all of it, the killing too? An innocent girl. A guy he'd been friends with his whole life. I pulled my gaze away, my chest tightening as I sifted through my memories: movie marathons and parties and childhood adventures. Davey had always been the type to take it, not to lash out. But maybe I'd missed something underneath. I'd somehow managed to not see how much I wanted Jena for a ridiculously long time.

"My dad's studio is soundproof," I said, distracting myself by speculating about where to stash Davey. Jena would alert us when he looked tipsy. "But he's in there all the time."

"My mom's leaving for a conference tomorrow morning, and she won't be back until Sunday," Vicky said, and hesitated. "Should we be talking about this?"

"What?" I said innocently. "About finding a place where we can have wild, noisy sex without being overheard?"

At least I could still appreciate the blush that spread across her cheeks even though no one was listening. But that didn't stop my gaze from darting over to Jena.

She was looking at me. She didn't look happy. I glanced at Davey's table, and my body went rigid. He was gone.

My phone vibrated in my hand. *Where did he go?* Jena had texted. *I only looked away for a sec.*

I shook my head at her, my pulse hiccupping. The way Davey could move these days…

"Oh, no," Vicky murmured.

We stood up and checked out his table surreptitiously as we brought our trays over to the trash. He'd left the rest of his fries, but the Pepsi was gone. He'd taken it with him? How much had he drunk?

There was a half hour of lunch period still to go. He was probably off sweet-talking one of those girls.

We'll search the first floor, I texted to Jena. *You take the second.*

Vicky stuck close to me as we set off. We peeked into every open classroom, surveyed both of the first floor bathrooms, and peered through the windows outside the office. Some of the kids hanging out by their lockers started to look at us funny. I tugged Vicky over to the stairwell and texted Jena to meet us in the basement.

He wasn't there either. The unsecured staff bathroom was empty. Jena caught up with us near the boiler room. I'd have looked in there too if it hadn't been locked.

"If he left school, it's going to be hell finding him," I said.

Jena grimaced. "I'm sorry. I was watching as closely as I could without everyone noticing. He was definitely drinking the Pepsi—I saw him. Maybe not the whole thing, but... I don't think he'd get very far. We put a lot in there."

"Let's hope we find him chilling on the front steps then."

We didn't. He wasn't anywhere on the lawn or the field out back. I started to wonder if maybe he'd just crouched under the table in the caf for a few minutes to see what we would do if he appeared to be gone. It sounded like something he might try just to mess with me.

"Come on," I said. "Let's go back in. We must have missed him."

Davey wasn't in the cafeteria now, so I asked a couple of the guys he'd been sitting with if he'd mentioned anything before he'd taken off.

"Yeah," Tyler said. "He had some project he needed to work on, something like that." But he couldn't remember for what class.

I kept waiting for a buzz to ripple through the halls as people heard some kid had passed out. But when I got to chemistry, all anyone was talking about was the pop quiz the Pecker had promised. There was still no sign of Davey.

I sank into my seat, answered the questions with only half my brain, and tried to figure out where Davey, this beast-possessed Davey, might have decided to go in the middle of lunch on a Tuesday. A jolt of panic shot through me—I hadn't seen Ash since the morning. I texted her, and she sent me a quick reply from her math class, saying she was fine. My edginess eased back only slightly.

At least, even if we'd lost him, he probably wasn't hurting anyone. We were all safe. If he had passed out, he had no way of knowing that had anything to do with us. We'd just try again tomorrow.

Unless he decided he'd had enough of us and never came back.

After final bell, Ash met the three of us by the front doors. We headed to the parking lot.

"Can you ask Joss to stop by Davey's house?" I said to Jena. "There's a small possibility he would've gone home. And if he's not there, we should search the ravine."

Jena nodded, and Vicky shivered. "I never liked it down there," she said. "Now I hate it."

The Mini Cooper stood near the end of the lot where we'd left it that morning. Joss wasn't waiting for us there. I glanced back, but he hadn't come out of the doors behind us either. "He does remember he's supposed to drive us, right?"

"He sometimes has to stay a little late in art cleaning

up," Jena said. "He'll be here in a—"

She jerked to a halt so suddenly the strap of her bag slid off her shoulder. I looked from her to the car, and my legs locked too.

From a distance, the dark splotch covering the pavement under the Mini had looked no different from the shadows beneath all the other cars. Now, closer, I could see the edge where the sun touched it. Where it shone with a red, liquid gleam. My chest clenched.

Vicky and Ash hesitated beside us. Vicky sucked in a breath, her hand rising to her mouth.

I left the others to circle the car. On the far side, the puddle stretched as far as the white line marking the edge of the parking space. A smell like sour rust filled my noise. I fought the urge to gag.

The same crimson liquid splattered the driver's side window and door, darker than the shiny red paint. It was drying, leaving a brownish crust on the glass.

Like blood would.

20

Jena's bag hit the asphalt with a thud. She crouched down beside it, her hands braced on either side of her neck as if she needed them to hold her head up.

"Is he there?" she said, so quietly I almost didn't hear her.

I swallowed hard. "No. There's no—there's no body. We don't even know the blood is his. It could be anyone's. It could be an *animal's*, just to freak us out." That was what anyone else who saw this would think: some sick high school prank.

I turned away from the car, but it wasn't any more pleasant to look at Jena. She stared up at me, her face chalky. Her voice shook.

"Davey didn't just *pretend* to kill Reuben or Ash's friend. Why would he start now? Did any of you see Joss after lunch?"

I hadn't. Vicky and Ash shook their heads.

"I didn't even think." Jena rocked back and forth on her feet. "It seemed like the people he went after had something to do with the party, with who was at the lake when he was attacked, and Joss was never there. I just assumed he was safe. But of course he wasn't. I told him about it. I made him get involved. He didn't *want* to."

"It's not your fault," I said.

She inhaled raggedly. "Maybe it's yours then. You're the one who said we should try to stop him ourselves, that we shouldn't tell the police. If I hadn't listened to you—"

"Max has been doing everything he can!" Vicky wrapped her arm around my mine. "Do you think he wanted this to happen?"

"Of course not, "Jena said, but I missed whatever words came after. Because Davey's voice ran through my mind like an echo. *Isn't this what you wanted, Max?*

My stomach listed queasily. That was what he'd say, wasn't it? *You never liked him, Max. You wanted him gone. Now he is. Why aren't you happy?* And he would smile that awful smile and laugh when I told him I *hadn't* wanted it.

Not like this, at least.

"No," I said out loud. The others went silent. I raised my head. "We've got to look for him. For Joss. Maybe he's still okay—maybe we'll find him before... We should go to the ravine, like we were planning to anyway."

Jena touched the pocket of her jeans, where the spare key to the Mini must have been. Her shoulders trembled. Before she could say anything, I stepped between her and the car.

"We'll walk. Come on."

I held out my hand, and she let me pull her to her feet. Her legs wobbled. She wasn't crying, but her face was still sickly pale. Vicky came up on her other side, steadying her by the elbow. Ash filled out our semicircle, her own face wan but determined.

Jena dragged in a breath. "Okay. Okay. Let's find him."

The closest end of the ravine was the one just past my house. I glanced up at the porch when we passed, half-expecting to find Davey there leering at us, but it was empty. Ash was looking at it too.

"I think you should stay with us until Mom or Dad gets home," I said.

She bit her lip and nodded. "I *want* to come."

At the ravine entrance, Vicky balked. "They got Reuben out, didn't they? He's not still..."

The Sunday newspaper had contained a brief mention of Reuben's death. They'd called it a freak accident, mentioning the levels of drugs in his blood and speculating that he'd climbed the tree and fallen very unluckily among the branches. It didn't appear that anyone had connected his death to Sofia's. But they'd definitely have removed the body. "He's not."

She shuddered. Finding Joss down there might be even worse. But when Jena strode on ahead, Vicky followed with me and Ash.

"Joss?" Jena's head whipped from side to side as she scanned the underbrush—and, now and then, tipped it upward to eye the trees. "Joss? *Davey*?"

Ash followed her lead, pushing aside the branches along the path and calling out both their names. Vicky and I came along more slowly, because Vicky had a death grip on my arm.

We reached the creek. Jena stopped, and her hand fell to her back pocket. She dug out her phone.

"They could track his, couldn't they?" she said. "You can do that with cell phones. If he left it on."

Her thumb tapped through her contacts. She held the phone to her ear, and her face brightened. "It's ringing!"

Then the light snapped out of her as if she'd been slapped.

My back stiffened. "What?"

She was pressing the phone so tightly against her ear it must have hurt. Her mouth flattened into a hard little line. After a moment, she lowered her hand and hit the End Call button. She dialed the number again and passed the phone to me without meeting my eyes.

I brought it to my own ear, my gut knotting. The line at the other end rang four times, sounding like any phone would. It clicked over to voicemail. But instead of Joss's low, arrogant tone, the voice that spoke was Davey's.

"I'm sorry," he said smoothly. "The person you are attempting to reach no longer exists. There is no point in trying again."

The dial tone droned into my ear.

Jena must have been waiting until she was sure I'd heard the message. As soon as my arm dropped, she turned toward the trees. Her hands clenched.

"Davey!" she yelled, so loud I winced. "Where is he? What did you do to him? Come out and admit it to my face! No? Are you too scared? You're not a beast, you're a fucking coward!"

"Jena." I grabbed her arms, but she shoved me off. I reached for her again, my heart hammering. He was going to kill her too if she kept calling him out like that.

She snatched her phone from my hand and hurled it at the creek. It bounced off one of the stones and pattered onto the muddy bank.

"Fucking coward," she repeated, and sucked in a breath like she was trying not to sob. Ash ran to rescue the phone.

"The message doesn't mean anything," I said. "We still don't know what's happened."

Her voice, when she managed to answer, was so weak, so not Jena, it made me want to pummel someone. Preferably the thing calling himself Davey.

"You heard it. Joss doesn't exist. There's no point in trying. What else could he mean?"

"If Joss is dead, where's the body?" I said. "Why the big game? Davey never went to much trouble to stop anyone from seeing what he'd done before. Why would he now, unless Joss isn't dead but Davey wants you to think he is?"

Even I didn't believe that. I just wanted her to stop looking like she was about to break into pieces.

Jena accepted the phone from Ash and stuffed it into her pocket. "He's not here."

We hadn't made it all the way through the ravine, but I felt the same way. This search was pointless. We might be caught up in a game, but it was Davey's game, and he was the only one who knew the rules and the playing field.

Vicky hugged herself. "So what do we do?"

I already knew what Jena was going to say. "We wait until tomorrow," I said before she could start. "This is a... a change in tactics. Maybe it means something. Davey will make another move, show his hand, and then we'll have something to work with. If we still don't know what to do then, we'll go to the police. But if we rush it, we might make things worse instead of helping Joss."

If Joss could be helped. If getting the cops involved wouldn't screw us all over even more. After the events of the last few days, I was even more convinced this monster could run circles around the town's police force—while juggling bloody hearts at the same time.

At the very least, waiting would give me one more day to figure out how I could save *Davey* before the only thing anyone knew him as was a murderer. Before the beast inside him decided it was bored of playing games and tore every other person in my life apart.

Jena was shaking her head.

Vicky drew in a rough breath. "It's true. If Davey hasn't really hurt him already, why would he now? He must want something else. We need to find out what."

Ash glanced at me. "The police might not even believe it's Davey who took Joss. They asked all those questions after you found Sofia. They might think it was you."

Especially if they realized the guy they'd found hanging in a tree a few days ago was connected to me too. "Yeah. Davey might encourage that."

"So it'd be bad for everyone!" Vicky said. "They'll accuse Max, or provoke Davey into hurting someone else, or—or *kill* him, trying to bring him in. And that'll be our fault."

"Why are you so worried about hurting Davey?" Jena broke in. "Do you really think there's someone in there worth saving? I'm *glad* you shot that thing by the caves, Vicky. I don't care how guilty you feel—all of this happened because of it, and I think…" She pressed her palms against her forehead and closed her eyes. "I don't know. Maybe killing Davey is the only option. Maybe we should have told the cops last week."

"Do you really think they would've caught Davey before he'd hurt anyone else?" I said. "We've done so much more than they would have—*you've* done more. We've got a whole list of stuff that should kill whatever's taking over him, stuff that could stop all of this, thanks to you."

"But none of it's working!"

"We've hardly had a chance to try. Who do you trust more with Joss's life: you, or some stranger who'll never believe Davey's capable of half the craziness we've seen?"

Jena wiped her eyes and scowled at the ground. "Me," she said after a moment.

"All right," I said, though I didn't feel half as relieved as I would have liked to. "So tomorrow morning, we'll see what we have."

I never heard Davey come. But when I opened my blinds the next morning, there was a message waiting for me—one nothing to do with Joss. A paper was stuck against the glass with a doodle drawn in scarlet pen.

Ash. He'd etched in the streaks in her hair and the bangles at her wrist, the careless way she often stood with her friends, one hand on her hip, the other dangling.

The pupils in her staring eyes were narrow ovals, and fangs poked from the edges of her smile.

I scraped at the glass, but the paper was stuck to the outside where I couldn't reach it. I spent five minutes trying to figure out if I could take the glass right out of the frame, and finally just slammed down the blinds again.

The real Ash, normal-eyed and fangless, was sitting at the kitchen table with a bowl of cereal when I came down. Mom was scooping scrambled eggs onto a plate—to take upstairs for Dad, I guessed. He must have hit the absinthe a little too hard after dinner last night, undoubtedly followed by drunken ramblings to Mom about how his talent had been squandered while she patted his shoulder and reassured him that he still had more opuses in him.

"Good morning, honey," she said without looking up. There was no way she could have thought anything was good if she'd seen my face.

Ash scooped a few bran flakes onto her spoon, considered them, and dropped them back into the bowl. I watched her do that three times before Mom finally finished prepping Dad's plate and whisked out of the room.

I slumped down at the table across from my sister. "Not hungry? I can't blame you."

She jabbed at a raisin and frowned. "What Kyle did to me, in eighth grade..." she said. "Did a girl ever do something like that to you?"

My gaze darted to her arms as if I might see fresh scissor-marks there. What had started her thinking about that prick again?

"Turn me down in a way that really hurt?" For some reason, my mind crept back to that New Year's morning, Jena pulling on her sweater over her stiff little smile. But that

didn't count. That had been mutual agreement.

Of course, there was also Friday night, when she'd pulled away from me before I could even try.

"Not exactly," I said. "But not every girl I've wanted to hook up with was into the idea."

"So what did you do?"

I shrugged. "I hooked up with someone who was."

"Because it didn't matter that much."

"Exactly. Well…" I was thinking about Jena again. I had to stop that.

"I saw Kyle yesterday night," Ash said in a rush. "A bunch of us went to grab some pizza. He came in while we were waiting for our order."

"Oh." I studied her expression. She didn't look too torn up, but it was obviously bugging her. "I hope you gave him a good kick where it hurts, then."

That remark drew out a sliver of a smile. "That's what you'd have done?"

"If I saw him? Hell, yeah. I've got no sympathy for that creep. He didn't say anything to you, did he?"

"Just, you know, hi and whatever."

She finally ate a couple bites of cereal, but when I looked at her again, her frown had come back.

"We should get going," I said. Since Joss wasn't around to drive us, Ash and I were taking a long route to school via Vicky's and Jena's houses so that none of us walked alone.

When we got to Vicky's, she was waiting by the door. It looked like she'd only gotten up a few minutes before and thrown on whatever clothes she could find fastest, regardless of how wrinkled they were. I smoothed my hands over her rumpled hair and kissed her forehead.

She leaned into me. "Jena sent me a text. We don't need to get her—she's with her dad."

Something about her phrasing sounded odd. "You mean he's dropping her off?"

"I guess." She hesitated. "You don't think we should be worried, do you?"

Jena's dad did sometimes drop her off at school on the way to the nursing home if the weather didn't look great. Maybe he'd noticed how stressed out she was. If Davey had been involved, I had the feeling he'd have sent the message to me, not to Vicky. But my nerves still prickled uneasily.

"Let's get to school and find her so we *know* we don't have to worry," I said. "And—can you call her, make sure she picks up?" If she'd rather deal with Vicky than me, I'd let her.

Vicky pawed through her purse for her phone as we hurried down the street. She finally found it and took about five hours pulling up Jena's number. She'd just lifted it to her ear when we turned the corner toward the school.

From four blocks away, I could see the police car parked outside, lights flashing. Panic hit me in an icy wave. Before I even thought about it, I was running.

My pulse thundered in my ears. My imagination drew a picture of Jena's body sprawled on the lawn, torn and bloody. I pushed my legs harder, my sneakers pounding the sidewalk.

Two cops were standing at the edge of the parking lot, talking to kids passing by. Caution tape marked off a square around Joss's Mini. I slowed and then stopped at the end of the drive. My chest heaved, but I couldn't quite catch my breath.

Vicky's shoes clattered over the pavement behind me. "She's fine, Max!" she called. "I've got her on the phone. It's hard not to be a little paranoid, right?" she added to Jena and giggled nervously.

A rough laugh tumbled out of me. I rubbed my forehead, willing my head to stop spinning.

Of course Jena was fine. Someone must have gotten worried that the bloody car wasn't just a prank after it'd sat here overnight and called the police. It made perfect sense.

"Yeah, there are a couple of cops, and they've taped off Joss's car," Vicky was relaying, as if Jena wouldn't have already witnessed the scene on her way in. We skirted the parking lot. One of the officers ended his conversation with the girl he'd been questioning and looked over at us.

I knew him. He was the cop who'd taken my statement about Sofia down at the station—Officer Fowley, my memory supplied.

He obviously recognized me too. "Max Weston," he said, coming over. "It seems I need to talk to you again, about your friend David Reeve."

"Sure," I said cautiously. "What's going on?"

"Something unpleasant happened here yesterday. We understand he may have been involved, and we'd like to ask him some questions. When was the last time you saw him?"

My skin went cold. They'd gotten information about more than just the car if they'd connected it to Davey. I glanced at Vicky. "At school yesterday. But only in class. He's been busy with end-of-senior-year projects, so we haven't been hanging out as much."

"Then you don't know where he is right now?"

I shook my head. "He should be coming to school if he's not here already. That's the best I can tell you."

One of the other cops ambled over to ask Officer Fowley something, and he turned away with a nod that was a dismissal. My mind was already someplace else. The pieces were clicking together. Beside me, Vicky hummed in agreement with something Jena had said. I plucked the phone out of her hand.

"Max!" Vicky said.

I gestured for her to follow as I stalked across the lawn. "You're not here," I said into the phone. "You're at home with your dad. He let you stay because you told them. You told them *everything*."

There was a moment's hesitation. Jena's voice crackled on the other end. "I had to."

"You didn't! We were supposed to figure it out together."

"That's what we've been trying to do all along. It didn't get us anywhere, Max. I didn't say anything about you, or Vicky, or Ash. I just told them I'd found Joss's car like that and that Davey recorded the message on his voicemail, and I was worried he might have been responsible for Reuben and the other girl, too."

And it wouldn't have taken the police more than two seconds to find someone who could tell them who Davey usually hung out with.

"So that's it?" I said. "You're washing your hands of it?"

"I'm sorry," she said quietly. "I just can't keep... playing heroes or detectives or whatever it was, with you. I let you get me all wrapped up again, when I knew— And now Joss is probably dead."

"Jena—"

"I've got to go," she interrupted. "I'll be careful. Don't worry about me. I hope you'll stay safe too."

Before I could say anything else, she hung up on me.

I lowered the phone. Vicky was staring at me. I handed it back to her without a word.

"Mr. Weston?" someone said behind me. Officer Fowley was walking toward us.

"I'm afraid I'm going to have to ask for a little more of your time," he said. "Would you come with me?"

21

"**A**nd how long did you wait after discovering Miss Russo's body before calling emergency services?" the new officer asked, as if she didn't have my statement about Sofia's death from last week right in front of her. Her sharp gray eyes stayed locked on my face.

"I didn't wait," I said, resisting the urge to shift on the hard police station chair. "I called right away. What else was I going to do?"

She pursed her lips. "Where did you go in the house after you called?"

"I went out front so I'd see when they showed up." *Like I already told you, and Officer Fowley and his partner before.*

This trip to the station had turned out to be even more unpleasant than my first. Fowley and his partner had asked me about ten times as many questions as last time, pausing and shuffling papers and asking in a slightly reworded way, as if I'd suddenly admit to knowing where Davey was if they found the perfect phrasing. It hadn't seemed to matter that I honestly had no clue.

Then they'd left me to this new woman who wanted to hash out Sofia's murder over and over again. The more she poked at my story, the more my skin crept with the impression that she thought I'd put someone up to pointing the finger at Davey, and that the real murderer was me.

At least repeating my answers, calmly and confidently, in the little white-walled room made it easier to avoid Jena's voice in the back of my head.

I can't, she'd said the other night, and when I'd asked what, she'd said, *You*. See me, talk to me, be in my general vicinity?

She hadn't just called the police because she was worried about Joss or because she felt guilty about Reuben and Sofia. She'd also done it because she didn't want *anything* else to do with me.

"All right," the new officer said finally. She signaled to one of her colleagues, who motioned for me to follow him. It was around noon when he dropped me off back at school.

I had Politics first thing after lunch—a class I'd normally shared with Jena. Her chair stood empty on the other side of the room. A dull ache filled my chest.

In the months since she'd had hooked up with Joss, I'd gone days without saying more to her than "Hi." I hadn't liked the growing distance, but that was the way it was, and anyway I'd had Davey and Vicky and the rest of the gang to distract me. This was different.

I missed her. I wanted her. And I'd utterly lost her.

Of course, I had other distractions now. I stayed over at Vicky's that night, because there was no way I was leaving her alone overnight with her mom out of town, and in the middle of the show we were watching, a special news bulletin started playing on the TV. Davey's yearbook photo from the beginning of senior year popped up on the screen.

"What do you think he's doing right now?" Vicky asked.

He hadn't shown up at school since the cops had turned up. But whatever efforts they'd been making to bring him in had been as successful as I'd expected—which was, not at all.

"Hiding out somewhere, I guess," I said. Or standing in the shadows, thumbing his nose at the police cars cruising the streets.

I stared at his photo as the reporter asked anyone who'd seen David Reeve to call in. There he was: the guy who'd been my best friend, with his regular brown hair and eyes, his hesitant smile, the slight slouch to his shoulders. I'd started to forget what he was supposed to look like. Who he was supposed to be.

"The police department will be enforcing a ten p.m. curfew," the reporter went on. "They request that everyone stay off the streets between then and five a.m. unless absolutely necessary."

Right. That would have been a *big* help to Sofia and Joss.

Any other time, playing house with Vicky would have been a lot more fun and a lot less nervously checking locks. She fell asleep against my shoulder while we were watching the least traumatizing movie I could find in her mom's collection, which was fine by me.

The next night, as we were getting in after a fast food dinner, a police car drifted past us down the street. Jena's voice echoed in my head. *I just can't keep doing it...*

Vicky slipped her arms around me and brushed a kiss to my mouth. It took a couple seconds for my mind to untangle itself enough to realize I should kiss her back. At least one second too long. She pulled away.

"You're worrying. Do you think Davey would really try to hurt you, or me?"

"I don't know," I said. "I don't know how his mind works these days."

"We'll still figure out a way to save him, right?" she said.

"'Course," I said, with a confidence I didn't feel. "It's just going to be harder now."

I tried to lean in to make up for my lack of response before, but Vicky's hand on my chest stopped me.

"It'll be harder because Jena isn't helping."

I shrugged. "And because we aren't even seeing Davey at school anymore. But we'll work something out. I just need a little more time to think." I sure as hell wasn't throwing Vicky into the line of fire again.

Her gaze lingered on my face. "You really freaked out yesterday when you thought Davey might have gone after her."

A sudden shimmer of tears filled her eyes. My stomach twisted.

"Why wouldn't I? Vick, she's one of my best friends."

"I know," she said. "But... You two never did anything that was more than friends, did you?"

"Of course not," I said automatically. "I swear." We hadn't in any way that had turned out to mean something.

She swiped at her eyes. "I'm sorry. I don't know why I'm thinking about that. Everything seems so messed up."

I hugged her and ran my fingers over her hair until her breath sounded even again. We meandered into her bedroom, and she turned to unbutton my shirt with a flirtatious smile that looked forced. I stopped her hands. Since I'd broken up with her in my head if not out loud, we hadn't done more than kiss, and I wasn't about to cross that line now.

"It might sound kind of corny," I said, "but tonight I want to just hold you. Okay?"

Her smile turned relieved. "Yeah," she said. "That would be nice."

I drifted off with her nestled against me, feeling like maybe I'd done one thing right.

"Those people are watching us," Ash murmured.

Two figures were sitting in the front of a beige sedan parked a couple houses down from ours. The man in the passenger side sipped from a coffee cup and nodded to us as if it were totally normal to be hanging out in one's car in the middle of the afternoon.

"Probably cops," I said. "I guess they're still not convinced I don't have Davey stashed away somewhere." Or that I wasn't the murderer myself.

Ash turned her head and made a face they couldn't see.

Inside, we both headed upstairs. Vicky had gone off after school to a big Friday night sleepover at Shannon's, which sounded safe enough, and I had one remaining paper to write tonight. It was hard to believe finals were going to start in five days. I sat in front of my computer, searching for the motivation to get started—and the hairs rose on my neck.

I wasn't even quick about it. I wheeled the chair around and glided to the window. There, I froze.

Davey was standing at the edge of the ravine on the other side of our backyard fence. He wasn't looking at me. His gaze was angled toward Ash's window.

For a few seconds, I just stared at him. I expected him to turn, catch my eye, and vanish, but his stance didn't waver. Holding my breath, I eased back from the window and turned to hurry downstairs.

The thought of the maybe-cops out front flitted through my head, but I had no doubt Davey would realize and take off if I tried to summon them. Me, he'd let get close.

I needed a tranquilizer gun. Or a Taser, maybe. But I didn't have either, and my spritz bottle of holy wolfsbane water had already proven useless.

I just had me. I hadn't really used *that* yet, had I?

Davey didn't shift his gaze to me until I'd crossed half the yard. Obviously it was no accident that I'd seen him. He'd been waiting for me.

"I remembered," he said conversationally. "That night by the lake, the moon was full. That seems significant somehow, doesn't it?"

I stopped by the fence. "I thought none of that storybook stuff made a difference."

He shrugged. "It could be a coincidence. But I expect next Monday will be interesting."

He looked up at Ash's window again. All that was visible was the back of her head over the top of her computer chair. My throat constricted.

"What would it take?" I said. "What would I have to do for you to stop this?"

"You're assuming there is something." He raised his eyebrows, still watching Ash.

"You know the police are looking to arrest you now."

"That's been exciting. I wasn't expecting that right now. Not even from Jena."

At her name, I tensed from head to toe. I kept my tone as casual as I could manage. "I suppose you've got plans to pay her back."

He dropped his gaze to me, suddenly intent. "Oh no, I've got no interest in Jena anymore. It's a funny thing. She took herself right out of the ring."

"What? What 'ring'?"

"You always told me I had to play the game if I wanted to get anywhere," he said. "But it wasn't a game, was it? It was more like a circus, with you as the ringmaster. 'Come when I say come. Jump when I say jump. Good boy.'" He mimed patting someone on the head.

Was that the beast talking, or was that what the real Davey thought? I couldn't tell the difference anymore.

We'd been *friends*, our whole lives. We'd joked and goofed off and had each other's backs. We'd made plans. I couldn't have been that wrong, could I?

"You know it wasn't like that," I said.

"Do I? Why don't we ask Sofia? Or Reuben? Or how about Joss?" Davey's eyes narrowed. "It was so simple to draw him in, you know. You never really wanted him to believe I was anything more than a screwed-up kid. You wanted him not to trust you."

I tried to think of all the times we'd talked while Joss was there, the way I'd talked *to* him. I hadn't wanted him with us, that much was true. I'd wanted one part of Jena to be mine alone.

"So whatever you did to him is my fault too?" My voice cracked, but I couldn't stop it. "And how did I make *your* life so horrible? Introduce you to girls? Make sure you didn't flunk out of school? Give you a place where your dad couldn't hit you anymore? If you're blaming people, isn't he the best candidate? He's the one who gave you hell every day. Why aren't you taking this out on him?"

Davey's lips twitched. "I considered it," he admitted. "But I think it'd make him happy to find out he was right and I really was a sorry excuse for a son. The kind of son who'd murder his own father. He doesn't deserve the satisfaction. It makes him much more miserable knowing I'm out here off his leash and there's nothing he can do about it."

I swept my arm through the air. "But you're fine with him and the whole rest of the world seeing you as some kind of serial killer?"

Davey paused. The glint in his eyes dimmed. "Nothing I can do about that now, is there?" he said. For just that instant, I heard more pain than bravado.

"Of course there is, Davey. If we—"

Any impression I'd had of the real Davey snapped away behind a flash of gold and a clenched jaw. "As for *you*," he broke in. "You never, even for a second, would've contemplated letting me make a pass at Ash. Would you?"

I faltered, remembering all too clearly my revulsion at his mumbled confession that night a couple weeks ago. "She's my little sister."

"And you've really taken her over."

"Davey."

His eyes flashed. "And 'Davey' is a five-year-old's nickname."

"You never complained before!"

"What would you have done if I had?"

I shut my mouth. I would have laughed, ruffled his hair like he really was five, and spent the rest of the day adding "Davey" to the end of every sentence I said to him. One friend hassling another, all in fun. If I'd known—if I'd *really* known…

"You should've said something. You can't put this all on me. If I was pissing you off so friggin' much, you should have told me."

"What makes you think I didn't try?"

"Well, you obviously didn't try hard enough," I snapped. "I think you weren't *that* pissed. I think you liked having me there to boost you up. You liked being around someone who could do all the things you were too scared to do and make you do them too. You were enjoying it way more than you wanted it to stop. If you're so angry at me, why don't you come after *me* for a change, instead of all those other—"

He moved so fast I didn't have time to brace myself. His fist slammed into my temple with the force of a Mack truck. I reeled backward, tripping over my feet, and sprawled on the ground. Pain radiated through my head and shot down my spine, sharp and dizzying. A choked gasp escaped my mouth.

All the anger washed out of me, leaving nothing but chilly uncertainty. I blinked, my eyes watering. There were four Daveys, then two, then only the one, staring at me as if he couldn't figure out how I'd ended up down there on the grass.

I gripped the side of my head. Davey looked down at his fist, opened it carefully, and lifted his gaze back to me. His chest rose and fell with short breaths.

"Wrong way." His voice came out slightly garbled, like a radio not quite tuned to a station. Despite the throbbing in my head, I could see him pulling back into himself. Any second he'd walk away. I shoved myself to my feet, staggered, and grabbed ahold of the fence.

"There," I said. "You got that out of your system. Now listen to me. I'll do anything. You want to make a pass at Ash? Let me try to change you back, and you can make as many as you'd like, the regular way. It's up to her in the end anyway."

"But it already is." His mouth twisted into a tight smile. "You're the one who needs to start listening, Max. Keep an eye on your girl."

"Don't!" I said, but he had already eased away from the fence. I jerked forward, and a fresh wave of dizziness rocked me. I closed my eyes for just a second.

When I opened them, Davey was gone.

I stood there a while longer, staring into the forest. The pain ebbed to a dull ache. I still didn't know what to do. With a grimace, I headed back inside.

Steam was whistling out of the kettle in the kitchen, but no one took it off the burner. I wandered over to the doorway.

Dad was jotting something down on a notepad, not even looking at Mom. "It'll only be for a few days."

"That's why I thought we could all go," Mom said. "I don't feel safe here right now, and I'm sure the kids would be happy to get away."

"Liz, you know I tap into the roots of the music better when I have my privacy. Do you have to push this?"

She went over and rubbed his back. "Of course I know that. You're right. With everything that's going on, I just wasn't thinking."

It had been a long time since I'd bothered to really watch them, I knew the parts they played so well. But now I saw the way Mom's shoulders inched up even as she tried to relax Dad's, the way Dad avoided meeting her eyes as he got up to grab the kettle.

How many things were hanging there in the air that they were never going to break role and say? *It's been so long since we went away as a family. I already told the latest girl I'd take her. I hate this. I'm sorry.* How the hell could they be happy like this?

Why did they do it if they weren't?

My stomach knotted. Because it was easy. Easier to laugh than to cry. Easier to kiss the girl who wanted you than to tell the girl who didn't how vacant your life was without her. Easier to bully a friend than to find out what he really thought of you.

Mom turned and noticed me. My face must have been something, because she hesitated, her eyes widening.

"Are you okay, Max?"

"Yeah," I said, forcing a smile and swiveling so the mark where Davey had hit me was out of her view. "Just tired." Because it was the easier thing to say. Then I fled upstairs to my room.

At midnight I was still lying awake on my bed. Every time I closed my eyes, Davey's voice murmured, *Keep an eye on your girl.*

Could I put Ash on a bus to the other side of the country? No, she'd tell me to forget it. I could stick her in Mom's car and drive us as far as I could get from here, but how far *would* we get before the police saw it as proof of my guilt and chased us down? Or before Davey figured out my newest trick and found us anyway? I had the sinking feeling the beast in him would actually enjoy the challenge, the chase.

And then I'd also have abandoned my best friend.

Ash's music seeped faintly through the wall. Her computer chair squeaked. I pressed my face into my pillow.

Davey had said Jena had "taken herself out" by calling the police. So maybe if I convinced Ash to go talk to those cops out front, tell them that he'd threatened her directly...

But if *I* convinced her, that wouldn't count, would it? He'd find some way to turn that against me. She'd have to decide on her own, like Jena had.

The curtains on Ash's window hissed over the rod as she pulled them shut. She slipped out to the bathroom. The pipes hummed. I sat up on my bed, resting my head in my hands.

Every plan I'd tried to carry out had gotten someone killed. Maybe if I stopped trying to out-manuever Davey, if all of us backed off and stayed out of his way like Jena was, he'd cool off. Maybe a little of the real-him would push its way back up.

Could I really hope it'd be that easy? He'd wanted me to see him today. There was backing off and then there was leaving ourselves wide open.

Finally, Ash padded back to her room and switched her light off with a click. The numbers blinked by on my clock.

He'd have to kill me before he got to Ash again.

Thirty minutes passed without a sound. I grabbed my sleeping bag and crept down the hall. Nudging Ash's door open, I stood still and listened. Her breath rose and fell with a slight rasp that wasn't quite a snore.

I eased inside and double-checked that the window was locked. Then I spread the sleeping bag in the middle of the floor and sank down onto it. The tension that had been wound up inside me since I'd talked to Davey loosened slightly.

I didn't expect to sleep even then, but sometime later my eyes popped open to sunlight streaming through the curtains. Ash was still curled up under her sheet, her arm tucked around her head. The window was undamaged. Davey hadn't come.

The clock on the wall said it was quarter to seven. Ash would probably sleep a while longer, but I didn't want to be here when she woke up. I suspected she wouldn't appreciate my protectiveness. I lifted the sleeping bag, crept back to my own room, and flopped onto the bed.

Across the room in the crumpled heap of yesterday's clothes, my phone beeped. Voicemail. A call must have come last night after I'd gone into Ash's room.

I dragged myself off the bed and rummaged through the clothes, my spirits lifting. Jena might have had some brilliant middle-of-the-night brainstorm and decided to help us after all.

It was Vicky's number. I tapped through to the message and raised the phone to my ear.

Vicky's voice wavered out. "Hi, Max," she said with a nervous giggle. "I know it's really late. I was hoping the phone would wake you up. Shannon got sick right after dinner, so we all went home. I thought I'd be okay, but I haven't been able to sleep, and like ten minutes ago I started hearing these... noises. It's probably just a tree or something. Everything's locked up. But I'm kind of freaked out. If you get this, could you call me? Or maybe even come over? I'd feel so much better. Miss you."

The message clicked off. I flipped to my missed calls list. My skin turned clammy.

Vicky had left that message around two-thirty, called again four times between quarter to three and three o'clock —and then stopped.

Probably the noises had gone away or she'd realized I was unwakeable and given up. But my finger skidded on the screen as I tried to dial her number. I closed my eyes and waited.

Her phone rang six times before voicemail picked up.

"I'm sorry I didn't hear you calling before, Vick." My voice choked up. "I'm coming now, as fast as I can."

I threw on yesterday's clothes and ran.

22

Vicky's house looked completely normal on the outside, but so had Sofia's. I sprinted up the front steps and tried the door. Locked. I jammed my thumb against the doorbell three times. The blinds on the living room window were shut. All I could see was my own reflection, wavering and panicked.

Vicky had told me where they kept the spare key one time when she needed me to pick up part of a project she'd forgotten. I punched in the code by the garage door and shifted impatiently as it hummed open. In the back corner, behind a can of motor oil, sat a cleaned-out baby food jar that must have been at least seventeen years old. The key lay at the bottom of it.

I dumped it out into my hand and hurried back to the front door.

The lock turned over easily, just like it had the other time. I kicked off my shoes on the mat out of habit as I went in. Vicky's mom was as committed to unmarked floors as she was to herbal medicine.

"Vicky?" I called. No answer.

I came around to the living room doorway and let out my breath. The back of Vicky's head was visible over the top of the suede couch, tipped to the side so her cheek rested against the cushion. A mug sat by the edge of the coffee table —probably hot chocolate. I'd teased her about drinking the stuff when the air outside was almost as hot, and she'd just said, "It always makes me feel better. It doesn't matter what the temperature is."

Beside the mug lay her mom's pistol. She must have come out here last night, curled up with the hot chocolate for comfort and the gun for protection, and ended up dozing off like she had with me the other night.

There was no point in interrupting her sleep. I'd probably scare her half to death. But she'd be happy to see me when she woke up on her own. I stepped closer, thinking I'd follow her lead and try to catch a few more Zs on the loveseat.

The rest of the coffee table came into view, and my legs stalled.

There were two mugs. The second one stood at the other end of the table as if someone had been sitting next to Vicky, drinking with her.

I lunged around the couch, my socked foot slipping on a damp spot on the floor.

Vicky's eyes looked at me sideways, unblinking. Her lips were parted as if she wasn't quite sure what to say. Everything below her mouth was drenched in blood.

A gash of ragged flesh gaped open on her neck from her chin to her collarbone. Her daisy-print robe was soaked through with red. Thin trails of it seeped down her tanned legs. A puddle had formed on the suede cushion where her left arm lay limply by her side, and spilled onto the floor. My sock had drawn a crimson smear across the polished hardwood.

The world spun. I found myself leaning over Vicky, my hands braced against the top of the couch, not remembering bending down. A tart, metallic smell clogged my nose. My breath hitched, raw in my throat. I tried to push myself upright, but my legs trembled. I bowed my head, squeezed my eyes shut, and listened to the staccato rhythm of the rasps of air I was dragging into my lungs.

When I felt capable of standing again, I opened my eyes and leaned a little further to kiss Vicky on the forehead. Her skin felt cool. She was still staring at me. I hesitated, my stomach churning, and reached to gently nudge her eyelids shut. Then I straightened up.

A figure was standing in my peripheral vision on the other side of the loveseat. He must have waited, watching the blood drain out of her, and slipped away into the dining room when he'd heard the key in the lock. My head felt leaden as I turned it toward him.

"It was easy," Davey said. For once, he wasn't smiling. "Do you want to hear how I did it?"

"I want to rip out *your* throat," I said. "If I didn't believe the real you is still in there, the one that must hate himself for doing this, I'd try."

"You wouldn't be able to," he said matter-of-factly. He rounded the loveseat and the coffee table, and sank onto the couch at the opposite end from Vicky.

"I called to her through the window. Begged her to let

me in. I told her I was fighting the darkness inside me and I wanted help, and I didn't think anyone would listen except her. I needed to know someone would try to understand. I was bedraggled and alone out in the night, and she was the one who could save me."

My fingernails dug into my palms so deep they stung. "And it worked." Of course it had. Vicky had never wanted to believe Davey had turned completely evil, that he might be beyond help. Just like she hadn't wanted to believe I might have touched any other girl while we were together. And she'd needed so badly to make up for the beast she hadn't saved.

"She opened the door and let me in. Made me a drink. Sat beside me on the couch and asked me what she could do. I told her to lean closer, and she did." Davey paused. His cold yellow eyes held mine. "She put out her neck, and I sliced it open. She really should've known better. But then, she'd gotten a lot of practice at buying into bullshit, hadn't she?"

I closed my eyes. "I would've come. I would have stopped you. I didn't know. I thought she was at Shannon's."

"I told you," Davey said. "I told you, but of course you didn't listen. You think you have it all figured out, Max, but you don't know anything. This isn't your game anymore. You're just too busy thinking in the same old ways to start *seeing*."

The sharpness in his voice made me hesitate. He'd told me?

Keep an eye on your girl.

My girl. Of course he hadn't meant Ash. What guy thought of his sister as 'his girl'? I hadn't even thought—but then, I hadn't realized Vicky would be alone. How could I have?

Davey was getting up. He headed toward the hall. I didn't think. My hand leapt for the gun.

He must have heard the clink as I picked it up off the table. He turned to face me. "Really?"

I pointed the gun at him, but my hand wobbled. Davey spread out his arms as if offering himself.

"Go ahead," he said quietly. "Do it."

In that instant, a quiver of desperation glinted in his eyes and wavered through his voice. As if there were someone inside the monster, deep down, who hated what he'd done so much he wanted to die.

"Davey," I started.

He dropped his gaze, and the moment broke. "I didn't think so." He ambled off down the hall.

It occurred to me then, too late, that I didn't have to kill him. I could do what Vicky had tried to with the other beast: shoot him in the leg to stop him. I didn't know what would happen after, but that didn't seem to matter.

I lunged forward, and Davey bolted. My sock made horrible tacky sounds on the floor as I dashed after him, leaving a trail of Vicky's blood. He was already at the back door by the time I charged out of the living room. He yanked it open and darted outside. I burst out onto the patio in time to watch him vault over the back fence into the opposite yard.

I stopped, swaying on my feet. My gut was a ball of nausea, my fingers slick against the grip of the gun. I drew them tighter around it.

One weapon was hardly even the beginning of a plan. But it was something I could use, and I wasn't going to let it go.

I walked back through the house. On the other side of the living room window, a police car was pulling up to the sidewalk beside a familiar beige sedan.

"Max," Officer Fowley said, "we're not accusing you of anything. Yet. But you have to know it doesn't look good. If there's something you're not telling us, this would be the time to spit it out."

I guessed he was the good cop in whatever routine the police were sending me through. I'd been at the station for most of the day. First the suspicious woman cop had talked to me, making me break down all of my movements since the evening before, followed by a youngish guy who kept scribbling on his papers even when I wasn't saying anything. Now I was back to Fowley.

"There's nothing else," I said. "I heard that message from Vicky and got worried, so I went over to check on her and found her like that." I'd played my voicemail for each of the cops several times. "Do you really think the killer would have stuck around to chat with me about it?"

I needed to get home. Davey could have headed straight there from Vicky's for Ash. Every five minutes I went through another silent debate about telling the cops as much.

Every time the debate ended with an image of ravaged bodies scattered around a smiling Davey, clutching Ash and grinning as he said, *You just had to try me, didn't you, Max?*

We were playing by his rules now, and I didn't have a

fucking clue what they *were*. But I did know the cops had been searching for Davey for four days without catching a glimpse, and he'd willingly given *me* a clear shot at him.

Officer Fowley studied me. He didn't look particularly pleased or convinced.

"And that bruise?"

I touched the tender skin on the side of my head where Davey had clocked me yesterday. He'd left me with half a black eye and quite a bit of purple-brown forehead too. "Like I said, I was taking down the blender from the cupboard, and my hand slipped so it smacked me in the head." Which was a totally reasonable story because I'd actually done it once, a few years ago.

"Making yourself a smoothie?" Fowley said, mildly sarcastic.

"What kind of drink do you think I'd be making?" I wasn't about to add underage drinking to the list of possible charges.

He shook his head and sighed.

"Look," I said, playing the best card I had. "My girlfriend just— I had to see her like that. I want to be home with my family. I've told you everything I know. Going over it again isn't going to do anything except make me feel even more sick."

It wasn't hard to work a quaver into my voice. I was literally sick of mentally revisiting my last memory of Vicky. I'd passed on every offer of donuts and vending machine food because I was so queasy I knew I wouldn't keep anything down. Maybe I should *make* myself eat something, so I could puke on him. That might convince him to let me go.

In the end, I think I was rescued by the same people who'd caught me. The plainclothes officers from the beige sedan had been watching the house all night, so they must have known I hadn't left until they'd seen me run off that morning. Late in the afternoon, the youngish cop stopped outside my room, gesturing toward me and saying something about "time of death" to a colleague. Ten minutes later, Officer Fowley came back and told me I could leave. For now.

"We may be back in the morning with more questions," he said. I shook his hand and thanked him.

The first thing I did with my freedom, after I'd walked a few blocks and determined no one was keeping an eye on me for the moment, was backtrack to Vicky's block to grab the gun. When I'd seen the police car that morning, I'd hurried out back and dropped it over the fence into the neighbor's flowerbed. If the cops had found it at Vicky's house, it would have been gone for good.

I snuck up the driveway, plucked the pistol from amid the lilies, and hurried home.

Mom was vacuuming the downstairs rugs when I came in. I don't think she even heard me. I dashed upstairs and headed straight to Ash's room.

She wasn't there. She'd made her bed like she always did, strangely neat in contrast with the clothes-strewn floor. It looked like she'd tried on several outfits before deciding what to wear. It was Saturday night—no doubt she'd gone out with her friends like last weekend.

Possibly I would crash that get-together. None of the

sophomores were likely to mind. And I didn't want to have Ash out of my sight between now and Monday.

I paused at my computer to look up the model of pistol and figure out how I was supposed to actually fire the thing without shooting off my foot in the process. Then I bounded back down the stairs. Mom was unplugging the vacuum.

"Do you know where Ash is?" I asked.

"Some boy came by to pick her up about an hour ago," she said. "She promised she'd be home by curfew or call if she was going to stay over at a friend's. Have you been at Vicky's all day?"

Bile rose in my throat. Obviously she hadn't turned the TV on. "Yeah," I managed. "Just some guy?"

"Oh, there were a couple of girls in there too. You know how they are. They can't go anywhere without the whole pack. I guess it's a good way to be right now—safety in numbers."

"Yeah," I said, with relief this time. "Hey, were you going to use the car tonight?"

"Do you have something special planned?" She smiled. "I guess your father's right—we have to keep living life no matter what else is happening. Go ahead, honey. Just be careful."

I sat in the driver's seat and called up Ash's phone. It went straight to voicemail. "If you think you're cool enough, leave me a message," her voice instructed with an edge of sarcasm.

"Ash, I need to talk to you about something important. Call me back ASAP, okay?"

I puttered through town, parking on one of the main

streets and roaming past the fast food places and restaurants, hoping to catch a glimpse of her scarlet-streaked hair. After an hour, I circled back. She still hadn't called. I skimmed through my contacts list until I found one of the other girls who hung with her crowd.

When the girl answered the phone, she had to yell over the music thumping in the background. "Yeah?"

"Hey," I said, "is Ash with you? I'm trying to track her down."

"Sure! She's right over there. Let me—oh, hold on, I've got another call coming."

I waited on hold for forty-five minutes, flipping restlessly through radio stations in the car, until the static finally cut out and gave me a dial tone.

It was getting dark, the sky dimming from reddish-pink to bluish-purple. I tried Ash's number again with no luck and determined that I didn't have any of her other friends programmed in. So I gave the first one a second shot.

This time I cut right to the chase. "Where are you?" I asked as soon as she answered.

"At the park!" She giggled, and I could almost smell the pot through the phone. "You should totally come."

I wondered if she even knew who she was talking to. "Which park?" I said, as patiently as I could manage. It wasn't as if there were a shortage in or around town.

"You know, the one with all the treeeeees." She giggled louder. I rolled my eyes and hung up on her.

The parks near downtown were non-ideal for hanging out, because it was too likely a bunch of adults would get annoyed by the noise and call the cops. So I ignored those and cruised around to the outskirts of town. Finally, by one of the old farmhouses that had been up for sale for years, waving sparklers glinted across the field. I parked by the side of the road.

I recognized a couple of the guys who were standing by the pond near the barn, trying to skip pebbles on it. "Hey," I said. "Is Ash around?"

One of them frowned. "Didn't she stay at Liam's?" he said to the other, who nodded.

"Where's Liam's?"

"You know," the second guy said. "On Marling Street."

I didn't know, but I figured it couldn't be too hard to find the house with the party going on. "Thanks," I said, and they raised their beers to me.

When I got to Marling Street, the stars were twinkling and the streetlamps filling the road with their hazy glow. Lights shone in most of the windows, but no music reached my ears and no kids had congregated in a front yard or on a porch. Maybe the thing at "Liam's" was a smaller sort of get-together. Maybe Ash was there with him alone. Or maybe those guys had been wrong and Liam didn't even live on Marling.

At the end of the street, I pulled the car over to the curb and turned off the ignition. The rumble of the engine faded away, leaving only the hum of the phone wires overhead and the breeze rustling the walnut tree on the lawn beside me. I sagged forward to rest my head against the steering wheel. My throat felt thick.

Davey was right. I didn't know anything. And there was no one left but me. Even Vicky… Fuck, fuck, fuck.

I swiped at my eyes. Nothing I'd done had made a difference. There was nothing I could do to bring Vicky—or any of the others—back. And now I'd lost Ash too.

23

I sat there for a long time in the dark. A few tears leaked out. When I was done being an idiot, I rubbed my nose on the sleeve of my shirt, dragged in a breath, and restarted the engine.

I drove aimlessly until a little after one, knowing the chances I'd stumble across Ash were miniscule, chafing at the thought of going home defeated. Then I turned the wrong corner at the wrong time and found myself facing down a police car on patrol.

The officer motioned me over. I slid down in my seat as she walked up to the window. I was running on about five hours of uneasy sleep, and my eyelids felt so heavy it was getting hard to keep them open.

She shone a light in my face and hesitated. I didn't recognize her, but she'd probably seen me at the station.

"Curfew started three hours ago," she said. "Where are you going?"

"Home," I said, because there wasn't really anywhere else I could go. "I'm sorry. I was looking for my sister."

Her mouth tightened, but all she said was, "All right. I'll escort you there. Next time you're worried about someone, you let us take care of it."

Like that had worked out so well before.

The cop sat outside in her car while I walked in. Mom had fallen asleep in the living room armchair, maybe waiting up for me. Or me *and* Ash. I slipped up the stairs.

Ash's bedroom door was closed. I crept over and eased it open.

Ash lay in a jumble of sheet, her hair scattered over the pillow. I closed the door behind me and sat down on the floor beside her bed. She stirred, let out a sigh, and snuggled deeper into the pillow. My chest tightened. For a moment I thought I was going to cry for the second time in one day, when even once was pretty much unheard of.

I put my arm on the edge of the mattress and leaned my head against it. I meant to sit there no more than a minute or two, until I was completely sure she was real. But somewhere in there exhaustion caught up with me, and my eyelids drooped shut.

The last image that floated through my mind before darkness rolled in wasn't of the dead or Jena or even Ash, but of Davey—drowning behind the gleam in those yellow-gold eyes, his arms spread wide, as the gun trembled in my hand.

Go ahead. Do it.

"Max. Max!"

A hand was nudging my shoulder. I blinked and swallowed. My mouth was as dry as if I'd been chewing on cotton balls. The muscles in my neck throbbed when I raised my head.

Ash was the one nudging me. She dropped her hand and sat back on the bed when I straightened up.

"What are you doing?" she said.

Good question. I looked around, absorbing the landscape of her room, while last night's adventure unraveled itself in my head.

"I was worried about you," I said. "I spent all night trying to find you. Why the hell did you have your phone off?"

She looked guilty for all of about an instant. "I forgot to recharge it. It happens. I was only a little late getting home."

"Well, you should be more careful! You have no idea how freaked out I was."

"You didn't have to be," she said. "I was fine."

"You were fine because Davey decided to leave you alone," I said, my voice rising. "If he'd come after you, you wouldn't have stood a chance."

She was silent for a moment. And then she blurted out, "Well, he could fix that, couldn't he?"

I stared at her. She dropped her gaze and started fidgeting with the corner of her sheet.

"Never mind. I didn't mean it."

"Didn't mean what?" I demanded. "What could he fix?"

"You having to worry about me." Her hands twisted the sheet and smoothed it out again. "If he changed me, no one would be able to hurt me. Right?"

A chill pooled in my gut. "Tell me you're not seriously considering this."

"Of course not. I was just... saying."

"Did he try to talk to you again?"

"No," she said, but the momentary hesitation betrayed her. I shoved myself onto the edge of the bed and grabbed her wrist when she started to pull away.

"What happened, Ash?"

"Nothing."

"*Ash.*"

"It's *nothing.*"

"I need to know," I said. "Ash, he killed Vicky yesterday." My voice broke in the middle of the sentence.

She looked at me finally, startled. "What?"

"Slit open her throat," I said as steadily as I could manage. "And then sat there and told me about how he'd done it. You can't listen to anything he says. He's manipulating everyone."

Her head drooped, her hair falling to hide her eyes.

"I did see him," she said quietly. "Last night, when I was waiting outside Liam's for one of the guys to give me a ride home. He was just there, all of a sudden. He said he had a dare for me. To go out to the lake Monday night, on my own. That he knew I could do it."

"Of course you could do it," I said. "Why would you want to?"

"He said the things he's done, it was people who deserved it. And he'd stop, if I was with him. If he had me, he wouldn't want to hurt anyone anymore."

"He was lying." But as I spoke, I understood how tempting it would be to believe that promise. *I* wanted to believe that there was a way he could stop. But Ash wasn't it.

"He wasn't lying when he came the other night," she

said. "When he said I could be as strong as he is."

"You're already strong."

"No, I'm not, Max!" She jerked her arm away from me. "You think I am just because you are, but I'm not at all. I felt so bad when I saw Kyle last week I had to run into the restroom to throw up. All those people I hang out with make their stupid, catty comments, and I laugh, but it still hurts. I don't know how to make it not hurt. I stood in the back of the auditorium and listened to the choir rehearse on Friday and I almost cried because I missed it so bad, but I know I'm not strong enough. I'm not who I need to be. I don't know what else to do!"

My lungs clenched. I groped for words, but didn't find them. None except Davey's, spoken across a fence. *You've really taken her over.*

I'd thought I'd known how to fix Ash. I thought she just had to be like me and she'd be okay, so that's what I'd made her do. But it hadn't worked. I hadn't fixed her at all; I'd only broken her more.

Davey had said that I needed to start seeing. He'd made it clear so many times that he was feeding on the things I'd said, the ways I'd pushed people. That he'd let Jena off when she'd stopped listening to me. Maybe all his little jabs weren't just taunting. Maybe the real Davey had been trying to tell me what I needed to know to end this.

Maybe Ash was only going to survive if she got rid of whatever parts of herself she owed to me.

"Stop playing his game," I said. "The beast in him wants you to think you're not strong enough, that you have to prove something. That's the only way he can get to you. So forget all that stuff. Do whatever it is you really want to do."

"What do you mean? Try out for choir again? Stay home instead of going to parties?"

"If that's what you want."

Ash laughed, a little desperately. "You were the one who told me to quit all that! Because it was hurting me."

"I was wrong. That can happen, you know. When were you happier, honestly? There?" I pointed to the photos of her new friends on the wall and then to the old concert poster by her closet. "Or there?"

Her eyes hazed with memory as she looked at the poster. She lowered her head into her hands.

"I've never been as happy as I was when I was singing for people," she said. "But I was sad a lot more then too, Max."

I touched her shoulder. "So maybe that's the price people pay for having a life that makes them happy."

What about mine? What was my life, without making over Ash and teasing Davey and playing a lovebird to Vicky? I'd thought I had a pretty good one, but I wasn't sure I had anything at all.

"But if he means it," Ash said. "If he only wants to let me have the powers he has, and I wouldn't have to do anything awful, and he wouldn't anymore either…"

"I don't care what he says," I said. "He's going to hurt you. He had to get torn apart before he turned into what he is."

She tucked her elbows closer to her chest. "Is it really that much worse than getting hurt the other way? Inside?"

I guessed we could have asked Sofia that, but she wasn't

available for comment. Guilt squirmed in my chest. It was my fault too that Ash didn't understand how dangerous Davey was, how beastly he was going to become. She hadn't heard him talk about Sofia, or Reuben, or Vicky, hadn't seen the bodies, hadn't faced the thing in the woods that had changed him. I'd tried to protect her by keeping her out of it, but I'd only made her more vulnerable.

What the hell could I say to her now that would undo the two years I'd spent indoctrinating her?

I thought about everything Davey had mentioned about Ash, all the way back.

"Do you know why he wants to save you?" After everything, it still made my gut twist to admit what I'd heard. "Why he killed Vicky and Joss and Reuben and Sofia, but he doesn't want to do that to you? He had a thing for you. And not because you wore cool clothes or acted tough or played hard to get. Because he heard you singing in your room. That was the girl he wanted: the girl who sang. That's the girl he's managed to protect from the beast that's taking over him, even though it's pretty much eaten *him* alive."

She ran her hands back through her hair and looked up at me. "I'm scared."

She didn't say what of.

I squeezed her shoulder. "I need you to promise me, Ash. Promise me you won't go anywhere on Monday. Stay home. We'll watch a movie. I'll even sit through a musical and listen to the soundtrack afterward. You get to pick. Just promise me."

Her eyes drifted to the window. Then she reached out to grip my hand.

"Okay. I promise, Max. You don't have to worry."

I didn't want to. I wanted to know it would all be okay. But something in her voice, in the determined way she held my gaze, made me think of all the times I'd held Vicky's hands, said, *I swear...* and lied.

24

On Monday I walked Ash to school, passed her in the hall between each class, and met her by the doors when it was time to go home. Walking up to the house, I nodded to the cops in the now-familiar beige sedan. Despite all my doubts, I felt a trace of relief knowing we weren't completely alone if Davey decided to break his own rules and came calling here tonight.

Inside, Ash turned to me. "You're not going to, like, run surveillance outside my room all afternoon, are you? I'm not going anywhere. I've got seven finals to study for."

"Of course not," I said, though I would have been tempted to if she hadn't brought it up. She headed into her room and cranked her music. I left my bedroom door ajar and picked up the one assigned novel I hadn't quite finished. Every couple pages, I glanced into the hall. Nothing stirred beyond my doorway. The music reverberated on through the wall.

I'd made it through about fifty pages when a siren wail cut through the music. A second siren followed. I dropped the book and hurried to my parents' room at the front of the house to peer from their big bay window.

The sirens were already fading. But the beige sedan on the street below was pulling away from the sidewalk. I watched it speed around the corner.

What the hell was going on?

I hustled to my computer. At first, skimming through local news sites turned up only vague mentions of massive police activity on the north side of town. Then I stumbled on a brief article that had just been posted.

The police had received a bunch of calls about several buildings out north… Traces of blood found in multiple sites… *"There was a splash of it, right on the door," a witness said.*

The words dredged up a memory of red liquid coating car windows. My stomach clenched.

Davey. Who else could it be? The north side of town was the opposite end from the lake. Of course he'd make sure the cops were completely occupied during the last part of his game. He wouldn't want them interrupting. And he was playing them as easily as he'd played the rest of us. It probably *was* animal blood this time, since it only had to look convincing. Unless he'd saved some from—

"Max?"

I suppressed a flinch at Mom's voice. I hadn't heard her get back from work.

She poked her head through my doorway. "Do you know where your sister was going in such a hurry?"

My pulse stuttered. "What?"

"She dashed right past me going out the door," she said.

"I didn't have a chance to ask her. She didn't even turn off her music."

I rushed past Mom to Ash's room. A document was open on her computer screen; a half-empty glass of iced tea sat beside the keyboard. She must have taken off the second she'd realized I was distracted.

My heart thumped, a frantic beat against the back of my skull. I ducked into my room, yanked out the bag I'd stuffed under the bed, and charged past Mom down the stairs.

"Is something wrong?" she asked, following me.

She'd dropped her keys in the dish in the hall, like always. I didn't bother working the car key off, just grabbed the whole ring. Mom caught up with me as I tugged on my sneakers.

"You're taking the car? Max, I try to be easy-going, but you are supposed to ask first. Especially right now. Where are *you* going now? What's happening?"

Wasn't it a little late for her to get concerned? *Well, Mom, your daughter's about to be turned into a homicidal creature of the night. How's that for family problems?*

"We can talk about it later," I said.

"No. Max, give me the keys." She held out her hand. "I can't believe you didn't say anything to me about Vicky yesterday—I had to find out from the news this morning. If something's going on with Ash, you have to tell me."

I looked at her, and all this anger I'd never known I had smoldering inside me flared up. "How about this, Mom? You tell Dad how you really feel about all his girlfriends and the music he's never writing, and then we can have an actual conversation. Until then, I need the fucking car."

I left her in the hall, staring at me. As far as I knew, she was still there when I backed the car out of the driveway.

Ash was nowhere to be seen. I headed toward the lake. For ten blocks, I drove at fifteen miles over the limit, my knuckles white where I gripped the wheel. Then my heartbeat slowed and my thoughts caught up with me.

I pulled over to the curb and reached for my phone. The police couldn't keep up with Davey, but my sister didn't have any supernatural skills to evade them with. If I could get through to them, if they found her in time, if I could convince them to put her in custody... Maybe I'd be setting up a massacre at the police station, but who the fuck cared when I might as well be handing Ash to Davey if I did nothing now?

I didn't even make it past the first *if*. The phone clicked through to an automated answering service. "All our dispatchers are currently engaged. Please leave a message with your concern and contact information."

My hand dropped to my lap. Who knew how long the cops would be caught up in Davey's diversion? A sense of inevitability rolled over me like a crushing wave.

I was on my own. Of course I was. How else could this have gone?

I dragged in a breath. The sun was only just grazing the nearest rooftops. Davey had told Ash to meet him at the lake at night. I had time before evening set in.

I'd already been planning to go out to meet Davey myself after Ash was asleep. To make one final attempt at curing him. Before, I'd been thinking I'd find him, get him talking, and then shoot him in the thigh or leg—somewhere non-fatal that would keep him from dashing off. Then I'd try every trick from Jena's bag that I could.

But if I couldn't get to him before Ash did, I might not even have that chance. If the beast in Davey thought she was within his grasp and I was going to get in his way, I was pretty sure he'd kill me.

There wasn't anyone else left, was there? What could possibly stop him? Not me, with my bag of antique knives and holy water and a pistol I'd never fired.

If he wanted me dead, I was. It was that simple.

My gut didn't recoil at the idea. I felt eerily calm. Only one thought pierced my resolve and hung there at the front of my mind until my chest started to ache. There was one thing I didn't want to leave undone if this was going to be my last night.

It wouldn't take long, and then I could put all my focus on saving Ash.

I texted Jena that I was on my way before I started the car, but somehow it surprised me when she opened the door as I came up the front steps of her house.

She stepped out onto the porch. Her arms were crossed over her chest, the lean muscles tensed beneath the straps of her tank top. Her face looked thinner and tired, the brightness gone from her gaze. It hurt, seeing her like that.

She frowned when her gaze stopped on the bruise beside my eye.

"Davey," I said. "I was asking for it."

How sickeningly accurate that statement had turned out to be.

Jena's arms tightened around her. "I heard about Vicky. I'm so sorry."

I swallowed thickly. "Yeah. So am I."

"What's going on?"

"I just— I needed to talk to you."

I'd known this conversation wasn't going to be easy, but I hadn't imagined standing here faced with the suspicion in her eyes, the skepticism in the slant of her mouth, would be quite this hard. The worst part was how quickly I spotted the chinks in her armor. She was leaning forward slightly, as if she wanted to step closer. When my mouth twisted, trying to find the right words, a flicker of sympathy passed through her expression.

She wanted me to convince her. Of what, I wasn't entirely sure, but I had the sense that if I got down on my knees and made a total fool of myself, groveling at her feet and begging for another chance to stay in her life, that'd do it. She wouldn't believe the Max she knew would embarrass himself like that unless he meant it.

The thing was, that was *exactly* what I would have done four weeks ago. But not because groveling was the best way to show what I felt—I wouldn't even have thought about how I felt. I'd have done it because it was the approach most likely to work.

I wasn't here to pull a con on her. I was here because I wanted to do one real thing before everything else went to hell. So I stayed on my feet and said what was actually true.

"I know you probably don't know if you can trust a single thing I say. I've been kind of an ass. No, not just kind of. I have been, and sometimes an idiot, and sometimes a straight-up jerk."

"Max," she started, but I shook my head.

"No. I want to say all of it. I've said a lot of things before that were bullshit. I've treated a lot of people like crap. But I really have missed you. I probably should have told you that sooner. I don't want to leave things with you thinking you were just another girl I tried to put a move on. I— You're more than that. A lot more. You always have been, I was just too scared to admit it to myself."

I stopped. She was looking at me, but I couldn't tell whether she believed any of it, whether she was glad to hear it or fed up. She exhaled, a little shakily.

"And the other girls? Vicky?"

"I have made... some mistakes. Some very big ones." Vicky, on the couch with her throat gaping open. I cringed inwardly. "I don't know what else to say, Jen. I have been one massive clusterfuck. I didn't know what I really wanted. I thought a lot of things didn't matter that did. But I know now. I don't want to be that guy anymore. I'm trying to do things right."

"Is that the reason you came over? To tell me that?"

"Well," I said, "I also came to ask—you can say no, obviously—but I would really, really like to kiss you one more time, without being drunk out of my mind."

She laughed like a release. "You never stop, do you?"

"I'm not—"

"I know." She studied me. Then she gave me an odd, crooked smile and let her arms fall to her sides. "Okay. I guess one can't hurt."

It took me a moment to realize she'd actually agreed,

and then I felt even more wound up than before I'd asked. I didn't have a shortage of practice. I'd kissed dozens of girls before, and none of them had complained. I'd kissed *this* girl before.

But it hadn't mattered the same way. This might be the last time I kissed anyone. I wanted her to remember this moment instead of the awkward one when we'd woken up next to each other and I'd done everything wrong. So I had to make it good.

I took a step forward and touched her cheek. She closed her eyes, her head tilting instinctively as I leaned in. Her lips parted against my mouth in a caress that sent a shiver right down to my toes. Her hot breath mingled with mine, and a little, soft, *wonderful* noise escaped her throat. My heart skipped a beat.

I slid my fingers into the heavy waves of her hair and kissed her more deeply. Her arms came around me, pulling me even closer, and for a good thirty seconds I wasn't thinking about much other than how magnificent it was to be me at that particular instant in time.

I only came back to earth when Jena eased back a few inches. Her shoulders trembled. She sucked in a breath that sounded almost like a sob, and I froze.

"Jena?"

"It's not—" she said. "It's only— Joss—"

I jerked away from her, heat flooding my face. I was such a moron. For fuck's sake, she'd just had her boyfriend disappear in a puddle of blood. Of course she wouldn't actually want this.

"I'm sorry," I said. "I shouldn't have asked. I shouldn't

have—"

I turned, meaning to go, and Jena grabbed the front of my shirt.

"No! I'm not upset at you. I just..." She lowered her head, and her voice dropped too. "I feel guilty. I sort of did all along. Because I never felt the same way about Joss that I did about you."

"Oh," I said. And then, "*What*?"

"Max, I think almost every girl in school has had a crush on you at one point or another, and you haven't exactly discouraged it. This shouldn't be a complete surprise."

It was, though. "Wait," I said, still struggling to wrap my mind around this new version of events. "Since when?"

"I don't know," she said sheepishly. "Sixth grade, I guess?"

"Sixth grade." How had I not noticed? "I had no idea."

"I didn't want you to. You were... you. Charming and confident, and taking some new girl for a spin every other week. You would have broken my heart, and then we couldn't even have been friends."

"But— New Year's. You acted like it shouldn't have happened."

"It shouldn't have," she said. "I didn't mean for it to. Do you really think things would've worked out if I'd said, 'Hey, let's start dating now'?"

I thought about who I'd been then. I wasn't sure I could do this properly *now*.

"No, probably not." But *my* heart felt as if it were breaking. In a good way, opening up and letting light and air into places where there hadn't been any before. A feeling so overwhelming I didn't know how to put it into words. So I did the only thing I could think of. I tugged her to me and kissed her again, trying to channel everything into the warmth between our lips.

Afterward, she tipped her head against my shoulder. I glanced at the sky. The sun was still gleaming over the rooftops, but night had crept a little closer. The exhilaration of the moment dimmed. I made myself let her go.

"I've got to go," I said.

Jena held my gaze. "It's the full moon tonight."

She must have known why I was doing this now from the second I'd texted her. Was that the only reason she'd said everything she had? Would she have *meant* all of it, otherwise?

I guessed I'd find out if I made it back.

"It is," I said.

"And you're going after Davey."

"Yeah."

Her mouth twisted. "Don't you think that's exactly what he wants? Don't give in. Stay here."

As if I didn't want to. "I can't," I said. "It's Ash."

I didn't have to say anything else. Her face fell, but she nodded in understanding.

"Do you want me to—"

"No. If anyone's going to get through to him, it's me. I can't drag you back into it." I swallowed hard. "If I can find her before he does, maybe we can just head home."

I didn't really believe it would be that simple, and I had no intention of abandoning Davey completely, and Jena probably realized both of those things. But she squeezed my fingers and gave me a little push. She stayed on the porch, watching, as I walked down to the car and got in. I raised my hand to her, and she raised hers back.

This might be the last time I ever saw her. My jaw tensed.

I dug the pistol out of the duffel bag on the passenger seat, wedged it into the back of my jeans, and turned the car toward the lake.

25

I parked around the same place I had the night of the party and stepped out onto the sandy ground, hefting Jena's bag over my shoulder. There'd been no sign of Ash along the road to the lake, but she'd know I'd be looking for her before dark. Even if Mom hadn't interfered, I'd have noticed her absence by dinnertime. She might be waiting, hiding, somewhere in town until it was late enough that she thought she could meet Davey as soon as she got here.

Did she really want him to change her? Or did she just want to prove to him and to herself—and maybe to me—that she was brave enough to come, strong enough to look him in the face and say no?

Either way, I suspected Davey wouldn't be giving her a choice once she was in reach.

The gun sat hard against the small of my back. I checked the hem of my T-shirt to make sure it was covering the grip and set off. While I still had the light, I might as well see if I could find the spot where Davey was planning to meet Ash.

I walked along the cliff face first. I recognized the cave

where we'd found the other beast before I saw it. The sour stench lingered. I peered inside, my heart thudding even though I knew that thing was gone for good.

The stone walls and floor were dry, barren. It didn't appear the beast had done anything but sleep there. No sense of a home or belongings remained—nothing to suggest the creature had held on to a shred of humanity.

Was that what Davey would become by the end of this full moon? Or would the change keep creeping in by increments, so gradually he wouldn't see it coming before he hit bottom? Before he was rambling through the woods like an animal, if one with superhuman strength and senses.

There was so much I didn't know. But maybe the answers didn't make that much difference.

I reached the field that stretched toward the river, glanced at the bridge the beast had fallen beside, and turned to wind my way back to the lake. I crossed the beach and circled the western side. After the sand ran out, the ground turned soggy. My shoes squished in the mud as I slogged through the reeds sprouting along the bank.

About a quarter of the way around the lake, I stumbled on a footprint.

I squatted down, careful not to damage the mark. The indentation was faint, only the edge of one side of a shoe, the rest lost in the damp grass. It pointed straight toward the lake, as if someone had walked directly through the forest to the water here.

I stood and hovered my own foot over the footprint. The person who'd left it had shoes a couple sizes smaller than mine. Like Davey did.

It could have been made by some kid playing around here—by anyone, really. But there would be something poetic about him living near the place where he'd been changed into whatever he was becoming that I thought might appeal to his new morbid sense of humor.

Trees filled my view everywhere I peered through the woods. I treaded into the underbrush cautiously. I didn't *think* Davey would attack me right now if he saw me. He probably had planned some spectacular showdown by the light of the moon. But as he'd rightly pointed out, I didn't know him anymore.

As I made my way deeper into the forest, the shadows darkened. A chill crawled over my skin. I edged around clumps of spiny bushes and clambered over logs until I wasn't completely sure the lake was still behind me. The sun was sinking fast, offering no more than momentary glints of light through the leaves. It felt as if I could keep walking forever and never find my way out.

I checked my watch. I'd give this route ten more minutes, and then I'd turn around.

It'd been five when my gaze caught on the edge of a log-lined wall. I stopped in my tracks. A cabin stood amid the trees ahead of me. The wooden slats of the roof blended in with the branches around them.

Nothing stirred by the small, squat building as I stole toward it. Waist-high saplings and jagged-leafed weeds cluttered what had once been a clearing around it. But the grass by the door was trampled flat. No one had taken care of this place in a long time, but someone had been using it.

I staked out a spot between the trees and watched the

filmy windows on either side of the door for several long minutes. If he was in there, Davey had probably heard me coming before I'd even seen the place.

He didn't emerge, so I edged forward and crossed the overgrown clearing. The doorknob turned when I tried it. I pushed it open, wincing at the hinges' squeal.

The door swung into a large room that appeared to have at one time been a combination kitchen/living/dining room. A row of dusty-coated cedar cupboards lined the opposite wall by a gaping space where a fridge would have stood. The oven had been left, the elements now rusted. A garbage bag was taped over a broken window.

On the side of the room closest to me, an air mattress sat against the wall, strewn with rumpled bedclothes. The twist of the blanket obscured the image printed on it. I tugged a corner, and it pulled back to reveal a fleecy reproduction of a *Star Wars* poster.

I dropped the blanket. Davey'd had the same one on his bed since he was six.

No, not the same one—this one.

The blanket wasn't the only thing he'd brought with him. A plywood table next to the mattress held two stacks of clothing: folded shirts and pants. A plastic bag underneath was stuffed with socks and boxers. He'd left his computer at home—no electricity here, I guessed—but the edge of his favorite issue of *The Amazing Spider-Man* peeked from under the bag.

My heart sank heavy in my chest. He was still Davey. Somewhere in there, he had to be. Here was the proof.

I walked to the door on the other side of the kitchen and

nudged it open with my toe.

Both of the windows in the room beyond had been pasted over with garbage bags. Only a thin light seeped in from the room behind me, across the bare floor to the small white shapes heaped in the back corner. My breath hitched.

The nearest skull looked the size of a dog's head, others cat or rabbit sized, one maybe a calf's. A jumble of femurs, ribs, vertebrae, and God knew what else crowded around them.

The comment Davey had made about the gerbils' bones echoed back to me, *nice and crunchy*. I guessed these had been too big to devour, and he'd hidden them... out of shame? To gloat over?

All of the bones were perfectly clean, whether because he'd washed them in the lake or because he'd sucked off every shred of flesh— I didn't want to know, didn't want that image in my head. Despite his comment about Sofia, her heart obviously hadn't made much of a meal. The beast in Davey was very, very hungry.

It occurred to me, as I stood there with legs locked, that if I poked into that pile I might find Joss's skull. My gut lurched. I jerked back into the main room, tugging the door shut in my wake. The walls spun. I doubled over, acid souring the back of my mouth.

Some part of the guy who'd chatted with me beside Vicky's body two days ago was the Davey I knew, but an awful lot of him was not. Just how much of the real Davey would survive if I did manage to banish the beast?

Well, I could worry about that problem when I came to it.

My vision steadied and settled on a different sort of white shape scattered in the corner near the door. Crumpled pieces of sketchbook paper. I picked one up and unfolded it in my hands.

The pen lines were dark and ragged, the paper punctured in places the nib had pushed right through. They formed a figure with a crooked neck dangling from a tree, but it wasn't Reuben. It wore Davey's scruffy hair and the Spider-Man shirt he'd drawn on himself in the picture he'd left in my mailbox.

I snatched up another and another, smoothing them out on the floor. Davey slumped, bleeding from a gash in his neck. Davey sprawled on his back, his chest gaping open. Davey's body wrenched into pieces, his face gouged out. My stomach flipped, and I shoved that one aside. I had a feeling I now knew what had happened to Joss.

Davey had drawn all of these images and then thrown them away. Which part of him had wanted to see himself in his own murders? Which part had rejected them?

"Davey," I said, as if he wouldn't have shown himself by now if he'd been nearby. The garbage bag over the window crinkled in the breeze. That was the only answer I got.

There was no point in staying. I doubted Davey would bring Ash here and risk her seeing his stash of bones while he was trying to convince her what a wonderful existence beasthood would be. So I headed back to the lake. A pink tinge was spreading across the sky with the fading sunlight. The moon hadn't risen yet, but it was on its way. I hurried along the bank.

The car was waiting where I had left it, all by its lonesome. I leaned against the hood, peering down the long, straight road into town. My hand reached back to rest on the pistol. I kind of wished I'd fired it a few times at a tree, like I'd told Joss I had, so I knew how the kick would feel. It was too late for target practice now. And maybe I would need those bullets.

I pulled it out of my pants, released the safety and re-engaged it, familiarizing myself with the motion and the catch. The moon, bloated and bright, peeked over the treetops. A yellowish haze still colored the horizon, but in a few minutes that would be gone.

Ash had to be coming soon. Should I try walking down the road? But she might be here already, waiting in the darkness beyond the nearest trees for the chance to slip past me.

The wind ruffled through the branches along the edges of the clearing and drew an unexpected smell to my nose. Wood smoke. I glanced reflexively toward the empty fire pit. For a second I could almost see Davey sitting there, poking at the logs, while the music played and our friends danced around him.

I stood. My skin prickled as I left behind the steel shell of the car and the protection it might have provided. The wind was carrying the smoke from somewhere to my right. Too far away for me to see the fire through the trees, but it wouldn't have been meant for me. It was probably burning within sight of the road, to signal Ash.

I walked toward the trees. They closed around me, and I waded on through the darkness. Streams of moonlight filtered through the leaves, ghosting the forest floor with a grayish haze. A smoky tang hung in the air, but I could no longer tell which way it was coming from. So I kept walking straight on, one foot after the other.

The first glint of firelight I thought I'd imagined. When I stopped and looked for it again, there was only blackness through the trees ahead. But I adjusted my course, and a moment later it flashed into view again. I hurried on, holding the pistol tight at my side.

The tree trunks surrounding the makeshift pit danced with orange light. Smoke swirled up through their branches. The flames crackled. I hesitated about ten feet away, searching the shadows around the fire for any sign of Ash or Davey.

A twig snapped. A thin figure eased to a halt at the edge of the fire's glow. Ash's face shone pale but determined. She took another step, and I headed for her.

She heard me coming and froze. Her right hand clenched where it was tucked behind the folds of her skirt.

"Ash," I said. "It's just me."

She turned at my voice, her lips parting, and another figure emerged from the darkness behind her. Even in the dim light, Davey's eyes glimmered like coins through water.

"Ash!" I launched myself toward her. She spun around, stumbling backward, and Davey sprang. He was closer to her and faster than me, but all I needed was to get in one shot before he grabbed her. Then I could get her out of here and come back for him.

But I miscalculated. He wasn't aiming for her. He brushed past Ash and charged straight into me.

I'd been tackled by Davey once before. That time he hadn't known what he was doing. This time, before I could even blink, he'd slammed the full weight of his body against my side. I reeled into a tree trunk, the muscles in my arm spasming. The gun slipped from my fingers and pattered somewhere amid the brush.

I whipped around and lashed out with my other hand, but I smacked only empty air. Davey's rush had thrown him past me. He whirled, his teeth bared in a grin. His pupils had narrowed into needle slits. The points of two curved fangs glinted over his lower lip. The voice that reverberated past them was cold and husky.

"I don't remember inviting you, Max."

I didn't want to take my eyes off him. My gaze darted to the ground and up again. Where the hell had the gun fallen? Between me and Davey, I suspected. The last thing my body wanted to do was move closer to him, but I had no hope at all without it.

Davey didn't look particularly concerned. When I didn't respond to his quip, he turned his head. Ash had edged toward us. The T-shirt she was wearing was fashionably shredded, showing glimpses of near-white skin across her shoulders and stomach. Her right hand was still braced by her skirt. She raised her chin.

"Why are you bothering with him? I thought you wanted me."

Davey's expression softened in a way that would have looked comical on his altered face if I'd been in any mood to laugh. It was the sort of daze that might have come over the nerdy outcast in some teen flick when the head cheerleader asked him to prom. He reached out.

"No!" I didn't have time to look for the gun. I flung myself at him.

He caught my head with the back of his fist. Pain shot through the tender, already-bruised skin. He knocked my feet out from under me as I staggered. I hit the ground rolling, crunching over twigs and pebbles, and wrenched myself onto my back. My fingers hit something hard and metallic, but it was only a squashed beer can.

Davey stalked toward me. "It's her choice. Isn't that what you said? Why take that back now, Max?"

"Take me," I blurted out before I knew what I was going to say. "Kill me. I won't even fight you if you promise you'll leave her alone."

Davey snorted, but he stopped. He eyed me speculatively. "It's not like I need your permission to kill you. And what makes you think I wouldn't take you up on that offer and then change my mind after you're dead? You won't be around to argue."

I pushed myself more fully upright. The damp of the soil tingled against my palms. I didn't think I could get to my feet before he'd be on me again.

Ash was staring at us, her hands balled, looking like she didn't know whether to run at us or bolt for the road. The firelight glinted off the shape in her hand.

My Swiss Army knife. The blade was open. As if that little piece of metal would be enough to stop him.

I would have shaken my head, but I didn't want to draw Davey's attention to her. Had she come out here intending to try to stop him the only way she could think of? Or was the knife only back-up while a part of her still considered his proposal? I didn't want either for her, beast or attempted murderer. It was all part of the same game—a game Davey never would have dragged her into if not for me.

And here I was, still playing it. Was it any wonder she hadn't listened to me when I'd told her to get out? She'd seen me strong and confident and don't-give-a-shit, but never really opening up. She was watching me now, wrapped up in the cat-and-mouse chase Davey had started, as if I didn't already know how it would end.

As if I didn't owe him at least as much truth as I'd owed Jena.

My stomach twisted. I sat up straighter, crossed my hands in front of my knees as if I didn't expect to have to go anywhere, and locked my gaze with Davey's.

"You're right. It was a stupid thing to say. But I've done a lot of stupid things since you've known me, haven't I?"

He cocked his head, his smirk faltering. His voice still slid out mockingly. "And it always looked like you thought you were so smart."

"I was really stupid about you," I said. "I was supposed to be your friend, but I pushed you around. I showed you up every chance I got. I guess I got a kick out of knowing that I could, but it was a horrible way to treat anyone. I wish I could do it over. *Look at me*," I demanded when Ash shifted and Davey's eyes flicked toward her. His gaze jerked back to me.

I thought back to the party on the beach, to my words sending him into the darkness beyond the trees, all the way through to the little pieces of Davey's life scattered in the cabin in the woods, and put every ounce of honest feeling I had into my next words.

"I'm sorry. I'm so fucking sorry."

My voice shook, and I let it. Davey stared at me.

Then he sneered. "Like you've ever cared what you did to anyone."

"Of course I care. What, do you think I've been letting you pull me into this charade for fun? I did it because it was you, Dave—" I remembered his protest at the nickname the second before I let slip the second syllable. "I didn't want to lose my best friend."

"Your best lackey, you mean."

I shook my head. "Maybe I treated you like that some of the time, but I never saw you that way. You were my friend first. The guy who could make me laugh so hard I'd almost piss my pants and quote lines from all our favorite movies with me. The guy I admired for taking so much abuse and still being brave enough to tell his dad he was getting out of here as soon as college came. That's the guy I came out here to bring back. If you never wanted to talk to me again after, I'd be okay with that, as long as I knew *you* were okay."

This time he just stood there, motionless. I couldn't see the person behind those beastly eyes, but something was making him hesitate. I pressed on.

"I think you know that. I think you don't want to be lost either. Every time you talked to me, you taunted me with the things I needed to know to stop you, didn't you? You were warning me what you'd do next and why. I was just too stupid to really listen. But I'm listening now. I want to get you out."

"And what if you can't?" Davey said, but it sounded more like an admission than a challenge.

"I don't believe that," I said. "You can fight it."

His mouth twisted and twitched, as if it were struggling with itself. "I tried." He paused, and his voice lowered almost to a whisper. "Maybe I didn't try hard enough, when it would have made a difference."

"We can still—"

"I'm not your friend anymore, Max. It's not just this thing inside me. It *is* me now." He took a step forward. "I'm a killer. I'm a monster. I liked it. Do you understand? I liked the killing more each time I did it. I'm going to do it again, and again, and I won't stop. I can't stop *myself*."

His gaze darted to the ground, only for an instant, but I followed it to a curved shape lying by a tree root a little more than an arm's length away.

The pistol. He'd probably known exactly where it was all along.

I looked up at him as his expression snapped back into its mocking smirk, and I understood. There was just enough of Davey left that he'd been able to tell me what he needed me to do and show me how. The drawings lying crumpled in the cabin, the plea he'd made in Vicky's living room, the fate he must have already wished a hundred times for himself. A chill flooded me.

No. I didn't want to.

But maybe what I wanted didn't matter anymore. When I admitted it to myself, the truth was that even if I shot both his legs, he would still grab me and rip out my throat before I could get close enough to try anything in Jena's bag. And then he would heal, even more beastly than before.

Maybe, just this once, we should do things Davey's way. Because he had asked. Because I had spent most of our lives assuming I knew better than him what was best for him, and I had been wrong. After everything, the least I could give him was the ending he wanted.

My fingers curled into my palm. The crack of Vicky firing the pistol echoed up from my memory, and I saw in a blink the flash of police lights, the suspicion on Officer Fowley's face. Resolve hardened inside me.

I could give Davey what he wanted *and* what he deserved. Maybe I couldn't die for him for real, but I could still trade my life for his in the only way I had left.

I tensed to lunge for the gun, and Davey hurled himself at me, snarling.

I shoved myself toward the tree with my heels dug into the dirt, throwing up my hands as if they'd do anything to protect me. The impact I was bracing for didn't come. The roar of blood rushing past my ears broke around a soft voice carrying a clear, high note.

Ash was singing.

Her voice dipped as it slid into a new line of melody. The words tumbled out a little rushed, a little halting. I didn't know the song—it must have been one she'd written herself.

I lowered my arms. Davey was standing a couple feet away, his legs spread as if he'd stopped in mid-stride, his body twisted toward Ash. His eyes had gone wide, the pupils dilated so they looked almost human-shaped again. A tremor ran through his body.

Ash launched into the chorus—louder now, more

confident. It pealed through the trees, her tone steady and pure. The sound reached right between my ribs and clamped around my heart.

You couldn't hear her and not know singing was what she was meant to do. Her face was still pale and her hands clenched, but she looked brighter somehow. Like she held a light inside her that she'd just remembered how to turn on.

I'd tried to take that light away from her.

Guilt wound around my stomach, but this wasn't the time to apologize. She was singing to save herself and me. I had to do my part.

I leaned over and stretched out my hand, careful not to brush a single twig or leaf. My fingers closed around the grip of the pistol. I drew it to me, easing the safety up with my thumb.

At the click, Davey's head snapped around. His eyes narrowed as whatever spell Ash had worked on him dissolved. Then he dove at me, his fingers like claws slicing toward my face.

"I'm sorry," I said, and pulled the trigger.

The gun jolted in my hand, and Davey's body jolted too. I scrambled to the side. He hit the ground shoulder first and sagged onto his back. A burst of blood spread across his shirt. The bullet had caught him square in the chest.

"Davey!" I bent over him. He blinked once, twice. His irises dulled to their usual muddy hazel. His lips moved, but nothing, not even a breath, came out. The arm closer to me tipped, his fingers brushing against the back of my hand. He managed to grasp my thumb, holding me there with him. His mouth formed a small, tight smile. I wanted to believe it was a thank you, but I couldn't know for sure.

His grip slackened, and his head lolled.

"Davey." My voice faltered. A lump had filled my throat.

Ash stepped between the trees. "Is he…" she started, but couldn't seem to finish the question.

I slipped my thumb carefully from his hand and touched his wrist. Not the threadiest pulse met my fingers. My vision had gone watery. I reached up to close Davey's eyes the way I had Vicky's and brushed a few strands of the hair that was once again fine and limp off his forehead.

"Yeah."

Ash sank down on her knees beside me. A sob wrenched out of her, and the knife tumbled from her grasp. "I'm sorry. I should have— I didn't know what to do."

I wrapped my arms around her and pulled her close. "No. You did good. You did exactly what he needed."

I held her tightly as her tears soaked into the front of my shirt. My own eyes brimmed. This wasn't any sort of happy ending. Davey should have been the one hugging Ash and me the one lying dead on the ground. If we added it all up, could anyone really say he'd been more of a beast than I had?

The one thing I could do for him now didn't feel like anywhere close to enough. But it was all I had.

Ash was only sniffling faintly now. Keeping my arm around her, I shifted to pull my phone out of my pocket. My finger trembled as I dialed the three numbers Davey and I had learned together in kindergarten.

"Hi," I said when the emergency responder picked up. "I just shot my best friend."

26

I told the police that Davey was a hero. That he'd followed me into the woods to protect Ash from me, and that it was only when I'd shot him that everything got clear again and I saw how messed up I was.

I don't know how much they believed my account. I didn't try to explain the other murders, just let them draw their own conclusions, sitting silent through their questions and only speaking to repeat that it was my fault. I didn't feel like lying anymore, and that much at least was true. The state lawyer they assigned to me shook his head after a while and stopped asking.

Shaky though the case against me might have been, Davey hadn't left any evidence behind, and the police already had their doubts about the tales I'd told before. It was obvious I'd shot Davey, at least. So they put me in a cell and the next day the story played on the news while I waited for someone to come and tell me what would happen next.

A picture of Davey filled the screen, the same one they'd used in the earlier bulletins, while the reporter lauded the young man who'd sacrificed himself to save his friend's sister. Watching, I smiled.

It was kind of a corny story, but it was a lot more what Davey deserved than the "facts." And in a way, it was true too. What *would* have happened to Ash if he hadn't made me see how I was hurting her?

The questions kept coming as the police moved me from one center to another and threw around words like judges and trial dates, but all of that felt very far off. Justice moved slowly. In the meantime I ate the tasteless food, kept my head low, and repeated my truth on cue.

I'd been in custody for a month when one of the guards told me I had a guest and escorted me down to the visiting room with all the booths and their fake telephones and walls of glass.

I hadn't allowed myself to feel a large variety of things since I'd turned myself in. I figured the best way to make sure I didn't break was to keep my mind completely focused on how I was making things up to Davey. But when I saw Jena sitting on the other side of the glass, my heart started to ache and the rest of me froze up. The guard had to nudge me to sit down.

"Hey," she said. Her voice sounded far more distant through the phone than she looked through the window.

"Hey," I said.

She rested her other hand on the table, her fingers curled tight. "I wanted to come before, but they wouldn't let me."

"It's okay. How've you been?"

"Worried sick about you. If you mean other than that, I

passed all my finals, and my parents are trying to convince me to come with them to Amsterdam for a week before college starts to get away from everything."

"You should go," I said helpfully. "I hear it's pretty awesome."

"Max…"

"Have you seen Ash around?" Dad was the only person who'd visited me before now, and he'd informed me gloomily that Mom had moved out and taken Ash with her. Which, I supposed, was good for both of them. But since I'd theoretically intended to murder my sister, no one planned on letting me chat with her any time soon.

"Yeah," Jena said. "She seems good. I ran into her when I was taking my last final. She said she's applying to a school for the arts in the city?"

Some fear I hadn't known I was holding tight inside me released. I exhaled. Jena eyed me through the glass.

"Max, you can't do this."

"Do what?"

"Keep telling them it was you. You know how long they could lock you up for—you could lose your whole life."

"I have to," I said. "I couldn't do anything else for him. So I'm doing this."

"It doesn't do him any good," she burst out. "He's dead, Max. The only person this changes anything for is you."

"It changes how people remember him. How they think about him. I think it'd make him happy if he knew. And it's not like I'm remotely blameless, Jen."

She sighed. "You can't believe you really deserve to be in here."

"I don't know." I closed my eyes. That was the one thing I tried hardest not to think about. Because somewhere in the back of my mind, I wondered if I didn't deserve worse.

What if I'd trusted Davey with my first suspicions instead of sneaking around on him? What if I hadn't been so sure I could handle the situation and he couldn't? Maybe it would have turned out we couldn't find a cure anyway. But maybe we could have stopped all of this before even one drop of blood had been spilled—him and me, together.

I was never going to know either way, and that was more awful than anything happening to me in here.

"They tell me I can take college courses in prison," I said. "I'll be very educated when I get out."

Jena laughed and clapped her hand over her mouth as if the sound had surprised her. She leaned forward. "I'm going to do everything possible to prove you weren't responsible for the other deaths. I'm going to try to make sure you really can go to college and all that. I'm warning you now, if I can manage it, I will. And I think, if I can, you should go along with it."

"Jena—"

"I know." She touched her hand to the glass. "I won't say anything that will point a finger at Davey. But there are holes in the case big enough to drive a bus through. All you need is reasonable doubt, you know. Then both of you could go free."

For a second, the dark part of my mind shuttered. Could this be enough repentance when everything was added up? It didn't seem quite right.

I lifted my hand and set my fingers over Jena's where

they pressed against the window. Funny, I'd spent an awful lot of my life like this, hadn't I? Looking back, so many of my memories felt fake. Always with that thin layer of distance that stopped me from having to notice how anybody really felt, how *I* really felt, while I watched them and nudged them where I wanted them to go.

"I'm not ready," I said. "I'm not done paying yet. Okay? But when I am… If I ever am… I know there isn't anyone I'd rather have on my side than you."

She didn't argue. She just smiled, blinking hard, and nodded. I tried to feel the warmth of her skin through the glass and wished I had the words to tell her what I was only just beginning to understand. What the simple act of her coming here was making me understand.

Maybe when I was done dying for Davey, I *could* start living again. For me and for him. It didn't matter how long it was before that happened. All the scummy apartments in New York City weren't going anywhere.

And if I got that far, then for the first time ever— wherever I was, whoever I was with—I'd make it an actual life

ABOUT THE AUTHOR

Like many authors, Megan Crewe finds writing about herself much more difficult than making things up. A few definite facts: she lives in Toronto, Canada with her husband and son (and does on occasion say "eh"), she's always planning some new trip around the world, and she's spent the last six years studying kung fu, so you should probably be nice to her. She has been making up stories about magic and spirits and other what ifs since before she knew how to write words on paper. These days the stories are just a lot longer.

Megan's first novel, *Give Up the Ghost*, was shortlisted for the Sunburst Award for Canadian Literature of the Fantastic. Her second, *The Way We Fall*, was nominated for the White Pine Award and made the International Reading Association Young Adults' Choices List. She is also the author of the rest of the Fallen World series (*The Lives We Lost*, *The Worlds We Make*, and *Those Who Lived*), the Earth & Sky trilogy (*Earth & Sky*, *The Clouded Sky*, and *A Sky Unbroken*), and *A Mortal Song*.